Contingency Jones
The Complete Season One

Books by this Author

Contingency Jones
Contingnecy Jones – The Complete Season One

Samuel Branch Novels
Falls (Revised and Expanded)
Turns
Rises
(Forthcoming) Runs

Contingency Jones
The Complete Season One

By Eric Dontigney

This book is a work of fiction. Names, places, characters and incidents are solely the product of the author's imagination or have been used fictitiously. Any resemblance to persons, living or dead, businesses, places or incidents is purely coincidental.

Contingency Jones: The Complete Season One
Copyright ©Eric Robert Dontigney, 2016
All Rights Reserved

ISBN: 1533025118
ISBN-13: 978-1533025111

Cover Design: SelfPubBookCovers.com/Fantasyart

Contingency Jones – the Original Flash Fiction, copyright ©Eric Robert Dontigney, 2013, first appeared in Challenge 11 of The Iron Writer Challenge

*This book is dedicated to my mother,
who didn't murder me in my sleep all those times
I so richly deserved it.*

Table of Contents

Bonus: Episode 0 – Truth and Consequences	7
Episode 1 - An Afternoon's Work	17
Episode 2 - Necromancy Blues	28
Episode 3 - Aftermath	50
Episode 4 - Threads of a Tangled Skein	62
Episode 5 - Enter the Demon	77
Episode 6 - Checks and Balances	95
Episode 7 - Small Mercies	112
Episode 8 - The Man in the Grey Fedora	137
Episode 9 - Witching Hour	156
Episode 10 - Godshead Revisited	183
Bonus: Episode 10.5 – Date Night	263
Bonus: Contingency Jones - The Original Flash Fiction	282

Bonus: Episode 0 – Truth and Consequences

1

I knew it was going to be a bad day, because it started with a noise that could only have been the bastard offspring of an air raid klaxon and the mating call of a pubescent water buffalo in heat. It was the third time I'd heard that noise, and I had no reason to think things would go any better this time. I reached out, picked up the device and hurled it at my bedroom wall. The device fell to the floor with a clatter. It knew it was unharmed. The thing looked like a smartphone, but was damned near indestructible. It made sense, since people in my line of work were hard on equipment. If you're going to give someone like that one of the most powerful computers ever created, you're going to make it tough. That also meant it continued making that appalling noise and would continue making it until I looked at it or the neighbors raised a fuss.

I rolled out of bed and tried to rub the fatigue out of my eyes. I hadn't been back at the apartment for more than a few hours. I was still wearing the blood soaked clothes I'd been wearing when I stumbled in, too tired for words, after one of the most brutal missions I'd ever been on. A lot of people died. I'd accomplished my mission, but the point of it, the necessity of all the bloodshed, was lost on me. Command moved in mysterious ways, I guess. I shambled over to the device and picked it up. As I straightened, I saw that the wall had a dent in it. Awesome. It seemed drywall wasn't made to withstand impacts from hurled objects. I looked down at the device, trying to focus on it, and punched in a code. Sweet silence descended on the room. I dropped the device on the bed without looking at it and peeled myself out of the ruined clothes. I'd have to dispose of them in some discrete dumpster. There was just no getting dried brain out of cotton. I looked at the bed and sighed. I'd also have to burn the sheets.

I dug through a dresser and selected clothes at random. I needed a shower. Not just to wash off the stink of death, but to try to wake up. There was only bad news on the device. There was only *ever* bad news on the device. Trying to face it half-conscious would have been counterproductive. Even with the water turned to a blistering heat, though, my mind remained sluggish and my body felt like I moved it by remote control. Every response was delayed. Every thought was murky. I was in no condition to work. I wasn't even fit to be showering. I needed rest, but whatever set the device off wasn't going to give me the opportunity. There was a good chance I'd kill someone, just for damnable inconvenience of it all.

"Serve them right," I mumbled around a face full of towel.

Cleaner, if no less groggy, I retrieved the device. I took a moment to muster all of my focus, then I looked at the screen. It took me the better part of a minute to draw the connection the device had made with its near-constant analysis of news and social media feeds. Inexplicable things were happening, which wasn't a cause for alarm in and of itself. The universe has a weird sense of humor. Still, it was enough to give me pause. The more inexplicable an event, the less likely it had a natural cause. When a number of those highly inexplicable events clustered in a small geographic area, it almost always meant magic was at play. Of course, it wasn't my job to stop magic. It was my job to stop magic from being used to rewrite history. The reason for the alarm finally scrolled across the screen and my heart nearly stopped. The blurb read:

"The FBI continues to be stymied in its investigation into the theft of the Edwin Smith Papyrus…"

It was that damned Smith papyrus, again. The stupid thing haunted me. These fools thought it was an Egyptian medical text. It wasn't. I should know. I was there when they wrote it. I hadn't understood the code at the time, mostly because there had been no reason to suspect there even was a code. By the time I figured it out, the damage was done and the papyrus was beyond my reach. I'd been banished to the temporal backwater of 21st Century America because of that failure. The priceless, apparently innocent, piece of ancient writing was a spell to summon Apep, the personification of evil. Someone was using it, and I had a sinking feeling about who.

2

By rights, I should have sent a message to Command as soon as I figured out what was happening. I didn't. I found myself sitting on the couch and staring at the wall, as I tried to flog my sleep deprived mind into functionality with caffeine. I needed to think through how much to say about my suspicions. I was already out of favor with the brass and hurling an accusation based only on my intuitions wouldn't win me any friends. No one in a command position wants to hear that someone in the organization has gone rogue, but that was the most likely explanation. I'd studied up enough to know that the Egyptologists at my current temporal location weren't savvy enough to have recognized, let alone cracked, the code on that papyrus. That meant it was either someone very, very old, or it was someone from my time that knew the details of my failed mission.

While the former option was a possibility, it wasn't a very good one.

There were a handful of quasi-immortals running around who called the lower Nile home in the not-so-good old days. I'd bumped into a few along the way. As far as I could tell, though, none of them had a vested interest in summoning Apep. That dark old god would probably destroy them on principle. I've been given to understand that gods take a dim view of human beings that achieve even imperfect immortality. Something about putting on airs. That only left the latter option. Another Agent was fucking around with the natural order and that pissed me off. We took an oath the day we graduated from training to stand in the gulf and hold the line against chaos. While an Agent going rogue wasn't unheard of, it happened so rarely that they could be counted on one hand.

Some little part of me knew that I wasn't contacting Command because I didn't want a brother or sister-in-arms to have turned traitor to the mission. An even smaller and more honest part of me whispered the real reason in the shadowed recesses of my mind. If someone had gone rogue, violated our oath and the law, I didn't want that person arrested. I wanted that person dead. More to the point, I wanted to be the one who drew the curtain on the miserable son of bitch. The innate ignobility of that sentiment no doubt accounts for why it was only whispered in the back of my head. If I did put down whoever it was, I didn't want to have to dance around my motivations during an inquiry. Even if I didn't share all the details, I needed to file some kind of report or there absolutely would be an inquiry into why I failed to do so. If it turned out to be who I thought it was, I'd need all the cover I could get. No one applauds the person who destroys a legend. Hell, people have been murdered for less. I sighed and picked up the device. It was my connection to my own time. I opened an application and started speaking. I detailed the facts, but kept my suppositions to myself. After all, I reasoned, it wasn't like I had any proof.

Command was unusually prompt in their response. I was ordered to investigate. According to history as we knew it, Apep did not manifest at this time and place. If someone did raise him, it would cause unspeakable damage to the timeline, if not time itself. If someone was trying to raise him, I was to stop the activity *at all costs*. I felt better about my decision to keep quiet. "At all costs" meant that I had the cover I wanted. I just needed to track the magical disturbances back to their source, preferably before an Egyptian god turned up, and survive a confrontation with someone I was pretty sure could kick my ass in ten different ways. I really wished I'd had more time to sleep. If I was going to fight a badass, I'd never choose to do it exhausted. On the other hand, there were billions upon billions of future lives in the balance.

I shook my head and pushed myself off the couch. "Sack up, Nancy. Sleep wasn't in the job description."

3

One of the pitfalls of operating in the past was that anything you did could, potentially, corrupt the timeline. Enough experience had taught us that minor disruptions would tend to self-correct, no doubt a defensive action on the part of time itself, but it was tough to gauge what was safe and what was dangerous. Asking a clerk where to find something in a store was probably safe. Basic purchases of widely available products, also probably safe. Beyond those limited interactions, though, there just wasn't a good way to tell. All of that meant that Agents had to go out of their way to minimize the changes they created. Rarely had I loathed that rule so much as I did when I got stuck in gridlock. The device could have smoothed the way for me by adjusting traffic signals, but at what cost? How many minor changes in the timeline would that create? Since I couldn't know what all those changes would add up to, I had to sit there, killing time as the evening rush hour traffic crawled along at two miles per hour.

I might have been less frustrated, but I'd already spent most of the day driving around. For all its incredible power, the device has its limitations. It could analyze the shit out of just about any kind of data, but magic was fundamentally irrational. It operated outside the order of natural law. Just because a manhole cover was mysteriously missing, and a child fell into the hole, and that child somehow survived without a scratch, it didn't mean that magic was happening nearby. Proximity, I'd learned, was a poor barometer for judging where magic was happening. That truth became more and more relevant the bigger the magic being attempted. Raising a god was about as big as it got, which meant that the probability altering effects of the magic would be spread out over a much larger geographic area. The only way to find the place where it was happening was to circle through the city, over and over again, and let the device gather a hundred kinds of data about subtle disruptions to weather, gravity, electromagnetic patterns and things I didn't even pretend to understand.

It was a slow, grueling process, made worse by the unusual heat of the day. I'd bought my car specifically because it was bland and innocuous. I hadn't considered things like whether the air conditioner worked. I'd left it off when I was able to keep the car moving. In the slow hell of gridlock, I turned it on. For twenty minutes, it spluttered and threw semi-cool, swampy smelling air at me. Then it died. As the heat rose in the car, my frayed patience and temper snapped. I punched the roof the car.

"Stupid piece of shit car! I don't ask that much from you! The one time I need the damn air condition and you punk out on me!"

I'd have bet I looked like I'd lost my mind. Then again, I doubted I was the only one hurling obscenities at malfunctioning air conditioners that day. So, in principle, I was actually doing a good job of fitting in and not altering the timeline. Yeah, sure I was. After a short geologic age, the gridlock started to thin out. I stopped at a gas station to gas up and buy a bottle of cold water, along with a huge cup of coffee. The clerk stammered at me like a petrified bunny rabbit while he rang me up. I couldn't figure out what his problem was until I turned to leave and caught my own reflection in the door. I looked haggard, furious, and dangerous. The effect was in no way mitigated by the long black coat I wore. It wasn't leather, but it looked like leather. The coat, like the device, was a tool. They also served as the closest thing to a uniform that Agents wore. They were our version of body armor. They were bulletproof, but that was just a nifty side-effect of their true purpose. The coats shed the shear forces that potent magic generated. Walk into the wrong room at the wrong time and those forces could tear a human being limb from limb. I'd seen it happen. In many ways, my job would be impossible without the coat.

I tried to put on a less murderous expression and looked at the clerk. "Thanks."

The clerk went pallid and started to tremble. Unintentional terrorizing – 1, me – 0. Sometimes, you just can't fix things. I pushed out the door and resumed my ceaseless circling of the city. It occurred to me later that I was lucky I needed to cover so much ground. If I'd zeroed into a specific neighborhood early on, the presence of my car on a loop would probably have caused some concern or drawn police attention. At the time, I was just too tired to think of those things. The sun was down and the traffic was comparatively non-existent by the time the device finally pinned down a location. I stared down at the address and map the device provided. Of course it was going down in the warehouse district. Lots of convenient, empty places to set up shop and do the work uninterrupted. I aimed my car in the right direction. Even as I drove, I hoped I was wrong about who I'd find there. It wouldn't change what I had to do, but it'd be a hell of a lot easier to do if I found a stranger.

4

I stopped the car about two hundred yards away from the warehouse the device had identified. There was nothing remarkable about it at first glance. A big, squat, two-story building, it was identical to dozens of others nearby. I wondered why it was that particular building, as opposed to any of the others. Was there some significance, or was it chosen at random because it was empty? I doubted I'd ever know for sure. The reasoning behind dark magic often eluded my grasp. Still, the device was sure that it was the place. It had never led me wrong before, so I got out of the car and walked toward the building. I felt telltale pressure on the coat as the fringes of the magic altered the fabric of reality. I stood outside the small door used by people entering the building, rather than the huge metal doors that opened for truck deliveries, and took a steadying breath. I didn't know what to expect inside, but I didn't imagine it would be anything good. I drew back a foot and kicked the door open.

I gasped a little as wave after a wave of dark power washed over me. The coat did its job, though, shedding the worst of it and leaving me mobile. I pushed forward and pulled out a fine piece of 20th century tech: a Smith & Wesson, Model 27 revolver. Sure, it wasn't regulation, but practicality matters. The shear forces intensified the closer I got, making it harder to walk, and the material of the coat grew hot. It was a little frightening. How much power was swirling around in that warehouse? Enough to summon a god? I couldn't even guess. No one had ever successfully used the spell to my knowledge, so information on what its use entailed was pure speculation. Still, the level of power staggered me. I'd never felt so much in one place, with one exception. For one mad moment, I thought about summoning *her*, but that prospect frightened me even more than the chaotic energies clashing around me. Also, once I looked around the room, I knew I couldn't. My worst fears were realized, but that made it family business. We clean up our own messes.

He stood there, body cloaked in a coat like mine, with the Smith papyrus in hand. He heard or sensed my approach and looked up. There was no shock on his face, or any other discernible expression. He was control embodied. I suppose that was why he was the legend and I was, well, infamous. Control wasn't my strongest suit. We faced each other across the empty floor of the warehouse, two men out of our time, and both of us blood-soaked killers. I expect that anyone who saw us facing off would have pegged me as the bad guy. I hadn't shaved in days and there were purple pouches beneath my eyes. Still, appearances mean very little in the grand scheme. The most beautiful woman I'd ever met had a dead stone where her soul should have been.

An expression of slight bemusement cracked through the rigid control on his face. "Contingency Jones. So, they really did send you here."

"Endgame Smith. You're two centuries out of your zone," I answered, pointing the revolver at his right eye. "Also, you're breaking the law. Summoning of deities is strictly forbidden. You know that."

"Oh please, you're not going to shoot me."

"No?"

"You've never had the stomach for that kind of bloodshed. Shoot a man in the head, in cold blood, it's too calculated for you."

I blinked at him. It seemed that Smith wasn't up on current events. He looked back down at the papyrus, seeming to dismiss me from his universe. The part of me that had hoped I was wrong seethed in righteous fury. He'd betrayed us, our cause, and that couldn't stand. I knew what I had to do, what I was required to do, but I hesitated. He was Endgame Smith. No Agent was more celebrated or more trusted. I supposed that was why he'd been able to get this far. Who would question it if Smith said he needed to go somewhere. If I'd been less tired or less emotionally raw from my last mission, maybe I'd have asked some questions. Maybe I'd have made a different choice. I'll never know.

5

I spoke into the device, reciting temporal and geographic coordinates by rote. "I need an extraction team."

I fired off the message. A few seconds later, I received a confirmation. *En route.* I reached out and plucked the papyrus from Endgame's hand. I reached into a pocket and pulled out a lighter. The ancient papyrus caught fire as soon as it came in contact with a flame. I dropped the priceless relic to the warehouse floor and watched it burn, simultaneously closing the book on my greatest failure.

The firelight danced in Endgame's pristine, left eye.

Episode 1 - An Afternoon's Work

1

"Wait," said Clea, "aren't we going to do something?"

"No," I answered, walking quickly from the scene. "It isn't our problem."

"A man is dead," she insisted, taxing the last, fragile threads of my patience.

"Yes, he is, but none of the indicators are here. That makes it, by definition, not our problem. I shouldn't have to explain that you."

Clea grabbed my arm and spun me around. Her black hair was short cropped and she glared at me with large, dark eyes.

"You," she said, incredulous, "Contingency Jones, of all people, are lobbing regs at me?"

"They exist for a reason," I said.

She was still gripping my arm and I gave her hand a pointed look. She snatched it back with an embarrassed look, but kept pushing the argument.

"Rumor is that you've violated regs more often than the rest of the service combined."

I counted backward from five in my head, reminding myself that being assigned a trainee was a sign of trust. I'd had to kill a man to earn that trust, which felt more than a little perverse.

"That isn't," I started, "entirely inaccurate, but it got me assigned to twenty-first century America. If I were you, I'd wonder if someone wanted me to fail."

She blinked at that. It hadn't occurred to her that having Contingency Jones as her training officer was an instant black mark. Of course, I expected her to fail. Very few people make it through preliminary training and fewer get through field training.

It takes a special kind of mind, or a strange one, to cope with the stress of living in the past. You need a psychological flexibility that most people lack. I suppose I should be thankful. That fact keeps me employed. As for Clea, mental flexibility wasn't her problem.

Empathy was her problem. She had too much of it and that led to problems exactly like this one. She wanted me, us, to intervene in a garden variety murder.

She gave me a strange look and said, "Are you telling me you don't want to help?"

"I'm telling you that it isn't necessary. I'm telling you that it isn't prudent. I'm telling you that it isn't safe. I'm telling you that it. Is. Not. Our. Job. You see all those people in uniform?"

"Yes," she said.

"It's their job and they actually get it done, more often than not."

"But it'd be an afternoon's work for you," she said, crossing her arms and glaring at me again.

"I'm sorry you feel bad for that dead guy, but this is another thing I shouldn't have to tell you: all of these people are walking corpses."

She winced.

I didn't let up. "Get right with that idea, fast, or you're done here."

2

I'd like to say that I shrugged off Clea's argument without another thought, but it'd be a lie. I'm not empathetic by nature. It's one of the things that let me live my life in almost complete solitude without going insane. Forget relationships. Clea was right that I'd broken a lot of rules and regulations in my day, but never that one. The part of the job that I take as sacrosanct is that my only function is to prevent people from using magic to rewrite history. Starting a relationship would be tantamount to the same thing. I wasn't about to screw up someone else's future because I get lonely sometimes. Except once, but we all screw that one up once.

That didn't mean I found it easy to accept the idea of letting a murderer get away. Even six hundred years into the future, murders still happened. Human nature is what it is, and emotions get the best of us. What the training can't prepare you for is how casual an act murder is in the past. Or the grossly stupid reasons it happened. I gave Clea a meaningless assignment to do and told her I'd be back later. An afternoon's work, she had said. I wanted to test that theory.

I went back to the crime scene, which was empty now, save for that strange yellow tape that cordoned off the area. What shocked me was how effective that ephemeral tape was at keeping out the morbid and curious. People would cross the street to avoid it, as if, somehow, the crime was still in progress and not long since over.

I pulled a device out of my pocket. It had been configured to resemble a smart phone before they'd sent me back to this miserable time period. I suppose I could have called someone with it, if I knew anyone, but it wasn't really a phone. The device in my hand had more computing power packed into its slim body than every computer on the continent combined and could process more trace evidence than any lab in the country. I walked down the street with the device aimed in the general direction of the victim's house and let it gather data.

By the time I'd walked a few blocks and was sitting in a diner, the device had finished its analysis. I closed the interface when the waitress walked up. I ordered a small lunch and a coffee. She smiled without really seeing me and told me it'd be right up. I waited until after she brought my coffee to open the interface back up. The device had accessed the police files and identified the victim as one Donald Garrison, a self-employed web designer. It had also identified the DNA of the probable killer, but couldn't match it to anything.

I suppose it would have been too easy for it to just give me the name of the murderer. I'd have to do this the hard way. I set the device to do a deep data gather on Garrison and set it aside. The waitress brought me my food and as I ate my lunch, I wondered why I was bothering with this task. Even if I figured it out, I wasn't going to tell the police where to look. It was a waste of time to pursue it, but I let the device continue its information search. I expect that the governments and banks of the world would have been horrified to realize how easily that device circumvented their security. Since I was the only person who had one, though, I guess it didn't make any difference.

I decided that it was simple curiosity. I wanted to know why a man was dead. Was it cold, hard business or was there something personal behind it all? A lover in the woodwork somewhere? Was it random? Maybe, I thought. It was possible that someone woke up, decided that today was the day to kill a person and Donald Garrison was the unlucky winner of a capricious lottery. I doubted it, though. Most murder victims end up that way for a reason. I should know.

I'd been pushing the memories away all day, but it was hard not to think about Endgame Smith. He hadn't been a friend, but he had been a colleague that I once respected. He was the guy we all wanted to be, the very best, right up until the moment he betrayed our basic mandate. He'd tried to summon one of the nastiest Egyptian gods and risked the future of billions and billions of people. So, I stopped him. Command called it justified, but I'm not sure that means anything in the big picture.

The device gave off a ding that sounded a little like someone receiving a text message. I jerked a little at the noise, glad to have a reason to leave my memories behind. I picked up the device and scrolled through the information it had compiled. I frowned. The device was absurdly powerful at compiling data, but a raw search on Garrison had left me with more information than I could process in a month.

I narrowed things down to the last six months, just to make it manageable. Several hours and many cups of coffee later, I'd plowed through the obvious with no results. He dated, but nothing serious. A few of his clients whined, but nothing homicidal turned up. I went back to his financial records and extended the displayed information back two years. His income was variable and from multiple sources, so it was hard to assess the norm, but the device turned up an anomaly running a pattern analysis.

Most of Garrison's income came to him direct from private clients and businesses. The anomaly was a series of payments from a shell company that only seemed to exist to pay Garrison. The shell company traced back to one Laurence "Larry" Barron, a real estate developer and occasional venture capitalist. Once I had two names, I put the device back to work to see where the men crossed paths.

The device dinged at me a second time and I looked down at the screen. Well now, I thought, that was interesting. It seemed that Clea's empathy was misplaced. Neither Larry Barron nor Donald Garrison deserved it. My curiosity satisfied, I paid my check and headed home.

3

I checked a sigh when I came into the apartment. It was customary for trainees to stay with their trainers during field training, but I was starting to question the wisdom of that. I didn't own much beyond the bare necessities. Clea, on the other hand, was fascinated by kitsch and had taken it on herself to fill the space with things I found useless, distracting, or annoying.

She also hadn't adapted to the social conventions of the twenty-first century. She was sitting on the couch, nude, and doing something with her own, much less sophisticated version of the device I used. I closed the door behind me.

"Put some clothes on," I said.

She looked up at me, a vague expression on her face. A second later the words seeped into her thoughts and she had the sense to look a little embarrassed.

"Sorry," she said, "I forgot."

She got up from the couch, grabbed some clothes from a bag and vanished into the bathroom. She reappeared a couple minutes later, tugging at the fabric of her shirt.

She looked at me and asked, "How do you get used to wearing this stuff all the time?"

"Practice," I said.

"Very instructive," she muttered under her breath.

I rolled my eyes at her and sat down at the small table that did triple duty as dining room table, desk and, thanks to Clea, home to an absurd looking lava lamp. I gestured to the other seat and she sat down. I pulled out my own device, locked down most of the functions and about half the information it had gathered about Garrison and Barron. I slid the device across the table to her. She looked down at it, but didn't pick it up. Strictly speaking, trainees weren't supposed to even touch the more advanced version, but I had a little latitude.

"Oh for God's sake, pick the thing up," I ordered. "Consider this an object lesson."

She swallowed and then picked up the device. She scrolled through the information I had left active. She caught her bottom lip between her teeth and chewed on it a little. Her expression went dark as she realized the obvious.

"Garrison was blackmailing Barron," she said.

"Yes."

"That doesn't mean he deserved to die."

"Maybe not," I admitted, "but you take your chances when you go down that road."

She scrolled through the information again, taking her time, really analyzing it the second time through. I was curious to see if she could pinpoint the things I'd left out on purpose. She didn't disappoint.

"Where did these two cross paths and what was Garrison blackmailing Barron with?"

"They went to the same university years ago," I said. "Barron got into an accident, killed someone, and crippled another. Garrison knew about it somehow. Barron's family paid him off to keep quiet. Barron went on to build himself a little empire."

"Garrison hears about it and decides that maybe the well isn't empty?"

"That'd be my guess," I said.

"I didn't see any of that in here," she said, flipping back and forth through screens.

"I know you didn't. That was the point."

"Another test?"

"Everything you do here is a test."

She didn't seem pleased with the idea, but let it go.

"So now what?" She asked.

"There is no what. Mystery solved."

"You know the police can't compile all of this on their own, even if they knew where to start."

"Like I said, it's not our job. Barron will get his. There are three separate investigations into him. It's only a matter of time before he lands in prison. Justice will be served. Even if it wasn't, we still wouldn't do anything. We can't get involved. Anonymity is the only thing that lets us operate safely."

"It doesn't seem right," said Clea.

"It probably isn't, but our mandate is clear. It's what you signed on for."

I got up from the table and "forgot" to take my device with me. Like I said, everything was a test. I went into the bathroom and took a shower that was just long enough for Clea to do something stupid.

4

For weeks, I'd been trailing Clea everywhere during her off hours. You can only train so much and people need downtime. She was paranoid and cautious at first, but I'd been at this a lot longer than her. It was covered up pretty well, but she took the bait and copied the information off my device. That act alone was enough to boot her from the program, but I don't care about stupid infractions like that. I wanted to know what she'd do with the information.

I was monitoring every aspect of the case. I knew who their suspects were, all wrong, and who was on the case. I also knew where those police officers lived, their professional and private email accounts, basically any method of electronic contact. Clea wasn't stupid. After all of her advocating, she'd know I'd put passive monitoring in place to make sure she didn't leak the information. If Clea was going to pass the information off to the cops, she'd have to do it in person.

It was grueling to watch her shop for more crap I didn't care about. Not to mention seeing her eat things that made my arteries groan in sympathetic pain. At least she was making the basic sociological and anthropological observations we needed to stay under the radar.

Either her patience wore out or she felt confident I wasn't paying attention anymore because one afternoon she slipped off to a residential neighborhood where the lead detective lived. She dropped a small, yellow envelope on the front porch of his house. She lifted her hand to door but, after a moment of thought, walked away without knocking.

Good, I thought, at least she wasn't stupid enough to expose herself directly. I retrieved the envelope from the porch and went home.

5

I got up early the next day, very early, and filed my report. I had no idea where the reports actually went. I'd asked a technician about it once and walked away with a migraine. However it worked, the reports always found their way to Command. I waited for Clea to get up. She stumbled out of the closet-sized space she was staying in, walked past me to get some coffee, and sat down across from me.

"Morning," she said.

I threw the yellow envelope onto the table and she rocked back in her chair.

"Let me explain," she said.

I pulled out my Smith & Wesson Model 27 and pointed it at her.

"I don't need an explanation," I said. "You failed."

"Are you going to shoot me?"

"Only if you run," I said. "The extraction team should be here shortly."

"Actually," said Clea, "they won't. I didn't fail, Contingency Jones. You passed."

Clea's entire demeanor changed in a moment. The youthful enthusiasm drained out of her and was replaced by a confidence that seemed to add five years to her appearance. She smiled at me and sipped her coffee.

"I beg your pardon?"

"Think it through," she suggested.

I did. I thought about her persistent nagging and pressing against the regulations. It was kind of obvious, if you were looking for it.

"It was a stress test," I said.

"After that debacle with you shooting Endgame Smith, Command started taking a hard look at everyone and everything. You can't be surprised they flagged you as the highest risk asset they had in the field, the one most likely to turn a blind eye to a flagrant disregard of regulations."

"I never ignored the important ones," I said, setting the revolver on the table … and feeling stupid.

"That's a matter of some debate, but things are about to change for everyone."

"How's that?"

"Command is of the opinion that solo field operatives are too big a risk, too susceptible to psychological and emotional fatigue," said Clea.

She looked around the apartment and I got a queasy feeling.

"That doesn't answer my question," I said.

"I've been assigned to you," said Clea. "We're going to need a bigger place, Contingency."

"Oh crap."

Episode 2 - Necromancy Blues

1

There were days, before, when I felt utterly, completely isolated from the rest of the human race. As a man out of his time, I was all but forbidden to interact with anyone, except to meet my basic needs and carry out my mandate. It was a lonely, friendless existence, bereft of all the normal human interactions that everyone takes for granted. Dear God, how I missed those days.

Clea gave me a disapproving look with a hand perched judgmentally on her hip.

I stood bent at the waist by a stitch in my side and wheezed. "Just give me a second."

"Honestly, Contingency, your cardiovascular health is appalling. Four miles and you're already out of breath? You clearly need to step up your fitness regimen."

I glared at her. "How often do you imagine we'll be in a four mile foot chase?"

"Probably never, but that's not the point. Preparation is the soul of victory."

The earnestness of her words horrified me in their naivety. "Spare me the catchphrases, Clea. Blind, stupid luck is the soul of victory, more often than not."

She didn't say anything, just turned and started running again. I gave serious consideration to the idea of just walking home before I started after her at a slow, limping jog. My legs burned and my right ankle was absolutely screaming by the time I got back to the little house we shared. I hated the house, mostly because it wasn't the little apartment I'd lived in for five years. It didn't matter to me that she was right that the apartment was too small for us. It had been mine and now it was gone.

I spared a little hate for Command. They saddled me with this regs-spouting, fitness-obsessed, inexperienced partner. Never mind that the whole reason this job appealed to me was it fit nicely into my loner psychology. Never mind that they knew that about me. Some other Agent lost his marbles and did something stupid. Why the hell was I the one paying the price?

I knew the answer, of course. I even agreed with it on some annoying, rational level, but it didn't scathe my ass any less in the day-to-day grind. Then again, I don't suppose I was Clea's first choice as a partner either. My reputation with Command wasn't exactly bright and shiny. Phrases like "black sheep," "social incompetent," "disregards authority," and "I'll quit if you ever put me in a room with him again," littered my periodic evaluations. A more socially competent person, or one without a reflexive disregard for authority, might be troubled by those evaluations. They just made me smile. Besides, Command didn't keep me around for my charming disposition.

I pointedly ignored Clea as I limped my way to the bathroom. The shower helped a little, but the ibuprofen helped more. By the time I got back out to the living room, Clea was curled up in her oversized beanbag chair – another in a long line of her kitsch purchases – and stared blankly at a reality show. It had something to do with singing, I think. I decided to take a pass on the television, as usual, and started for the kitchen. I almost made it before someone pounded on the door. I traded glances with Clea. We didn't get visitors and the "no solicitation" sign by the door scared almost everyone else off.

I made my way to the door and shot Clea a look. "Be ready."

I looked through the peephole, but all I saw was the top of someone's head. I sighed, unlocked the door and opened it a little. At least, I tried to open it a little. The weight of a full grown man using the door as a support tore it free from my hands. He staggered forward and I caught him under the arms.

The man rasped out a word. "Jones."

I pulled back enough to get a look at him. "Sonafa...Clea get over here and shut that door."

Clea followed orders while I dragged the man to the couch. She came over and did a basic check of his vitals. She frowned.

"This isn't good. He's got a fever, weak pulse and," she pulled his jacket back to reveal a tattered shirt, soaked in blood. "Who is he?"

I didn't answer her. Instead, I opened a panel I installed in one of the walls after we moved into the little house. It contained a few things I'd rather didn't fall into primitive hands. I grabbed a med patch. It was about the size of a fifty cent piece and twice as thick. I hurried back to the man, tore open the remnants of his shirt and slapped the med patch against his chest.

Clea stared at me in disbelief. "What are you doing? You can't use that on someone from this time!"

I gave her a hard look. "He's one of us."

"No he isn't."

Clea made a grab for the med patch. She was fast. I was faster. I grabbed her wrist and twisted it into a painful joint lock. Say what you want about my cardiovascular health, my reflexes are top shelf.

She gasped a little at the pain, but still found the breath to berate me.

"I know every Agent in the field. He isn't one of them."

I shook my head and released her wrist. "Different program. He's a floater."

Clea blinked at that. "I thought that was a myth."

I rifled the pockets of his coat and came up with a device, identical to the ones Clea and I carried. I held it up and let her take a long look. "Not a myth, just classified. Like I said, one of us."

"If it's so classified, how do you know about it?"

I looked down at the man on the couch. "He saved my life once."

"When?"

I kept staring down at him. Something was off. Those med patches were like an instant hospital. He should have come around within moments. "Check his vitals again."

Clea went through the routine a second time. "His heart is a little better, but he's still running a fever. Shouldn't he be…"

"Yes."

Dread boiled in my stomach. I sent Clea to get me a damp cloth, gloves and some rubbing alcohol. I slipped the gloves on and gently washed the blood away from the wounds on his chest. There was ugly puckering around them, as if an infection had settled in days before. My dread feelings transformed into near certainty. My profession aside, I'm not a spiritual man. Yet, to my shock, I realized that the words muttered under my breath sounded a lot like praying. I poured the alcohol all over the cloth and my hands. I handed the bottle over to Clea, who took the cue and went to work on her own hands.

I hated to do it, but I needed to know. I grabbed the man and shook him. "J'adoube. J'adoube! Open your eyes!"

The man's eyes fluttered open, closed briefly, and then snapped open. "Contingency. Thank God." The effort of speaking seemed to drain the man, but he fought on. "It's bad."

I closed my eyes, but I couldn't avoid the question. "Necromancers?"

J'adoube nodded. "Archan."

"He's dead."

"Thought so too. Here. Now." J'adoube fumbled in a pocket and pressed something into my hand. "Stop him."

J'adoube took a shuddering breath and passed out.

Clea looked at me with terrified eyes. "Necromancers?"

"Apparently. Go wash your hands, right now. Keep the water as hot as you can stand and leave them under for at least 3 minutes."

For once, Clea didn't even pause. She ran for the sink. She was right to be terrified. I was terrified for me, for her and for J'adoube. I grabbed his device and said something I had never imagined would ever be necessary. "Contingency Jones. Clearance code seven, seven, five, two, six, eight, violet. Priority code, absolute."

There was a brief pause and then I was connected, live, to someone 600 years into the future. "Jones, there had better be an extraordinarily good reason why you're contacting us through that device. You aren't even cleared to know we exist."

"J'adoube Green is here, unconscious, and soon to be dead if you don't come get him."

"Use the damn med patch."

"I did. It was necromancers."

That voice from the future went silent and then I heard the sound of a woman screaming orders as only a person with near supreme authority can. After a minute, she remembered I was still on the line.

"Jones, emergency extraction, one minute. You know the protocol."

"Yes, ma'am." Even I stand on ceremony sometimes.

The line went dead and I got to do something else I never imagined I would need to do. I punched in a five digit code on J'adoube's device. A seam opened along all four edges. I spun the face 180 degrees and pressed the face back down. The screen started flashing bright red.

I placed the flashing device on his chest, next to the med patch, and ran toward the kitchen. "Clea! Cover your eyes!"

I got there in time to drag her down to the floor and then covered my own eyes. Even so, the light was blinding.

2

I tried to blink away the afterimage of that blinding light. The smell of ozone was thick in the air, like an electrical spark the size of an SUV had arced across the house. I heard dozens of car alarms going off all over the neighborhood. Lovely. Nothing said circumspect like a shrill orchestra of anti-theft devices. My vision cleared enough that I saw Clea. She blinked and squinted and then blinked again as she also tried to get her sight back into working order.

She spotted me through all the visual noise. "What was that?"

I rubbed at my eyes. "Emergency extraction. It's never pretty. You should finish washing your hands."

I walked back to the living room and heard the sound of splashing water behind me. The only evidence that J'adoube Green ever set foot in the place was a bloodied cloth and the discarded gloves. I hunted up another latex glove, bagged the bloody cloth and then bagged it again. I took it out to the garbage bin and dropped it in. It wasn't an ideal solution, but it was the best I could do short of burning the soiled rag.

Clea was drying her hands when I came back inside. She still looked shaken by everything that happened. Smart kid. I went into the kitchen, turned the water on blistering hot and took my own advice. You didn't screw around with necromancy-fueled bacteria. I could feel it as Clea hovered behind me. She wanted answers or direction or comfort. I didn't have much to offer on any of those fronts.

She positioned herself in my peripheral vision. "I thought necromancy was gone."

"You can't kill an idea, Clea. It's like trying to kill algebra. All you can really do is stop the practitioners. The principles that drive the practice, however evil, can be rediscovered."

"Your friend, J'adoube, said a name: Archan. Who is Archan?"

I leaned against the counter and regarded my partner. God, she looked so young. Chronologically, I only had about seven years on her, but a lot can happen to you in seven years. Archan was one of the things that happened to me. "A lot of people consider him *the* necromancer. No conscience. No pity. Power mad. Though, I guess that all probably goes with the necromancer job description."

"You and your friend both thought he was dead."

I nodded.

"Why did you think that?"

"Because we killed him. I guess we didn't quite finish the job."

Clea's jaw tightened. "None of this was in your file."

I snorted. "No big shocker there. Don't worry. Your official file will be more fiction than fact inside a year or two. That's how you know you've arrived."

I tilted my head back and closed my eyes. The last time I'd squared off against Archan, I'd been in the field less than a year. I was still too green, then, to understand the magnitude of the danger he posed. Plus, I'd had J'adoube on hand to pull my hide out of the fire. I wasn't green anymore and I understood all too well the danger Archan posed.

This time, I'd be the one who needed to watch out for a green Agent. At least she was smart enough to know, intellectually, how bad it could be. It still wasn't the same as being face-to-face with resurrected corpses and some psycho who wielded magic so black you could feel the evil in your bones. I wasn't sure I could actually stop Archan, let alone stop him and keep an eye on Clea. I'd have to figure out a way to do both, though. Unless, I realized, I didn't take her.

That idea appealed to me on a lot of levels. I was used to working alone. It's what I was trained for. When you worked alone, the only back you needed to watch was your own. The only life you were responsible for was your own, as well. I could leave her behind. She'd hate it, but it would keep her clear of a firestorm she wasn't ready to face.

"I can hear the gears spinning in your head, Contingency."

I didn't even open my eyes. "You're going to sit this one out."

I expected a tantrum or righteous fury or indignation. What I got was silence. It lasted long enough that I opened my eyes to make sure she was still breathing.

Clea was so pale she looked gray and her hands trembled. "No."

"What?"

"I said no. This is my job too. It's my responsibility."

"Clea, I appreciate the sentiment, but *you* are my responsibility. Keeping you clear isn't about letting you off the hook. You aren't ready for this. There is no shame in that."

"Can you beat Archan by yourself?"

"That is the question, isn't it? I don't know. Maybe. I guess it depends."

Clea frowned. "On what?"

"On whether blind, stupid luck cuts my way today."

The struggle was clear on Clea's face. I was giving her an out, and she wanted to take it. I wanted her to take it. Whatever I might have thought about her naivety or her blind acceptance of the rules, I'd give her this much. Clea wasn't a coward.

Her face settled into staunch defiance. "That isn't good enough. Maybe I'm not ready. If you aren't sure you can do this alone, though, you need to take me."

I weighed her words. If she'd been a superior, I'd have ignored her on principle. It's just how I'm made. As much as I wanted to believe that I didn't need her help, or someone's help, I didn't believe it. I could call for backup but, necromancers or not, that backup could take a week to arrive. I couldn't wait a week. I gritted my teeth and nodded. I hoped like hell I wasn't sentencing Clea to death.

A thought struck her and she gave me a look. "Why did J'adoube come to you? I mean, of all the people to reach out to, why you?"

I grimaced. "How do you think I got my name? Why do you think Command tolerates me and all my regs violations? I'm the contingency plan."

"I don't understand."

"I have an unusual skill set. I get things done. It isn't always clean, but sometimes results are what matter."

The implications of that weren't lost on Clea.

"Oh," she said.

"I bet you're wishing they'd told you the whole story before they stuck you here."

She didn't meet my eyes. "Doesn't matter now. So what do we do?"

I fingered the business card J'adoube had pressed into my hand. "We go to work."

3

I didn't like it. The card led us to a little blues club with the uninspired name of Frank's Blues. Clubs, bars, restaurants, anywhere people congregated, were a nightmare for people like me. There were too many bystanders who could get caught in the crossfire and, if they didn't, could act as witnesses. It was a no-win scenario. Yet, it was the only clue we had. The usual data mining failed to expose anything interesting. The club hung on to existence through a shockingly thin, but reliable profit margin. The owner and staff appeared to be standard-issue normal people. There was nothing about the place that would draw anyone's attention, except for die-hard blues fans.

"Maybe that's the point."

I glanced over at Clea. "What?"

"Like you said, it doesn't draw attention. Maybe that's point. I doubt your necromancer is looking to make a big splash, at least, not until he's ready."

I pretended that I'd been talking out loud on purpose. "Good point."

We sat in the car, the beigest and most non-descript sedan I could find when I first arrived, for another three minutes. I was procrastinating. Archan frightened me. Not the knee jerk fright of a sudden noise, but the deep fright borne of the rational acknowledgement that your next step could be your very last. I closed my eyes, tried to lower my heart rate, and forced the fear and uncertainty down as best I could.

I looked at Clea again and gave her what I hoped looked like a reassuring smile. "Let's go."

We got out of the car and walked the half-block down to the club. I reached out and took her hand in mine. She gave me a shocked look.

I resisted the urge to laugh. "We're just a couple out for the night. Listen to some music, have a few drinks. Nothing to see here."

"Right."

She laced her fingers through mine and sort of leaned into me a little. It was a closest I'd been to another human being I didn't plan to kill in years. The bouncer barely glanced at us before he gave an impatient head jerk toward the door. We went inside.

The place was maybe half full, with a bar to left and small stage off to the right. There were booths along the far wall and small tables scattered throughout. I ignored the stench of cigarettes, cigars and old liquor. The acrid scent would fade into the background before too long. The lighting was poor, except on the stage. It created an atmosphere that hovered between intimate and gloomy. I led Clea to one of the booths, so we could watch the entire space. I felt a nervous tingle on the back of my neck that didn't inspire confidence. Something was off. I just couldn't put my finger on it.

A waitress came over and took our order with the mechanical boredom of the chronically overworked. I ordered a domestic beer. Clea ordered a mixed drink. While we waited on the drinks, the house band geared up and launched into a song. Clea stared at the band, eyes wide and mouth hanging open a little.

"Clea."

She jerked her eyes to me and blushed a little. "Sorry. What are they playing?"

"It's an old blues standard called *Five Long Years*."

The waitress walked back with the drinks. I picked up my beer and, every once in a while, lifted it to my lips without drinking. Clea took her cue from me and pretended to sip at her drink. I kept scanning the club, confident something wasn't right. Every instinct in my body screamed at me to get the hell out of that building.

Clea glanced around. "What are you looking for?"

"The thing that doesn't make sense."

"Such as?"

"If I knew that, I wouldn't be looking for it."

We sat through decent renditions of *Catfish Blues*, *Mean Old World* and *Key to the Highway*. My nerves were taut as guitar strings at that point. I forced my leg to stop bouncing up and down beneath the table. The singer, a grizzled blues crooner, stepped back and handed his microphone off to a young woman. I recognized the tune even before she started to sing. *Trouble in Mind*.

How apropos, I thought.

I glanced around again. My mind tried to curl up into the fetal position when I finally saw what I had missed. The singer fixed her gaze on me and I recognized a sympathetic terror in her eyes. Clea was watching me and saw my posture stiffen. She didn't panic, just reached across the table and took my hand, like someone out for the night might do. I'm glad one of us wasn't panicking.

She squeezed my hand, hard. "What it is?"

"God, I'm so stupid. We need to get out of here. Right now."

In my experience, evil never gave itself away with the obvious. It was always in the little details that your brain overlooked because it saw what it expected to see, not what was actually there. The club was a fraud. No, not even a fraud, but a tiger trap, and I'd walked myself and Clea right into it. I'd have bet J'adoube did the same thing.

The other patrons went through the right motions. They lifted glasses and mugs to their lips. The tips of cigarettes burned. Waitresses cleared away bottles and brought fresh ones. Only, no one inhaled from the cigarettes. The bottles and glasses were full when the waitress cleared them away. Everyone in that club, with the exception of me, Clea, the young woman on stage, and possibly the band, were corpses. Fresh corpses at that, based on their appearance.

Clea looked around, more casually than I would have managed. "What did you see, Contingency?"

"This is a trap. They're all dead."

She looked around again and, now that she knew what she was looking for, Clea saw it. Her hand clamped down on mine. I pushed back the thought that I'd killed us both. It wasn't over, yet.

I squeezed her hand back. "Did you do what I told you to do before we left?"

She nodded and pulled a cross from beneath her shirt. The pale silver gave off a dull gleam in the low light. She reached into her coat and I heard the click of a safety switched from on to off. "Now what?"

"We make for the door. Be casual about it, like we're heading home. If things go sideways, though, you run. Don't wait for me. Don't look back. Run like hell and tell Command exactly what happened."

"What about you?"

It's not something I do much of but, in the clutch, I can lie with the best of them. "I'll be fine. The thing about a trap is that they cut both ways. You ready?"

"Is anyone ever ready for something like this?"

I shrugged and stood up from the table. I dug around in a pocket and tossed some cash on the table. I threw my left arm around Clea and buried my right hand in the pocket of my work coat. I felt the smooth handle of my Smith & Wesson Model 27 against my palm. I closed my hand around it, drew back the hammer and pretended to whisper something in Clea's ear. She played along and laughed.

A voice rang out from the stage. "Going somewhere, Jones?"

I didn't turn. I calmly drew the revolver. "Go!"

Clea bolted toward the door and all that cardio time she put in paid off. She was fast. I wasn't taking chances though. I put bullets through the heads of the four animated cadaver's most likely to stop her. I drew the hammer back one last time and waited a split second. The bouncer's head appeared in the glass of the front door. I put a round through his head too. Clea slammed through the door and vanished from sight. I gave myself one millisecond to feel relief that I hadn't gotten her killed and then vaulted over the bar. I felt it as something grabbed at my coat, but momentum worked for me and the material pulled free.

I dropped the revolver, with a bit of regret, but I needed both hands free. I grabbed the first two bottle of high proof liquor I saw. I popped over the bar and smashed one of the bottles against the face of some poor bastard Archan had resurrected. I smashed the other against the bar. I dropped down, grabbed the revolver and sprang back up. I grabbed the zombie covered in alcohol by the hair, slammed it's face against the pool of booze on the bar and fired off the last round in the Smith & Wesson next to its face. There was enough of a spark to ignite the zombie's head and the liquor on the bar.

I jerked my hand back, but not before it caught some of the fire. It hurt, a lot. If I'd had more time and fewer enemies closing on me, I might have stopped to plunge the hand into some ice. I didn't have time, though, or didn't feel like I did. I crouched behind the bar. I'd bought myself a few seconds at best. I shoved my hand into my left pocket and grabbed a fistful of salt. I sincerely wished that hand wasn't burned when I grabbed the salt, but sometimes you have to take a lot of pain now to avoid a lot of dead later.

I took a deep breath, did a sideways shuffle away from the flames and sprang up again. Despite the relative hours that had passed in my head already, there was a still a lot of confusion. The corpse I'd set afire was lurching and flailing around as the flames disrupted the necromancer's magic. It had even managed to set another one on fire. Sadly, the flames on the bar had started to die. That's the problem with liquor, it burns hot and fast. Still, it served its purpose. The other corpses that were closing in on the bar steered clear of the fire. That left them in a nice tidy cluster in front of me.

I whipped my left hand across my body and salt flew in an arc. Fire is great, but when it comes to black magic, there is just no replacement for good old salt. Salt of the earth, it cured what ailed me. As soon as the salt came in contact with the corpses, they collapsed. I dropped back down, a few more seconds bought. I crawled back, grabbed the revolver and flipped open the cylinder. I emptied the spent shells onto the floor and managed to load two more rounds.

"Jones. Enough of this foolishness! Show yourself, or this girl dies an ugly death."

I was out of time and options. I needed another edge. I closed the cylinder and slid the revolver into my coat pocket. I had a feeling I was done using it, one way or the other. I looked down at my left hand. The burns weren't as bad I expected, but the skin was red and blistered in places. I reached out and grabbed a piece of broken bottle. A little more pain wasn't going to matter. I held the glass over my left palm and vacillated. I wasn't sure I could still do it. I hadn't in a long time.

"I'm losing patience, Jones."

I heard the girl cry out in pain. That made the decision for me. I opened my palm with the glass. "All right, all right! Keep your panties on, Archan. I'm coming out!"

I took my time standing, and started to chant beneath my breath. The grizzled blues crooner had the girl by the hair and a switchblade pressed to her throat. That explained why I hadn't recognized him. I added body snatching to the list of Archan's crimes. If there was a limit to the ways in which that man could violate the laws of nature, apparently we hadn't found it. I held my hands up. If Archan gave any notice to the blood dripping off my palm, he didn't seem to care.

He smiled at me across the room. "I have to admit, Jones. I never expected to find you here."

I shrugged, but didn't break the pace of my chant. The cut on my palm was growing hot, almost painful. Just the way I remembered.

"I recall you being a bit more chatty, Jones. Full of smart talk. Has age finally taught you to respect your betters? Or maybe you're just not so brave without your friend? Tell me, did he survive? If he did, I'll have to pay him another visit."

I shrugged again.

Archan must have sensed that something was off because he gave me a hard look. "What the hell are you muttering about over there, Jones?"

I gave him a little smile. "Lords of Order, I beseech thee! Cleave the unnatural life from the dead flesh!"

Archan pressed the tip of the blade hard against the girl's throat. "Stop it! I'll kill her."

I couldn't have stopped if I wanted to. At a certain point, magic always took on a life of its own. "Set to peace the lost souls and guide them to their just ends! I offer the blood of the living to balance the pain of the dead! Come forth!"

4

Even among my colleagues, there was a false conception that magic was inevitably accompanied by special effects. If there wasn't thunder and lightning, they assumed something went wrong. I've never understood why they think that. In my experience, the most powerful magic was always accompanied by silence. In that blues club-turned-necromancer den, silence fell. A figure that had not been there a moment before stood in the center of the room. She peered around at her surroundings and gave a disdainful sniff.

Archan looked at her in stark terror. "Kill her!"

The reanimated corpses, the ones that weren't on fire or stilled by salt, threw themselves at her. She opened a hand and swept it downward. Archan's hench-zombies crashed bodily into the floor and twitched. She gave Archan a looked that chilled my soul and then strode toward me. The look she gave me was difficult to describe. Friendly wasn't the word for it. I doubted friendship, as human beings understood it, was part of her emotional vocabulary. Whatever the expression, it didn't leave me wanting to pee myself. I took the win I could find.

"It has been long years since last you called me. I wondered if, perhaps, you had forgotten me."

There was mild reproach in her words and, unless I misread her entirely, a little hurt. That was a problem I needed to solve immediately. You never, ever, not even for a second, want celestial beings wandering the universe with a grudge against you.

I gave her my most winning smile. "I didn't want to tax your patience. I call when the need is great and the innocent are at risk."

I wasn't sure if my words mollified her or not, but she inclined her head to me in a generally non-threatening way. She turned her attention back to the zombies she'd pinned to the floor. I didn't need the Moron's Guide to Celestial Beings to understand the disgust on her face. I felt the same disgust. Archan had bound living souls to those dead bodies. The souls provided the raw fuel that kept the bodies moving, but they had no choice, no free will.

They were like batteries, along for a horrific ride. If Archan kept those souls bound for long enough, it would use them up. There would be no afterlife, no great beyond, just nothingness. It was easy to feel disgust and I focused on that. Focusing on my disgust helped me avoid glancing at the movement by the side of the stage. I should have known Clea wouldn't actually leave, but there wasn't a lot I could do about it.

Archan was silent through my little exchange with the angel. At least, I assumed she was angel. It's never entirely clear where one type of mythic being leaves off and another begins. I suppose she could have been some kind of goddess, or a very powerful fae, but she didn't seem quite manipulative enough for that. When she turned her attention from me, though, Archan found his voice.

"You have no business here, vile thing. Begone and leave mortal affairs to the mortals."

"Speak to me such again and I will rip the poisonous tongue from your head."

She delivered the threat in an offhand voice, as if she'd announced she was running out for eggs. It was a little like taking an instant master class in intimidation. I don't know if the angel's intent was to keep Archan focused on her for Clea's benefit or not, but it worked. Clea didn't gloat. She didn't even speak. She just pressed the little .22 caliber pistol behind Archan's ear and pulled the trigger. He blinked. Clea grabbed his arm and dragged the knife away from the captive girl as Archan fell.

I had no idea if that was Clea's first kill. I hoped not. The first one was always the worst, even when it was someone as unrepentantly evil as Archan. The angel walked over and stepped up onto the stage. She stood next to Clea. If the angel spoke to Clea, I couldn't hear it. The angel's hand shot out and grabbed what, to my eyes, looked to be a piece of thin air. She smiled the kind of smile that I knew would haunt my nightmares for a long time.

She pulled the thin air closer. "There you are, Archan. It would have displeased me greatly were you to miss what happens next."

She went back to the center of the room and uttered a few words I couldn't understand. There was a momentary glow around the poor dead people Archan enslaved. The false life drained from their bodies and they all went still and gray.

The angel glanced at me. "You called for just ends, Contingency Jones. I heed your call."

She let go of Archan's, well, soul. Nothing in the room manifestly changed, but I felt it nonetheless. You get a sixth sense for the presence of violence in my line of work. Violence was happening, even if it was behind some veil the eyes of mortal man do not pierce. I was glad I couldn't actually see it. I didn't want to watch a soul die. I doubt I ever would have slept again. I watched the angel's eyes flicker back and forth, as she observed the actions behind that veil. After what felt like a very, very long time, she nodded.

"It is done."

I came out from behind the bar and approached the angel. I was never quite sure about the etiquette. I held out my bloodied hand to her. She reached out a finger and took a solitary drop. It vanished into thin air.

I'd asked her, once, what she did with the blood. She had given me an astonished look and then answered, as one might address an inattentive student, that she used it to "balance the equation." I hadn't known there was an equation, let alone how a single drop of blood balanced it, so I refrained from asking her more questions. I had also stopped calling on her help.

Once Archan put that girl's life into play, though, my reticence became meaningless. I don't know if the angel read my thoughts or if I was always transparent, but she smiled and wrapped her hands around my burned and lacerated palm. The pain that I'd already started to mentally block faded away as sweet coolness washed over the damaged flesh. Her ministrations left the skin healthy and pink.

I nodded to her. "Thank you."

She stared at me for a long moment. "I will always come when you call."

Then, as abruptly as she arrived, she was gone. I looked around the club. The bar top was still smoldering, courtesy of my handiwork. There were bodies everywhere, several with bullets in their brains. The absence of police cars surprised me. I stared at the floor for a while. I was tired. The fight was short, really, but the physical toll was always high. I just wanted to curl up and sleep. I pushed through the lethargy and dragged the device from my coat. I once more uttered something I'd never imagined needing to say out loud.

"'Contingency Jones. Clearance code seven, seven, five, two, six, eight, violet. Priority code, absolute."

5

We didn't stick around after the cleanup team arrived from the future. I confirmed their identities, ordered them to wipe that poor singer's memory of the entire day, and then hustled Clea out of there. I wanted to get her away from the killing field. The longer she stared at Archan's body, the more she'd second guess her decision. We rode back to the house in silence. I unlocked the door and we tramped inside. I started to ask Clea if she was hungry, but I felt the muzzle of her gun press up behind my ear.

"Clea?"

"Talk, Contingency."

"About what?"

"How about you start with who you really are?"

"You know who I am."

"I saw what you summoned, what it could do. Who are you, really?"

"Clea, remember earlier when I said I have an unusual skill set? That's one of my skills."

"It's too much power for any one man to control. You have to understand that."

I sighed. I had a pretty good idea what she was working herself up to.

I'd killed a man for trying to do something that was all of one split-hair different from what I actually did. Although, it was one of the rare instances that a split-hair made a big difference in practice. Since I wasn't going to let her shoot me, I showed Clea one of my other skills. I took her gun away. I wasn't gentle about it.

I crouched down next to her. "Clea, you've had a rough day, so I'm going to let this slide. Here's the thing you need to remember. I don't control that power. Not really. I can summon it, but I can't compel it to act against its nature. I couldn't get it to, I don't know, kill a bunch of bystanders or nuke an office building. Well, I guess it might depend on the office building. My point is this. I'm not like Archan. I don't have the stomach for it. I don't love power or pain. I've got no taste for empire building. In the end, I'm just me."

She glared at me and massaged her jaw. "Doesn't that take us back to the original question?"

"I suppose it does. I'm a guy with a strange job, a problem with authority and, I'm quite certain, some shaky ethics. I've got some skills that you can't get off the rack, but I rarely use most of them. If you're really worried about it, consider this. I've been living in the past for the last decade or so. If I'm such a bad guy, why hasn't everything gone straight to hell?"

Clea opened her mouth and then frowned. "You have a point."

I stood up and offered her a hand. She took it, grudgingly, and I pulled her to her feet. I gave her a neutral look. "I'm making food. You're going to eat some of it."

"I'm not really…"

"You put a gun to my head. If I say you're going to eat, by God, you're going to eat."

She blushed and nodded. "There is one other thing."

"What it is, Clea?"

"What do I call that thing you summoned in my report?"

I shuddered at the very thought of paperwork and shook my head at her. "We'll talk about those lies tomorrow."

Episode 3 - Aftermath

1

"We never talked about it."

Clea went very still at those words. "There isn't anything to talk about."

I checked a frustrated noise before it could escape my lips. It wouldn't be helpful. "You killed a man, Clea. No one shrugs that off."

"You don't seem too bothered by it."

"Is that what you think?"

"As near as I can tell, you haven't given a thought to Endgame Smith since you put him down. Why should I spare a thought for Archan? He had it coming."

I looked away for a moment and tried to get my emotions in check. "Did you know that, in this time, most major police departments require every officer who kills someone in the line of duty to visit a psychologist?"

Clea blinked a few times. "No. I didn't know that."

"They don't do that on a lark. There's a price to pay for taking a life. It sticks with you. It changes you."

"Is there a point coming?"

"That point is that you're thinking about it. You're having nightmares about it. It's haunting you. I know that's all true for two reasons. Reason one, you're not a psychopath. You have empathy. That means that no matter how much Archan had it coming, and God knows he did, it's eating at you."

Clea shuddered and closed her eyes for a moment. "What's the other reason?"

"I think about Endgame Smith every day."

"But you never…"

"Talk about it? Of course I don't. It's not my nature. He also wasn't my first kill. I've been through this a few times. I know what to expect and that, eventually, it gets less awful. But you can't wish it away, or pretend it away, or talk your psyche into acting like there are no consequences."

"So, you're saying you don't have to talk about it, but I do?"

I'd expected Clea to be defensive, but soft skills were never my strongest suit. I sipped at my water and worked very, extremely, extraordinary hard not to roll my eyes at her. "Not really. Talking helps some people. If you need to talk about it, I'll listen. If talking isn't part of your process, I'm fine with that. The point is that you need to stop trying to repress it. Repression is what wrecks you in the long run."

"Is that the voice of experience, Contingency?"

I shrugged. "I've seen it happen to people. It's not pretty. Honestly, though, I just don't want you coming unhinged during a crisis. I'm very attached to being alive."

She shot me a dark look for that little crack. "Your empathy is overwhelming. So glad to see my well-being is your top priority."

"Spare me. I'm not your dad or your big brother. We play for keeps in this business. You need to be functional, or you need to be gone. I'm giving you the information and the options. It's up to you to decide how it plays out."

She opened her mouth, but bit back on whatever she planned to say.

"Right. I get it. This is a job with a high risk factor. If I can't hack it, it puts us both in danger and jeopardizes the mission."

"Pretty much. Listen, Clea, you made a hard call. For whatever it might be worth, I think it was the right one. Archan was a bad guy doing unbelievably awful things. He wasn't going to stop until someone stopped him."

"Yeah. I bet you're hoping that I decide to cut out and go home. It'd sure make your life easier."

I'd been waiting for some little bon mot like that since the conversation started. It shocked me that the words still stung a little. "I doubt it. They'd just send someone else I'd have to break in. At least I don't have to remind you about social conventions anymore. Besides, I've gotten sort of used to you."

Something almost like a smile broke through the haze of emotional pain on Clea's face. "Contingency Jones, I think you just admitted that you like me."

"Yeah, well, let's not get ahead of ourselves. I'm cranky and liable to change my mind at any second."

An actual smile shone through for a moment. It was hard not to pump my fist in victory. It took a moment before I realized that, in some way, Clea's well-being mattered to me. When I signed on for the job, I did so with the full knowledge that it meant isolation. You learned to harden yourself to that, to live without investment in other people. There was no other choice, but madness. Mandated by Command or not, her presence peeled back some of my emotional plate armor. I debated whether to be pleased or distressed by that revelation. Investments often proved a double-edged sword.

Her smile faded as quickly as it appeared. "Do you ever wonder if all of this is worth it?"

I refrained from giving the rote answer and thought it through. "In the end, I have to believe it is. The dangers are real. Someone has to be on the line, fighting in the trenches. What's the alternative? Do nothing? How many lives would that cost? Millions? Billions?"

"I wouldn't have pegged you for a humanitarian."

I snorted. "Believe me, I'm not. I'm just practical. The job has to get done, and I can do it. It was either that or be an accountant. This seemed more interesting."

"Accountant?"

"Long story. Remind me sometime and I'll," I heard a ding from my work coat.

Clea and I both looked at the long black coat that hung by the door. We traded a glance. I frowned and walked to the coat. I pulled my device, a terrifyingly powerful computer made to look like a smartphone, out of the coat. I took in what I saw on the screen and felt a telltale shiver of concern at the base of my spine.

Clea peered at me from across the room. "Trouble?"

I pursed my lips and shook my head. "I don't think so. I just need to go check on something odd. I'll touch base if I need some backup."

"You sure?"

"Yeah, it's probably nothing. Something tripped a sensor I left in an old hot spot. Since it's in an alley, I'm guessing it's probably just the ghost of a stray cat or dog."

"That sounds so very thrilling."

I gave her a half-smile. "Believe it or not, this is the job most days."

2

I parked the Beige Monster, as Clea dubbed it, a few blocks away and fed a fist full of quarters into the meter. It was probably more time than I'd need, but it was cheaper than a parking ticket. I walked with my head mostly down and watched the other pedestrians with my peripheral vision. It was a trick I picked up that discouraged people from engaging me in casual conversation. Even small changes in the timeline could add up to something bad in the long run. I cut down an alley and managed to frighten a few rats.

There were only so many places in the world that could accommodate the transition I needed to make. In the twenty-first century, people still referred to them as ley lines. For my purposes, I needed a spot where two ley lines intersected. The common belief was that ley lines carried mystical energies and, as far as it went, that was true. Of course, it was only partly true. They also served as a kind of nexus point in time-space. With enough magical power, the right technology, or a savvy combo of the two, you could use ley lines to do some pretty amazing things. You could transport yourself laterally to another spot in the world. You could also use them to travel through time. It was how Agents like me monitored an entire century.

You can't be everywhere at the same time, so Command spent more than a little time and a staggering amount of resources setting up a network that enabled Agents to shift around a given century without direct intervention from the future. It minimized disruption to the fabric of reality and drew a lot less attention. In the early days, Agents monitored several hundred years. It was a mistake with a monstrous price. Agents were simply lost in the ley lines, never to be seen again. There were the usual rumors about ghosts in the ley lines. Senior Agents used those legends to regale or frighten recruits. After the better part of a decade in the program, though, I'd never seen one and I'd had reason to look.

The thing that I worried about was bumping into myself one day. While a lot of fail safes were in place to prevent exactly that outcome, technology has hiccups from time to time. It had happened. There was awkwardness. The temptation to ask yourself questions or give yourself advice would be overwhelming and the possible consequences hard to imagine. Much like the ghosts in the lines, I had never accidently bumped into myself.

I pulled the device from my pocket and pressed it up against an apparently random brick. This was the one task where all of the immense computing power of that device was put to use. Transporting someone through space and time was no mean feat. It wasn't a three-dimensional problem of getting my body from here to there. The earth was hurtling through space as the universe expanded. The device needed to make sure I that got to the right physical position that the earth was at in the universe at the exact moment I was going to appear. Get that wrong and I could appear in the cold vacuum of space or in the molten core of the earth.

Much like how sausage was made, I found it best not to think too hard about the process. The device gave off a little beep to let me know it was ready and, after a glance to make sure no one was watching, I tapped the screen to activate the network. Traveling in the ley lines wasn't like anything else. It didn't feel like flying or driving or running or swimming. The sum total of existence broke down around you in a prismatic explosion of light. All notions of linear time vanished and you became, for lack of a more appropriate term, unanchored from normal reality.

Everyone I talked to experienced it a little differently. Some people fought to impose a sense of order on it. Others embraced the non-linearity of the experience with an aim to glean insight into the nature of reality. I guess I wasn't contrary enough to fight the experience and, perhaps tellingly, not imaginative enough to try to get something out of it. I treated the whole thing a bit like a carnival ride. It's scary, because you're sure the whole thing will come apart at the seams any second, and thrilling because it doesn't resemble anything else.

Tangible reality coalesced around me again and I took a shuddering breath. That first second or two after arrival were dangerous for Agents. The disorientation made you a motionless target. Needless to say, neither Command nor the Agents themselves advertised that fact. The mortality rate was high enough. I shook off the disorientation and looked around. It was dark and the architecture was mostly hidden in shadow. I caught the smell of sea air, though.

A soft voice called out from the shadows, perhaps ten feet away. "Jones."

The Smith & Wesson, Model 27 was out of my pocket and aimed at that shadow before my brain had time to issue the command. There was something to be said for muscle memory. "Who are you?"

A figure stepped out of the shadow and I recognized a long coat like mine. There weren't many of those coats floating around, but a few had gone missing over the years. I didn't lower my weapon. The figure reached up and pulled back the hood that obscured his face. I heaved a sigh of relief and dropped the revolver to my side.

"Mother of God, J'adoube, that's a good way to get shot."

"My apologies, old friend. I wished to ensure that it was you before I revealed myself."

"You could have come to my house."

"I felt this conversation required more privacy than your new partner would afford us."

I blinked at that. "Clea's okay."

"Perhaps."

I let that one go and glanced around again. "Tangier?"

"It seemed appropriate."

I backtracked. "I'm glad to see you survived."

"Yes. I'm told I have you to thank for that."

"You were told? You don't remember?"

"No. I tracked a necromancer to your zone. I found him, but I was overwhelmed. I don't remember anything after that. It was Archan."

I pushed down some phantom fear. "Yeah, I know. He's dead."

J'adoube fixed me with a piercing gaze. "We thought so once before."

I frowned, not sure how much to reveal. "I made sure this time."

"Then some good came of it. That man was a pox on creation."

It felt like J'adoube was stalling. "Not that I don't enjoy a little pleasure trip to Tangier now and then, but why the cloak and dagger routine? It's a bit much, even for us."

J'adoube crossed his arms and stared down at the ground. "I was some time in recovering. It was the longest I'd spent at home in years. I find myself troubled by what I saw."

"Okay? What did you see?"

"There were many new faces at Command."

I shrugged. "That's bound to happen. People come and go."

"True, but not like these people. They were civilians."

I took a second to process that piece of information. At the core, our entire program fell somewhere between law enforcement and a military unit. We answered to a political authority, but the last time I checked, only the Premiere and ex-Premieres even knew we existed. There was just too much at stake to let that information become public knowledge. The potential for abuse merited a healthy level of paranoia. "Has the political situation changed that much?"

"I discovered that no one was interested in discussing the new arrangement, at least with me."

That wasn't a cheerful thought. I was a black sheep, so I couldn't expect to be kept in the loop about sensitive information. J'adoube was another matter. On paper, at least, he was as clean as they come. There was no good reason not to talk to him. After a gentle cough from J'adoube, I noticed I was pacing. My body was ahead of my brain again. "What do you think it means?"

J'adoube lifted his hands to either side of his body. "It may be, as you say, a change in the political situation."

"You don't believe that, do you?"

"No."

There weren't a lot of other places for that line of thinking to go. "You believe the entire program has been, or is in the process of being, compromised."

"I do."

"You think Clea is part of that, don't you?"

"I don't know, Contingency. It's possible. Endgame Smith gave them an excuse to change the status quo, but I believe those changes were coming regardless."

"I don't see you saddled with a partner."

"I suspect it's only a matter of time."

"If you believe that the program is compromised, why tell me? I might be part of it."

J'adoube laughed. "You aren't capable of treason. It's not in your nature. The answer to your question is simplicity itself. You are Contingency Jones. You're the one we turn to when traditional solutions fail us. If I'm right, our problem will require a non-traditional answer. Also, you haven't shot me yet."

I glared at him. "Did you consider that maybe I don't want to be responsible for any of this?"

"I might be wrong. You can choose to ignore me."

"Yeah, sure I can. The lives of every Agent in the field, not to mention history as we know it, might hang in the balance. Somehow, I'm supposed to ignore that."

"I didn't say it would be easy to ignore me."

I counted backward from fifteen. "You're a piece of work, J'adoube. This is a hell of a way to thank me for saving your life."

"I am grateful for that."

I poked and prodded at the problem in my head. Even if there was some kind of conspiracy at Command, there wasn't a lot I could do about it. I couldn't investigate it directly from the past and no one would trust it if I abruptly asked to be pulled out of active field duty. There was always the other possibility. "What if you are wrong about this?"

"Then you have nothing to worry about, since there will be nothing to discover."

"You know as well as I do that there are always secrets to find. Even if you're wrong about this, it doesn't mean we won't stumble onto something that could get us both killed."

"You've risked your life for less, Contingency."

He was right, though it galled me to agree with him. "Let's say I'm even willing to entertain this madness, what do you expect me to do?"

"For the moment, the same thing I plan to do. Be vigilant. I'm free to roam more than you are, so I'll use that to my advantage. If I were you, I'd take a hard look at your new partner. Watch her behavior. Test her loyalties."

"Well, that sounds like about as much fun as setting myself on fire."

J'adoube grinned at me. "At least that much fun."

"I hope to God you're wrong about this. If you aren't, I'm not sure we can do anything to stop it."

"I fear much the same, but what else is there to do but try."

3

The drive home wasn't a pleasant one. On the one hand, I wanted to do something. The implications of a third party, one without a neutral agenda, making decisions about how we carried out our mandate was deeply frightening. That fear made me want to lash out. On the other hand, J'adoube was right. The only thing we could do was wait and watch. There was no proof that anyone had actually violated any of our rules. Unless some kind of evidence appeared, it was just a hypothesis. I pulled into the driveway and sat there for a moment to compose myself.

Until I knew where Clea fit into the hypothesis, if she did at all, I couldn't tip my hand. I prepared my lies, put on a vaguely grumpy face and went inside. Clea was half-watching something on the TV. She looked at me when I came in and tried to give me a smile. "I see you aren't bleeding. I take it nothing interesting happened."

I shook my head. "Just some kids playing around with magic. They managed to summon a ghost. Probably stupid of them, but it's not really our problem."

I put my coat on the rack by the door and got a beer from the fridge. I didn't want the beer, my stomach was knotted, but it was what I would have normally done. I opened the beer and sat down on the couch. I forced myself to sip. Clea continued to half-watch the TV and snuck a look my way every so often.

After a few minutes of silence, she turned off the television and looked at me. "I thought about what you said earlier."

"Come to any conclusions?"

She hugged herself a little. "I think I do need to talk about it."

"Fair enough. Like I said, I'll listen if you need me to."

She was quiet for another minute and then the words seemed to explode. "I keep going over it and over it in my head. I keep wondering if there was something else I could have done, some other way to deal with it. I know there wasn't, but I keep seeing it. I keep seeing him die." She trailed off.

"It's like that sometimes. You wouldn't be human if you didn't second guess yourself."

"At night, though, I dream about it. I don't always kill him. When I don't, he kills me. Or he kills you. Or he kills that girl. Or he kills all of us! I know I did what I had to, but it feels like I did something wrong. It feels like I should be punished…"

As the pent up grief, guilt and apparent self-loathing poured out of Clea like water rushing over a cliff, I wondered if it was all an act. Was I being played?

Episode 4 - Threads of a Tangled Skein

1

I dragged Clea around a corner. "They knew we were coming."

"How?"

"I don't know."

"So what do we do?"

She posed the question as though I would actually have an answer. So much of what we did depended on the element of surprise and there was no backup to call in. We operated, for the most part, independently. Every once in a while, though, orders came down the pike and directed us to intervene somewhere. Until an old friend showed up and posed the possibility that our unit was compromised, I'd never questioned those orders. After arriving at what should have been a simple snatch-and-grab and finding a fistful of men with machine guns waiting for us, I was on my way to.

If I'd known the men would be there, or even suspected it, I could have prepared and brought the right equipment. Instead, we were stuck inside an abandoned office building with nothing to defend ourselves but my Smith & Wesson, Model 27, and a little Luger .22 that Clea had picked up for herself. Both were very effective weapons in the right situation. None of those situations involved the other team wielding AR-15s. I had other options, a set of decidedly non-regulation skills that I could deploy. I found it curious, though, that I'd needed to call on those skills more times since Clea arrived than I had in the previous five years. It made me paranoid. I wasn't about to let that cost me my life, though.

I reached into the pocket of my work coat. It was a long, black coat made to look like leather. It wasn't leather. It was some artificial material that let me survive the colossal forces that magic could produce. As a useful byproduct, it was also bulletproof. I fished out a shell for my revolver. It was pretty clear to me that one shell wasn't going to make the difference in the fight. At least, it wasn't going to make a difference if I used it as a bullet. I closed my hand around the cartridge and muttered a spell under my breath. I felt the spell draw energy in from the environment.

Clea gave me a perplexed look. "Did you just do something?"

"Trade places with me."

Clea slid down the wall and I moved to crouch at the corner. I did my best to lower my heartrate and listened. I could hear footsteps creeping closer. I looked at Clea. "You'll want to cover your ears."

I counted to five and then flung the enchanted shell around the corner. I jerked my arm back as the men reflexively fired off a few rounds at the motion. I covered my own ears. There was a long pause. Long enough that I was worried the spell had failed, then an explosion shattered every window on that floor. I hoped that our target wasn't in the blast radius. The orders were extremely explicit on two points. The target wasn't to be harmed. Clea was to be kept on a need to know about the details. Not there had been many details. Really, all they provided was an address, a picture of middle-aged man and an implicit timetable of immediately.

I was up and moving before the room stopped shaking. Three of the men were dead. I felt a momentary twinge of guilt about that. I didn't want to kill them, but there were only so many choices when people aimed automatic fire at you. The first live one I saw was down on the ground and I kicked him in the head. He went still. The other two were still on their feet, if only just, and tried to train their weapons on me. I'd hoped it wouldn't come down to it, but I put a round through each of their heads. As it was, I still needed to dive out of the way when the one on the left spasmodically jerked the trigger.

I shook my head at the carnage. It was not how we were supposed to do things. "Clea!"

Clea stepped around the corner, weapon raised, and took it all in. She went a little pale. She lowered her small pistol and walked over to me. "So much for in and out, quiet as a mouse."

"Best laid plans and all of that. Sometimes these things go sideways."

"Quite the trick with that shell. Care to share where you picked that up?"

"London, 1939. Let's go."

2

I found the stairs and we hugged the wall as we made our way up to the next floor. I hadn't thought about London in a while, or the woman I met there. Abigail knew things about magic. She'd also known things about me that she couldn't possibly know, like where I came from and why I was there. I stayed with her for three months, violating about a hundred regulations and my own code of ethics in the process. I think I would have stayed with her forever, but the day came that she told me I needed to leave.

She didn't explain, just insisted that I go. I was furious and left without a word. It wasn't until years later that I finally looked into it. Abigail died the next day when a Luftwaffe bomb leveled her building. She must have known, impossibly, that bomb was coming. She knew me well enough to know I would have insisted she leave, save herself. I don't think I would have had the courage to face certain death the way she did. At least, I don't think I could with her kind of foreknowledge.

I felt a lump in my throat and pushed the lid back down on that Pandora's Box. I stepped across the doorway that let out into the second floor and flattened myself against the wall. Clea followed suit on the other side. I pushed the door open with my hand, taking care not to expose my head or body to view. Bulletproof coat or not, it didn't pay to take unnecessary chances.

Clea turned an annoyed expression on me as I moved through the door to look around. "We're wasting time."

I mentally bemoaned the lack of practical tactics taught to Agents before Command turned them loose in the field. No wonder so many got themselves killed. "It looks that way right up until we get boxed in by the gunmen we didn't know were there, because we didn't bother to look."

Clea blushed at the criticism. "Oh."

"Make sure no one tries to sneak past."

I swept the empty space and kicked open the doors to the enclosed, corner offices. I didn't find anyone, which made me feel more, rather than less, unsettled. By rights, we should have needed to clear armed security from every floor. There were three possibilities. One, the bad guys were stupid enough to believe we'd never get past the goons on the first floor. Possibility two, the rest of the hired help was concentrated somewhere above us. The last and least cheerful possibility, our target wasn't there at all and the building was a trap.

As an added bonus, the clock was running down. Automatic weapons fire and explosions meant the cops were probably en route. The fact that it was an abandoned building might pad the response time. Still, I gave it five minutes, ten on the outside, before a contingent of flashing LEDs lit up the ground floor light a Christmas tree. I made a command decision. I pulled a device that resembled a smartphone out of my pocket and spoke into it. "Lock."

I tossed Clea my device. It's officially sanctioned name was the Quirt. I thought that was a stupid name and refused to utter it. To me, it was simply the device. It was the most powerful piece of computer equipment on the planet, several hundred years ahead of its time and capable of facilitating travel through time. We got them when we transitioned to the field. As the quintessential tool of my profession, I felt naked without it. I couldn't afford to let it fall into primitive hands. "Clea, fall back to the car."

"What?"

"There's a good chance I'm going to have to bluff my way past local law enforcement to get out of here. If they don't buy it, I need someone on the outside to backstop my lies. I'll use the Homeland Security ploy we talked about."

She didn't like it. The problem was that I didn't know why she disliked it. It could have been rookie displeasure at not seeing more action. What worried me more was the possibility that it meant she couldn't carry through some order I wasn't privy to, given to her by someone that had no business tinkering with the past. I needed her on the outside for the exact reason I said, but it also gave me a chance to test her. As the senior Agent, I was authorized to order her out of the line of fire at my whim. She was obligated to take the order.

She shook her head at me. "Don't let it come to that. I don't like messing with government computer systems. I'm always worried I'm going to launch a nuclear weapon on accident."

"Duly noted."

3

I waited until the door banged shut a floor down. There were four floors above me and not nearly enough time to search them all. I hated to do it, but I really didn't want to get caught on the police cars' cameras. Facial recognition was still painfully primitive, but it could make my life hard enough that I'd need to relocate me and Clea to another decade. I took the stairs two at a time, pausing on each floor to listen for a few moments. I was surprised by the absence of any sign of life. I had a bad feeling that I was going to find the top floor filled with armed men. There was no going back, though. I had my orders.

I stopped outside the top floor door. I listened hard, for a lot longer than necessary. I rechecked to make sure I loaded fresh rounds in my revolver. I prepared another spell, one Abigail taught me, and I opened the door. I dashed into the room at an angle and then switched course after a few steps to make it harder to shoot me. It needn't have bothered. The space was all but empty, save the target of the operation.

A middle aged man regarded me with a cool expression from across the room. He wore a custom-tailored pinstripe suit. One of the really nice ones with a vest, though he opted to go without a tie. His hair was short-cropped and silver, with hints of white at the temples. Dark eyes flickered behind wire rim glasses. He pulled a pocket watch from his suit vest and flicked it open.

If he was impressed by either my entrance or the gun in my hand, there was no visible evidence. "Contingency Jones, I presume."

"You presume correctly."

"I expected you two minutes ago. I suppose you stopped to sweep a floor or two, before you determined there wasn't sufficient time before the police arrived."

I frowned. I wasn't sure what I expected, the orders were thin on details, but the man's attitude wasn't sitting right. "Do I have you to thank for the welcoming committee downstairs."

"Don't be absurd. I'm a prisoner. You're here to extract me, not arrest me."

"If you're a prisoner, where are you guards?"

The man waved a hand in the direction of a darkened office behind him. "I left them in there."

I circled wide around the man and opened the door to the office. There were three men in pile. They didn't look to have died well. I turned to him. "It doesn't seem to me that you needed any help. Why didn't you just deal with the men downstairs?"

One of his shoulders lifted in something that might have been a shrug. "You Agents are so temperamental. I didn't want to wound your ego. We should leave. By my estimation, we have three minutes until the police arrive."

"Who the hell are you?"

"My name is August Worth, I'm…"

"I know who you are, Director. Let's go."

4

I did my best not to let my shock or curiosity show. I knew Worth by reputation. In the organizational hierarchy, he was the biggest of big fish. Frankly, he was not a man I wanted to know me on sight. Careers evaporated at his word. Rumor had it that a few people had evaporated on his orders as well. He was, even when I was still a raw recruit, in charge of dozens of classified operations. In other circumstances, I might have been amused to be in the same room with him. There was absolutely no reason for him to be in my zone, or anywhere out of his own time for that matter. That he was in my backyard didn't bode well.

I took us down the stairs fast. He didn't seem to have any trouble keeping pace with me. We hit the ground floor and I held up a hand. I cracked the door and peeked out. There were no flashing lights. I motioned him forward and we walked past the aftermath of my little parlor trick. He glanced around and raised an eyebrow at me. "Your handiwork?"

"My orders were short on details. I worked with what I had."

I don't think he meant me to hear it, but I caught the word under his breath. "Adaptable."

We went out the front door and I heard sirens closing in. "We need to go."

He nodded and I took us east, cutting through a big parking lot and a small park. Once we were under cover of some darkness I brought us to a stop and crouched down to observe. Worth raised no objections, just crouched down next to me. We watched for a few minutes as half a dozen police cars swarmed the front of the building. I shook my head. "Sloppy."

"They seem to be adequately disciplined to me."

I spoke without considering the recipient. "Not the cops. Me. When I do things right, the police never even know there was a reason to show up. Nothing to be done now."

As we walked through the park, Worth gave me the occasional sidelong glance.

It started to bother me. "What?"

"I was wondering if you were planning on letting them know you achieved your objective."

"I will when we get back to the car."

"Why wait?"

"It's where my," I choked the word out, "Quirt is."

"You left your Quirt unattended in a car?"

"Now who's being absurd? I left it with my partner. I figured it was even odds I was going to get arrested. I couldn't risk that technology getting dissected."

A ghost of a smile crossed Worth's face. "I must say, Mr. Jones, you are not at all as advertised."

"How am I advertised?"

"Do I really need to tell you?"

It was my turn to smile. "Probably not. I can guess the gist. I'm just curious what words they use."

"Ah, of course. Common terms applied to you include reckless, anarchist, deviant, and unreliable. One person referred you to a soul-less hellspawn, although I assume there was some hyperbole in play."

"I see you spoke with Janet."

Worth offered me an expression of mild surprise. "How did you know?"

"She called me that to my face."

"Might I inquire as to why?"

"I told her that I would prefer to drink battery acid and swim through rusty razor blades than be forced to watch her eat a meal."

Worth's mouth dropped open. "My God, why would you say such a thing?"

"The evaluations aren't wrong. I have a problem with authority. She was the authority in the room at the time."

"I'm an authority. You seem to have your behavior under control right now."

I grunted a non-committal noise. "It's different. This is work. Those evaluations get conducted in pristine white rooms, by people who have clearly never spent a second in the field. They have no idea what we really do out here or the costs involved. If they think they're qualified to judge me, I'm happy to return the favor."

"I see."

"At least now I know why they were so adamant I bring you in unharmed."

"Adamant?"

"They repeated it three times in the orders."

Worth rolled his eyes. "They do fret over my well-being."

I gave the man a sidelong glance of my own and decided to roll the dice. "If I can ask, how did you wind up here?"

5

Worth stopped walking. He gave me a look that left me feeling like I was under a spotlight. It was disconcerting as hell. "That, Contingency Jones, is a question I intend to see answered in full. As to the details, I'm afraid I wasn't conscious for most of it."

I nodded and didn't press the issue. Either he told me the truth or he lied outright. I suspected the latter, but opted to not take it personally. It was, after all, way above my pay grade. I led us the rest of the way through the park and we stepped out onto a sidewalk. I saw Clea sitting behind the wheel of the Beige Monster. I waved a hand and she slumped back in the seat before raising a hand in return. I turned to walk to the car, but Worth put a hand on my arm.

"Your partner, Clea, what do you think of her?"

I thought for a second before I answered. "She's inexperienced, which isn't a sin in itself. We all start somewhere. She's smart, intuitive, and maybe a bit too idealistic for her own good. Assuming she doesn't get herself killed in the next year or two, I expect she'll make a good Agent. She isn't someone who will have evaluators calling her hellspawn, though, more is the pity."

"I suspect one Agent like that is more than sufficient to keep the evaluators on their toes, don't you agree?"

"Yes, sir." I didn't try to hide my grin.

We walked down the sidewalk and then Clea stepped out of the car. I saw her face light up and she sprinted toward us. She flung herself at Worth with a nearly incoherent scream. "Grandpa!"

I watched the old man hug his granddaughter with dawning horror. The ways in which everything could go wrong in my life started to grow exponentially. I buried that horror as fast I could. "Clea, we should get the Director off the street."

The word "Director" seemed to jar some common sense loose and Clea let go of the man. She did her best to put her professional face back on. "Right. Director. We should go."

I got my device back from Clea and told her to drive. While she sat up front and talked with her grandfather, I sent the message that I'd retrieved the target, *unharmed*, and needed further instructions. A message sprang up a few seconds later. "Clea, take us to the alley."

She glanced at me in the review, a little hurt. "Already?"

"Orders."

Worth stepped in to save me. "They need to debrief me, Clea. There will be a great many questions."

His words mollified her. I felt for Clea. I didn't have any family in the future to miss, so the psychological toll on that front wasn't as harsh for me. Command wasn't merciless, though. They allowed Agents to exchange messages with loved ones, but those messages were vetted. It was a security protocol and probably necessary, but I always thought it must temper everything that Agents said. To have her grandfather sitting right next to her, only to know he would be gone within the hour, must have felt like a cruel tease to her. I still didn't know whether Clea was a traitor, but she was a human being. I made a mental note to do something nice for her. I kept quiet and let the old man and Clea share their limited time. When we approached the alley I told Clea to park about thirty yards away. I opened the door, stepped onto the sidewalk and spoke back into the car. "I'll scout it out."

It wasn't much, but it was the best I could offer them. I scouted the alley and the surrounding area. I took my time with it. When I ran out of ways to run up the clock, I went back to the car. Clea and Worth stood next to each other on the sidewalk, and I finally saw the resemblance. It was subtle, more an implication of resemblance, but there in the jawline and the eyebrows. Worth looked to be telling a story, with huge gestures and the most animated expressions I'd seen on the man. Clea was laughing hysterically. As I watched them, I realized that I wanted J'adoube to be wrong. I wanted to believe that someone who could laugh with that much abandon couldn't be a traitor. I knew it wouldn't stop me from looking for the truth, but it would hurt.

I put on a neutral expression and walked toward them. "The position is secure, sir."

Worth nodded and pulled Clea in for a hug. "It was good to see you, Clea."

"You to, Grandpa. I wish you didn't have to go so soon."

"We all answer to some master. I need to go answer to mine. I'll message you soon."

"Okay. Be careful."

He gave her a little nod and turned to me. "Lead the way, Agent."

I suspected he knew exactly where to find the nexus point. That was his way of extending me a little respect in front of Clea and cementing me in role of senior Agent. I found myself a little surprised and grateful.

Worth waited until we were out of Clea's earshot. "I appreciate you dragging out your reconnoiter of the area."

"I appreciate you not undermining my authority with Clea."

Worth fell silent for a moment. "I was acquainted with your father, a long time ago. You remind me a great deal of him."

6

I almost tripped over nothing, but managed to recover before I embarrassed myself too much. No one had so much as mentioned my father to me in over fifteen years. "I'm sorry to say that I never really knew my father."

"No, I suppose you would have been a child when, well, at the time. He was insubordinate, as well. He took every opportunity to tweak the nose of authority. Most people thought that was all he was, because they never saw him in a crisis. Then, oh my, Jones, then he was all business and profoundly good at his job. Another thing I believe you share in common with him."

I felt a touch of embarrassment at the praise and the comparison to a man I knew only through stories my mother told me. "Thank you, sir, but why do you say that?"

"You were faced with an impossible scenario. You didn't have the information you needed or the time to gather it, so you came in without the right tools. Yet, you overcame a heavily armed opposition. You didn't have enough time to sweep the entire building, but you needed to accomplish your objective. Doing that required you to make a potentially life or death choice, for you and for Clea. You chose to take the risk for yourself, but, for the second time, you ordered an inexperienced Agent out of harm's way. You made a series of tactical and strategic decisions on the fly that would have left most Agents paralyzed."

I hadn't really thought it through, but what he said made a certain kind of sense. We cut down the alley and approached the brick that served as the touchstone between my relative present and the future. Worth turned an appraising eye on me. "You seem to have an innate facility for two things: success and survival. These are things I hope Clea will learn from you."

I took a mental step back from the situation and really thought it through. "Jesus, you arranged all of this, didn't you?"

"Agent Jones, are you suggesting that I, a high ranking officer with unparalleled access to classified operations, arranged to have myself abducted and transported through time simply to ensure that I'd made the right choice in having my granddaughter assigned as your partner?"

I straightened a little and looked Worth in the eyes. "Yes."

He smiled at me. "I knew I was right about you. Which brick?"

I pointed and then a thought struck me. "Sir, do you have a Quirt?"

He smiled and pulled out his pocket watch. I raised an eyebrow. I never would have thought to take the watch off of him. It was old, worn and looked like stainless steel. Not valuable at all, unless you knew what it was. Worth turned to the wall and lifted the watch to the brick I'd pointed at, but his hand stopped short.

"Agent Jones, I noticed that you spent several months in London, circa 1939, I believe."

"Yes." It wasn't precisely a secret.

"I took a special interest in that period. It's fascinating from a historical perspective, but also from a temporal perspective."

"Sir?"

"It's in a state of near-permanent flux. The sheer enormity of the violence and magical forces unleashed then give it a unique quality. If, for example, the life a young woman were to be inexplicably saved, when it should have ended, I doubt it would so much as create a temporal blip. I thought, given your own fascination with the period, that such a fact might prove of interest."

Worth pressed the watch against the brick. He looked back at me. Right before he vanished from sight, he winked at me.

I stared at the brick wall. "Mother of God."

Unless I'd totally misunderstood his intent, August Worth had just given me tacit permission to change history for my own benefit.

Episode 5 - Enter the Demon

1

Clea stopped next to a bench and, a few moments later, I came to a much more out of breath stop. She gave me a long-suffering look, but she didn't say anything. I thought that was fair, since we were at the six mile mark and I wasn't limping or on the verge of passing out.

"You're doing much better."

I gave her a wry look. "Thanks. I still maintain there is zero benefit to acting like we're training for a marathon."

She sniffed. "If you really believe that, why do you keep doing it?"

"There are worse ways to spend a morning than jogging behind a pretty girl in tight shorts."

As Clea turned about thirteen shades of red and started to sputter, I held my straight face for as long as possible. That turned out to be around a heartbeat or two. "Dear God, you have got to work on your banter. The correct response was to call me an evolutionary defect and threaten me with a lawsuit for creating a hostile work environment. Or maybe throwing a shoe at me."

For a split-second, Clea looked stunned and then her eyes narrowed. "Are you saying I'm not attractive enough for the great Contingency Jones to notice?"

I gave her a little nod. "Much better."

"What's been with you lately?"

I raised an eyebrow at her. "What do you mean?"

"You've been preoccupied with something, which has made you even more taciturn."

"Has it?"

"It's like you're trying to elevate being laconic into an art form."

"Oh."

Clea waited for longer than necessary. "You're messing with me again, aren't you?"

"Little bit, yeah."

She looked up at the sky and then back at me. "Keep it up, funny guy. I know where you sleep."

"Much, much better." I decided to give Clea enough truth to keep her satisfied. "My mom died about fifteen years ago. She's been on my mind lately. Her and the things I never thought to ask her."

I neglected to add that I'd been worrying about the possibility that Clea was part of a conspiracy to undermine the entire purpose for which we were living in the past. I also neglected to add that I was weighing the possibility of changing history for my own benefit with, I believed, the permission of her grandfather, August Worth. The more I thought about what had happened, the less plausible I found it. If I was right, and Worth had certainly implied that I was, the man arranged to be abducted and transported through time. His purpose seemed to be to get a read on me.

Of course, I didn't believe for a second that a man like August Worth ever did anything for a single purpose. He was extraordinarily powerful and the man in charge of the entire program that supported me and the other Agents like me. He had also struck me as the kind of person that very little escaped. If there was a conspiracy to undermine the program, I sincerely doubted that Worth didn't know about it. If he did know about it, that left a lot of open questions.

Was he actively working against it? If so, his little jaunt into the past might have served a two-fold purpose. He could see if I was doing my job where his granddaughter was concerned, which he appeared satisfied with, but it also gave him a chance to decide if I was the kind of person that might fight against such a conspiracy. If he was part of it, though, his implicit offer to let me change the past could be a test or a means to establish blackmail. The most troubling possibility was that he honestly had no idea. If he didn't know, I had a moral and, arguably, legal obligation to tell him.

The big problem was that I wasn't sure that the conspiracy actually existed. J'adoube Green thought there was and I trusted J'adoube's judgment, but I hadn't heard anything from him since our little tete-a-tete in Tangier. I needed proof. Clea had failed to provide me anything solid to connect her to a conspiracy, but that was tricky ground. In the right context, traitorous behavior looked an awful lot like inexperienced decision making. The whole thing served as an ongoing source of lost sleep.

Clea stared at me. "Fifteen years ago? You couldn't have been more than, what, sixteen?"

"Something like that. My stepfather looked after me, in a way, until I joined up. By the way, that man truly has elevated being laconic into an art form. I learned it from him."

"Do you keep in touch?"

I rolled my shoulder. "We trade messages a few times a year. Hi. How's work? You going to be on the right continent for the holidays? That kind of thing. We get to together every few years for dinner."

"Sounds, kind of empty."

"It's convenient, is what it is. Think about all the lies I get to avoid. I honestly don't know how people with families can do this work."

Clea didn't say anything for a moment. "You do what you have to."

"Fair enough. Come on, there's three miles to go."

"Maybe I'll let you lead for a while." Clea directed a wicked grin at me and I wondered if I'd created a monster.

As we rounded the corner on our block, I saw a man in a black suit walking down the steps of our house. He was short and pear-shaped, but moved with unlikely grace. He paused by a sedan and turned to look straight at me. He raised a hand to the brim of the gray fedora perched on his head, almost in a salute, before he slid into the car. I didn't get a good look at the license plate before the sedan sped off.

We stopped in front of our house and Clea turned to me. "Who was that?"

"I have no earthly idea."

"Seemed like he knew you."

"I know, but I'd lay money that I've never set eyes on that man before today."

We turned and walked up to the house. There was an envelope taped to the door. Clea grabbed it and pulled it free. She looked down at it and her eyes narrowed. She lifted her eyes to meet mine and then handed me the envelope. Written across the envelope in neat cursive were two words: *Contingency Jones.*

2

"You're positive you don't know him?"

I ground my teeth. "For the fourth time, Clea, I am positive I do not know him."

"Then this is a pretty serious problem."

I reigned in a snarky comment. She wasn't wrong. "I know. I just don't know what to do about it, yet."

By rights, no one within fifty years in either direction should have known my name. I entertained the notion that the note represented some obscure means of communication on J'adoube's part, but rejected that out of hand. He wouldn't have risked a method of communication that Clea could so easily intercept. The other people who knew my actual name, not to mention when I was, could have communicated with me via the normal methods. The man in the gray fedora was either a new player or represented one.

Clea tapped her finger on the table. "Are you going to open it?"

"I'm still thinking about that."

Among its other features, the device possessed very sophisticated forensic analysis features. The device found the envelope and its contents to be innocuous, at least from a biological health point of view. There weren't any viruses, chemical agents or explosives hidden inside. That wasn't really a surprise. There are far simpler ways to kill someone, even me. What I did find distressing was that the device wasn't able to identify a manufacturer for the envelope and, despite all odds, there were no fingerprints. There were very few good explanations for that information gap.

I contemplated simply burning it without looking inside. The odds that the contents were something I wanted any part of seemed nil. It was my own curiosity that won out in the end. I picked up the envelope and tore it open. There was a single, folded sheet of paper inside. It was covered in neat, cursive handwriting.

Contingency Jones,

I regret that we can't meet in person at present, but there are events in motion that threaten us all. I suspect that you are already aware, in general or specific, of some of those events. Do not be lulled into a false sense of complacency or mistake it for idle speculation. It is fact of the most deadly kind.

There is another matter, however, that requires your immediate intervention. An agent provocateur is working to incite a mob war between the Westies and the Gambino crime family by orchestrating the assassination of James Coonan, circa September 21, 1978. If this ploy succeeds, it will ignite a bloody conflict that will result in the premature end of dozens of lives and send significant temporal shockwaves into the future. You understand the potentially catastrophic results of that outcome.

Sadly, I do not know the identity of the agent provocateur, nor the precise methodology he or she intends to employ, but I strongly suggest that you take immediate action to put a stop to his or her actions. If you wait to receive official word of the disturbance, you may arrive too late.

I hope you do not hesitate out of fear that this is some sort of elaborate trap or, worse still, the belief that this is a hoax. It is neither. My knowledge of your existence and your purpose should prove sufficient to allay any notions that this is some form of fraud. As to whether this is a trap, I can prove nothing. I can only hope that your instincts lead you to accept my words at face value and act on them.

If all goes well, we will meet soon enough and I will be at liberty to speak with you openly about all the many questions you must surely have.

Sincerely,

Your Friend

I handed the letter to Clea without comment and watched her expression. Her eyes scanned through the first paragraph and, if it triggered some form of guilt, there was no sign of it. She read through the entire letter twice and then set it down.

She frowned at the letter and then at me. "What do you think?"

"About what you'd expect. Trap or hoax."

"It seems like a lot of trouble to go through. If someone wanted to kill you, they could do it here and now. Sniper rifle, car bomb and about two dozen poisons I can think of off the top of my head."

The ease with which she rattled off the ways I could be killed sent a shiver down my spine and ratcheted up my paranoia another notch. "All true, but maybe the game is the point. I'm so clever that I can make you dance."

"Setting aside the obvious and glaring problem that someone knows who and what you, well, we are, let me play devil's advocate. What if it's exactly what it claims to be? What if this letter is for real?"

"That's the question that has me worried too."

Clea picked up the letter and read through it again, more slowly, and shook her head. "What is this business about events being in motion and not mistaking it for idle speculation? Do you have any clue what that's supposed to me."

"I have no clue. That's part of what makes it seem like a hoax to me and a paranoid one at that." I resisted the urge to check and see if my pants were aflame.

"Whatever this is, we need to report it to Command immediately."

"No."

Clea's eyes went huge. "What do you mean, no? Are you kidding me? We can't keep this to ourselves. Someone knows who we are, Contingency! I am not going to get trapped here because you find protocols inconvenient."

"It's not about that. Think about it. Let's say, for argument's sake, that we report this. What do you imagine happens then?"

"I don't know. We relocate to some other decade."

"Not even close. The two of us get pulled in for the longest, most excruciating, most anal probe-like debrief of our lives. They will put us under a microscope and make us recount every second of every minute of our lives since you arrived here, maybe even longer for me. Then, in a month or two, if we're lucky and they actually believe that neither of us exposed the program, they'll send us back here."

"Then what do you suggest we do?"

"We take a trip to see if what the letter says holds water."

Clea gave me a pensive frown. "What if it's a trap?"

"Then you run like hell and send a report."

"While you do what, exactly?"

I looked away. "While I buy you enough time to run."

She shook her head. "This is a bad idea, Contingency, for about a million reasons. Not the least of which is that you're treating your life like it's disposable."

"Clea, we are disposable. I know they don't ever spell that out during academy training, but it's a fact. Like it or not, though, I'm the senior Agent. That means it's also my job to keep you alive. If that means you get to walk away and I don't, then that is how it is. Now go get your gear."

3

Most of the time, I'd do almost anything to avoid New York City in the 1970's. It was gray, bleak and felt like death. The West Side of Manhattan was particularly ugly. Dock work was drying up and people were desperate. The resurgence of the 1980's and the gentrification that would follow were nothing more than fantasy in those days. Still, we went and it was as bad as I remembered it being.

I stepped out of the dingy bar with palpable relief. It had been a necessary, inevitable stop, but one I didn't relish. I'd made Clea wait in the car. She hadn't been happy about it, but she obeyed the order. I slid behind the wheel, fired up the engine and pulled away.

"So, why exactly did I have to wait in the car? Who were you talking to in there?"

"Ironically, the answer to both questions is James Coonan."

"Wait, you met with Coonan? Why?"

I let out a long breath. "Nothing goes down in this area without him knowing about it. If this is a trap or it's a real play against him, we're probably going to end up making some noise. I needed him to know we weren't here for him."

"I still don't see why I had to wait in the car."

"He's a murderer, Clea. Ice cold. He's also the kind of person who can smell fear and uncertainty. You're coming along, but you weren't ready for that. Plus, I didn't know how he'd react to you."

"I don't understand."

I winced. I'd hoped to avoid the conversation. "Your complexion, Clea. I don't know if he's a bigot."

Clea blinked in momentary confusion before the comment hit home. What followed was a hard to process combination of righteous fury and naked disgust. "You didn't take me in there because my skin is too dark."

"Take a breath, Clea. It's not about what I think. It was about what he might think."

She closed her eyes and took a shuddering breath as she pushed the anger down. Intellectually, I knew the historical causes and fallacies that drove racism. I found them incomprehensible as a person. It was utterly irrational and the actions carried out in the name of that so-called cause were enough to turn the stomach of any sane person. Yet, like it or not, it was a real problem in the Big Apple of the 1970's. I couldn't ignore that fact. Pretending it wasn't so could get Clea killed.

I offered an olive branch. "I'm sorry."

"Don't be an idiot. I know it's not you. We're just so insulated most of the time. I forget how it can be. Where are we going?"

"The waterfront. Coonan told me some odd things were happening down there at night."

"What kinds of odd things?"

"The usual. Weird lights and sounds, people seeing ghosts or thinking they're seeing ghosts, at any rate. It's a place to start."

Clea looked out the window for a moment before she directed a disgruntled look at me. "No offense, but don't you ever eat?"

"What?"

"It's bizarre. Once you're on task, it's like you lose complete touch with all things normal. I'm hungry. We should eat."

"Oh, right. I guess that's true."

I drove around aimlessly and slowly in the late afternoon traffic until we found a fast food joint. We ate our "food" in the parking lot out of creepy Styrofoam containers. Apparently, the environmental movement hadn't caught up with the food service industry in '78. Clea slurped the remains of her soda and then put the empty cup on the floor.

She turned to me. "I know I've already said this, but I think we're making a mistake."

I ground my teeth. "No, I'm making a mistake. If I'm wrong about this, I'll take the blame."

"I don't care about the blame. I don't want us getting killed because we got fed bad intelligence."

I stared at the steering wheel. "I don't either."

"Then why are we doing this?"

"I've seen what happens when history gets changed. We're temporal anomalies, so when we go home, we can see the changes. A friend of mine just ceased to exist. Wars appear out of nowhere. Kill the wrong person in the past and it can wipe out a million lives, in a second. Every time a big change like that happens, it strains reality."

"I know all of that."

I shook my head. "You know it, but it's gray matter knowledge. I know it in my bones. I'll chance being wrong to prevent that kind of damage."

"Does it ever bother you to play god like this?"

The paranoia that had been building in me for months swung into high gear. "What?"

"We're playing god with billions and billions of lives. I wonder if we have the right or the wisdom."

I thought hard for a second. I needed to play this just right. "I suppose it does bother me a little. I'll never be a candidate for wisest man alive. Still, do you have a better solution?"

Clea pressed her lips into a hard line. "No. It just seems like there ought to be."

"Listen, take it for what it's worth, but I wouldn't go repeating those thoughts to anyone but me."

Her eyebrows shot up. "Why?"

"It'd be pretty easy to interpret them as a prelude to betrayal. Bare minimum, it'd probably get you pulled out of the field. Just some friendly advice."

"You can't be serious."

"There isn't a lot of room for self-doubt and second-guessing in the field. If they think you'll hesitate or that you're not on board with the program, well, you'll find yourself fast tracked into a go nowhere admin position."

"Unbelievable. Seriously, Contingency, how have you lasted in this job for as long as you have?"

I gave her a wink. "People like me. Just can't seem to help themselves."

4

The docks were quieter than I expected. They weren't empty by any stretch of the imagination, but I'd dummied up some FBI badges for us. It never ceases to amaze me how many questions those badges prevent. It also helped that I made it clear we were there to look into the oddness. Everyone got real tight-lipped about that, but some gentle pressure sent us in the right direction.

After we were out of earshot, Clea asked me the question I'd been waiting for since we arrived. "Why didn't we use our Quirts to figure out if something out of the ordinary was going on down here?"

I waved a hand out at the water. "Something about all that moving water messes with the readings. This close to the water, we pretty much need to be right on top of something to pick it up. Hence, the legwork."

Apparently, Clea didn't believe me, because she pulled out her device and started keying in commands. Then, she shook the device. Then she hit it. "Come on you piece of junk, work."

"I told you. Supposedly the tech guys are working on a patch, but I think this is one of those things without a soluti…"

I stopped in my tracks. I felt the residue of powerful magic in the air, a kind of coldness and static electricity. Clea took a couple more steps before she realized I wasn't walking anymore.

"What's with you?"

"I don't know if the intelligence is bad or not, but someone called down some serious power near here."

Clea looked down at her device, shook it again, and then back up at me. "How can you tell?"

I drew my Smith & Wesson, Model 27 out of my work coat and flipped up my hood. "I can feel it."

Clea took her cue from me and pulled her own hood over her head before she drew a compact 9mm pistol from her coat. I'd insisted she get something with more stopping power after we walked into that office building to find half a dozen guys with machine guns.

Clea looked over at me, her face shadowed under the hood. "One of these days, Contingency, you're going to tell me how you got to be such an adept with the magic. No way you picked all this up from the training we got."

"Focus, Clea."

"You don't think it's relevant?"

"Right now, no."

I moved past her and did my best to block out the distractions. I held out my left hand and used it like a dousing rod, waving it back and forth until I could start to zero in on the origin point of the magic.

"What are you doing?" Clea demanded.

"Shhhh."

I closed my eyes until they were bare slits, opened just enough that I wouldn't walk headlong into something. I followed the sense of cold and static. It took a while and a few backtracks, but we finally found ourselves in front of a smallish, by dock standards, building. There weren't any lights on inside, which did nothing for my sense of well-being. If there were lights on, it would have meant there were janitors or some other kind of human life inside.

I glanced around, saw a door and walked over to it. Clea ghosted in my wake, silent as death. I regarded the plain knob with more than a little apprehension. It was a worst case scenario. There could be anything inside. I heard a zipper and looked back at Clea. She had a small black case in her hand. I saw small tools inside the case that had only one purpose.

"What are you doing, Clea?"

"I'm going to pick the lock."

"Don't bother." I reached out and twisted the knob. The door swung open.

"How did you know?"

I shrugged. "Instinct. I think we're expected."

"We should go. This is obviously a trap."

"If it is, we're already inside it. Turning back now might be worse than just moving forward."

Clea started to object again, but I walked into the building. Confronted with the choice of following me or waiting outside, Clea opted to stick close. In my heart of hearts, I knew she was probably right that we should fall back. Still, someone had gone to a lot of trouble to get my attention and bring me here. I wanted to know who it was, and I wanted to know why. There were far too many people taking far too much interest in me.

I pushed deeper into the darkness and, once my eyes adjusted, saw it was a basic office. Desks were arranged into a grid-esque pattern. I shivered and then held out an arm to stop Clea.

"Whatever happened, it happened here."

"Quite right, Jones," said a voice that emanated from everywhere and nowhere. "You really did miss your calling. Ah well, too late to change your mind now."

Clea spoke in a tight voice, "Who was that?"

I closed my eyes. It was a trap. "Not a who, Clea. A what."

"Jones, I'm wounded. I most certainly am a who."

I was already tired of the smoke and mirrors. "Show yourself."

"And why would I do that?"

"I won't ask again. Show yourself or I'll make you do it."

I felt Clea move closer to me. "What's happening?"

"Later," I whispered.

"Oh, the great Contingency Jones thinks his parlor tricks are enough to compel me. So be it, mortal, compel me."

I hadn't expected it to call my bluff, but there was no other way. I held my hands out to either side, palms facing toward the room. All I needed was my own cross to complete the picture. "Servant of darkness, denizen of the shadows, wanderer of the forsaken places, I compel and command thee, come forth. By the ancient compacts and the laws of the First, by the sacred rites and the blood that fell to the cup, in the names of the wounded ones, I command thee to come forth."

I felt it rising in me, the fever of gathering power and the sure knowledge that the commitment was made. I would either succeed or die.

"Terrible thing that knows no love and fears the light, fallen from the path, fallen from the world, fallen from the embrace of the First, I command thee to come forth. By power of the silent guardians, I ward the living from your power and bind you to my will."

In some distant corner of my mind, I noted that wind was howling through the office, whipping paperwork in every direction. While light spilled from my hands and illuminated every square inch of the room.

"In the name of the Lords of Order, I command and compel thee, come forth!"

There was a scream of pure, unadulterated agony that should have cut straight through my nervous system, but it broke against me like the waves against the cliffs. It appeared before us, not three feet away. In other circumstances, I might have felt some shred of pity for the malformed thing. It was huge. Had it been able to stand upright, it would have towered over us, but its body was a hunched, twisted parody of a human being. It threw itself at me, broken claws at the ready. Light flashed from my hands and it screamed again.

It tried to scramble away and hide its face from the light that continued to pour off my hands.

I was still lost in the fever of the magic and spoke without understanding why. "You demanded it. So it is done. You are compelled!"

I heard Clea behind me. "Oh my god."

I directed my words to the misshapen thing. "We will speak. Speak quickly and I will allow you to escape back into your precious darkness."

The thing pushed itself back another foot away from my hands. "Ask. Ask!"

"Who sent you?"

"I was summoned by the Red Cord."

"What is the Red Cord?"

"Time travelers, sorcerers, men and women like you."

I felt a spike of fury. "They aren't like me! I don't summon demons!"

The light from my hands flared and the thing howled in pain.

Clea grabbed my arm. "Contingency, for God's sake!"

I glared at her. She looked terrified, but she didn't back off. I ground my teeth and pushed the fury away. I looked back at the thing. "Why did they send you?"

"To start a war between the criminal factions."

"Why?"

Its skin was starting to blister and crack in the light. "I don't know."

"Why involve me?"

"I don't know," it wailed. Smoke began to pour off of it.

I had a sense that if I didn't let it go soon, it might actually die. It was tempting. If I asked, it would no doubt tell me how many souls it corrupted and lives it ruined. Clea saved the miserable thing in the end.

"Contingency, send it back where it came from or kill it. This is beyond cruel."

I spared a glance for her. She looked like she was ready to vomit. I closed my eyes and lowered my hands. "Return from whence you came and remain there, without reprieve or parole, until the end of all things. I command this in the name of the Lords of Order."

The thing vanished and the light that poured so blindingly from my hands flickered and winked out. For a moment, I was rendered blind. Maybe that was best, though, since Clea picked that moment to puke.

5

I helped Clea outside. Her eyes were wide, frightened, still seeing the foul thing.

"Jesus, Contingency, that was a demon."

"Yes, it was."

"A fully fledged, straight from the freaking Pit, demon."

"Yes, Clea, I was there. I saw it."

"A consume your soul, cursed in the eyes of God…"

I sighed. It was always like this the first time people saw a demon. I grabbed her arm and shook her a little. "Clea! Get a grip!"

She snapped out of the litany of descriptions and turned a wary eye on me. "That wasn't just a demon, was it?"

I shook my head.

"An arch-demon, then. One of the original fallen angels. You *compelled* an arch-demon! Mind telling me how long you've known you could do that."

"About five minutes, but you're missing the point."

"Oh, am I? You pulling off a stunt that maybe five damn people in all of recorded history have done is missing the point. Then do tell, what is the point?"

I gave her a steady look. "Red Cord. Somebody out there is actively messing with history and now we have a name for them. That is the point."

Clea just stared at me for a long moment. "Arch. Demon."

I sighed. It was going to be a long night.

Episode 6 - Checks and Balances

1

I gave Clea my sternest expression. "What are the rules while I'm gone?"

"Do not engage the bad guys in direct conflict and, if something happens, contact you immediately."

"And if nothing happens?"

"Contact you in twelve hours with some imaginary crisis that requires your immediate return."

"Good."

Clea fixed me with a stern look of her own. "What are your rules while you're gone?"

I rolled my eyes. "No unnecessary aggravation of authority figures."

She raised an eyebrow at me. "And?"

"Don't make anyone cry. Why do you care, anyways?"

"Because, for all your aggravating qualities, I suspect I'm learning a lot more from you about actually surviving this job than I would from anyone else. Call it self-interest on my part."

I nodded. She was probably right. "Fair enough."

"You're really going to wear that? At least take that ridiculous thing off your head."

"Not a chance. If I can't make anyone cry, then I get to wear this."

Clea sighed. "Fair enough."

"Twelve hours," I repeated.

"Yes, Contingency, for the fiftieth time, I'll give you an excuse."

I glanced to the mouth of the alley and pressed my device against the right brick in the wall. There was a longer than usual pause as the device connected with Command's mainframe, hundreds of years in the future, and then I was pulled into the ley lines. I felt the familiar loss of linear time and overwhelming sense that I was everywhen and nowhen. Reality crystallized around me and, after a few moments of disorientation, I looked around. A technician stared at me, mouth hanging open, and I smiled on the inside.

A slightly more disciplined man that I vaguely recognized shook his head. "Jones?"

I gave the man a surly look. I hated annual reviews. "Reporting, as ordered."

"Follow me."

I stepped off the platform and followed the man out of what was probably one of the most secure rooms in the world. We stepped into a sparsely populated hall and I stopped short. I shook my head and tried to readjust on the fly. I'd been in the past too long. The casual nudity of my own time now seemed somehow foreign and even a little libertine. I trailed after the man and tried to remember his name. Laurence, Lenny…

"Lester?"

He gave me a surprised look. "I'm shocked you remember me."

I shrugged. "I remember you were smart, seemed like an up and comer. You piss someone off?"

"Sir?"

"I can't imagine retrieving me is some kind of honor. Any lackey could do it."

"Ah. No, I didn't piss anyone off. She wanted me to make sure you got there promptly."

I nodded. Of course *she* did. Why wouldn't *she*? Getting me in and out as fast as possible would make *her* life a lot easier. I shook off another wave of disorientation. There were no straight lines in sight. The hallway was all smooth organic curves. It made me feel like I was on the verge of tipping over at any moment. We passed by a number of classrooms where bright, shiny trainees sat in rapt attention as complete morons supposedly bestowed invaluable knowledge and wisdom. We passed a large open gym where hand-to-hand combat training was, at least in theory, being taught. I don't know exactly when the decision was made, but by the time my brain caught up with my actions, I was inside the gym, stripping off my work coat and removing the object of Clea's disdain from my head.

I heard my own voice. "No, no, no! What the hell is wrong with you? Are you trying to get these kids killed someday?"

The instructor, Fleming, was someone I remembered. I hadn't liked her much back during my training. I liked her even less once I got into the field and realized how piss-poor her training had actually been. The feeling was apparently mutual, given the look of utter hatred that crossed her face.

She snarled. "Jones, this is none of your concern."

"Like hell it isn't. My life might depend on one of these sorry sacks one day."

"I'll pit any of my students against you."

"Pick four."

I heard a garbled noise and glanced over my shoulder. Lester stood there and I saw the realization on his face that *she* would hear about this. He had probably been ordered to make sure I didn't do something exactly like what I was doing. I gave him a big, cheery smile and threw him a double thumbs up. He looked a little green, but he wasn't crying. Fleming picked out her four favorites and they formed a loose ring around me. The rest of the class was clustered off to one side, looking both confused and a little excited.

I pointed at them. "And now, for your viewing pleasure, competence."

2

Fleming's favorites were sprawled on the floor around me, rubbing bruised jaws, aching ribs and sore joints. The rest of the students stared at the spectacle. Most of them seemed a bit overwhelmed. It had happened fast. I glared at Fleming.

She stared back in utter shock. "Where did you learn that?"

"Brazil, 2130, during the Capoeira Uprising. Korea, 1895. Beijing, 1900. So help me God, Fleming, if I find out one of these kids dies because you couldn't be bothered to learn your craft, I will come for you."

I put my discarded attire back on and headed for the hall. Lester fell into step beside me.

He gave me a pained look. "Was that necessary?"

"That woman is incompetent. She should have been fired years ago. I can't control that, but at least those kids will have some sliver of understanding of what they might come up against."

"Is what you said true, about being at the Capoeira Uprising."

"Yeah. I wish it wasn't."

"What was it like?"

I glanced at him. He looked genuinely curious. "It was bloody, Lester. A bloody, ugly mess that didn't need to happen."

Lester frowned, but didn't press the issue. He led me into the administration wing and I was immediately cheered up by the collective response to my clothing. Clea had lobbied hard against it, but I opted to wear a pair of scuffed combat boots, jeans that were torn and bloodstained, a t-shirt with the phrase "I'm the Bad Thing That Happens to People" emblazoned across the chest, and a pair of mirrored aviator sunglasses. With the addition of the absurdity perched on my head, I drew stares and gasps. What passed for fashion in the future reminded me of the scrubs that doctors and nurses wore back in the day. I became much less cheered when I noticed all of the extra personnel wandering the halls. J'adoube was right. They were civilians everywhere. Worse still, they all had an air of secrecy and lies that blanketed them like fog. I pushed it aside. My immediate problem had to take precedence. I blinked when Lester took me straight past the debriefing rooms where Agents were given their annual performance reviews.

"Lester, I think we missed my stop."

"Change of plans, at least for you."

I felt a tremor in the pit of my stomach and slid my hand into the pocket of my work coat. I was reassured by the presence of my Smith & Wesson, Model 27. It was beyond archaic, a museum piece really, in the halls I walked. Halls built with a combination of magic and technology so complex that it might as well have all been magic. Still, surrounded by futuristic technology or not, the revolver would kill just fine. Lester waved off a few busybodies and took me straight into the lion's den. He paused outside a door and gently knocked. From inside the office, I heard *her* voice.

"Bring him in."

Lester opened the door and I followed him into the office of Captain Marguerite Kane, my boss and all around pain in my ass. She was faced away from us, talking into screen I couldn't see. No doubt, she was putting out some bureaucratic brushfire that meant absolutely nothing in the big picture, but seemed all too important to the bureaucrats who create them. Kane talked for another minute or so before the screen went dark. Lester gently cleared his throat. She turned her chair to face us and gave Lester a dismissive wave of the hand.

I eyed Kane. I hadn't been this close to her in half a decade. In a lot of ways, she was nothing more than a name on orders to me. I was surprised by what I saw. She was only a few years older than me. That had seemed like an infinite gap in the long ago days of my own training, but no more. She graduated from the academy and went into the field around the time I was finishing my first year. Somewhere along the line, she got dropped into the Command track. She looked tired, but what my animal brain was screaming at me was that this woman was *attractive*. It wasn't a vague, fashion model attractiveness, but something subtler, an air of confidence and competence and of raw vitality. She finally looked at me and blinked.

She pointed at my head. "What is that?"

"It's a fez. I saw it on a TV show. The lead character said they were cool."

"That character lied."

I smiled and took the fez off. I placed it with great care on her desk. "Technically, it's 700 years old, give or take. I think that makes it a priceless relic."

"Take those sunglasses off. For God's sake, why are you dressed like that?"

"I thought it'd put whoever was doing my review off their stride."

Kane closed her eyes, appeared to count backwards for a while, and then pointed at a chair. "Sit and take off those sunglasses."

I slouched in the chair and took off the sunglasses. "By the way, why am I here? Shouldn't I be in a white room being questioned by some idiot?"

"I'll be conducting your review, Jones."

I sat up in my chair. That wasn't protocol. She looked at little self-satisfied at my momentary surprise.

"Might I ask why you're conducting it?"

"Orders, from the top. The very top, Jones."

It seemed that August Worth was taking an active interest in me. That created some mixed feelings. That kind of attention cut in both good and bad directions.

Kane gave me a knowing smile over the desk. "I'm glad to see the implications aren't lost on you. You've just become political."

I stood up and walked over to her window. It looked out over the entire complex. In many ways, Kane was responsible for the lives of everyone inside it. Some part of me made idle note of the bodies moving back and forth on the ground several stories below, but most of my thoughts were on how to escape the new grenade Kane had lobbed at me.

I didn't look at her when I spoke. "I'm not political. You know that."

"When August Worth comes to my office, in person, to tell me that I'm to conduct your review, you're political. More to the point, everyone knows it now, too. You're his anointed one."

"That man just painted a target on the back of my head."

Kane let that hang in the air for a moment. "Speaking of the back of your head, I'm tired of looking at it. Please, sit down."

I shrugged out of my coat, draped it over the back of the chair and sat down. Kane was watching me. Then it hit me. She wasn't watching me, she was checking me out. That animal brain reiterated to me that she was *attractive*. We sat there, looking at each other while the charge in the air built to an uncomfortable level. I looked away first.

"So, there is something we need to discuss. There are some discrepancies between your reports and Clea's."

I shifted gears with a head shake. "Oh?"

"Your little day trip to New York City, for example. Your report reads as follows: Stopped aberrant mob war."

I nodded. "That's about the size of it."

"Jones, given the particular role you play in this organization, I usually find your lack of details a relief. However, the term arch-demon played a prominent role in Clea's report. According to her, you managed to compel one. Is that true?"

"Yes, I suppose that is accurate."

"You didn't feel that merited a mention."

I worked to suppress a smirk. I failed. "I did not."

"Do you care to explain why?"

"Frankly, I didn't feel like getting sucked into trying to explain to those tools over in Magical Practices how I did it."

Kane frowned at me with a thoughtful expression. "How often do you leave things of that magnitude out of your reports?"

I gave her a flat look. "On the record, once."

"Off the record?"

"It happens."

"Jones, I get why you'd do that, but other Agents could learn from you."

I shook my head. "No, they couldn't. It's not the kind of thing you can teach, at least not what I do. It's part experience, part intuition and part aptitude. I can't train people to have aptitude or intuition. I damn sure can't teach them the kind of judgment you only get through long practice."

"So you've decided for everyone? What gives you that right?"

"I haven't decided for everyone. I decided for me! What gives you the right to demand that I try to teach people things could cost them their souls?"

"How self-righteous are you to think that only you know what's best, Contingency Jones!"

The door to the office swung open and Lester stepped inside. "Captain Kane, is everything…"

Somewhere along the way Kane and I had both stood and started yelling at each other across her desk. In unison, we looked at Lester and yelled. "Get out!"

3

For a second, I thought Lester might actually cry, but he wisely slunk out of the office without another word. I turned to face Kane again and wondered if the yelling would continue. She just stared at me, blank-faced for a second, and then she snickered. That set me off and we spent a couple minutes trying to not laugh.

She sat back down and shook her head. "Poor Lester."

"Bet that he doesn't do that again."

"At least not when you're in the room. The point still stands, Jones. You're holding back knowledge that could help all of us."

"Some knowledge isn't meant to be public. You, of all people, must realize that. Look at the secrecy we work in. When it comes to higher order magic, if you can't get there on your own, you shouldn't know it. Even then, it isn't always safe."

"Yet, you felt it was safe enough for Clea to know?"

"Clea has an unusually accurate awareness of her own limits. I doubt she'd ever even attempt something like what I did. Not anytime soon, anyways. More to the point, I bet she gave a full accounting in her report."

"She did."

"An accounting I'm sure you passed along to the boys over in Magical Practices."

"Also correct."

"How far did they get with it?"

"They couldn't make heads or tails of it."

I raised my hands in a there-you-go gesture. "I rest my case. If they couldn't do it with the information Clea provided, then they aren't ready."

"I don't get you, Jones."

"How's that?"

"Every year, you come in for your reviews and it's like pulling teeth from a chicken. Why are you being so chatty with me?"

"For the same reason Worth told you to do my review. You've been in the field. You understand how fast things can happen, how split-second the decisions are. You might not agree with all of mine, but I'd bet you can guess how I came to make them. I refuse to justify myself to some bureaucrat that's never had to make a choice with billions of lives hanging in the balance."

"We're overpaying our psychologists."

"Sorry?"

She rolled her eyes. "They really don't understand you at all. You should read your psych evaluations some time."

"I'm sure they're entertainingly wrong. I went to a lot of trouble to make sure they would be."

"Most people don't have the skill to game those evaluations. It makes me think I should be worried."

"I only game the parts that don't matter."

"How can I know that's true? I've only got your word on that."

I smiled. "I'm super trustworthy. I promise."

She smiled. "Red Cord."

Lying becomes second nature in the field. It's a survival skill. If you can't learn to control your body language, learn to sell the words with the behavior, you're useless. I sold it. I gave the obligatory furrowed eyebrows, cocked head and confusion.

"What's that?"

Kane pulled a gun that looked a lot like mine out of her desk and pointed it at me. "You're a frighteningly efficient liar."

I sat very still. "Okay?"

Kane circled around her desk and made her way to the door. She locked it. The barrel never wavered.

"Look," I said. "I know I'm not your favorite person, but all of this seems a little dramatic, don't you think?"

"I don't take treason lightly."

I'm used to thin ice. Hell, I practically live on thin ice, but the ice was thinner than I liked. Either she legitimately thought I was a traitor, in which case she might actually shoot me. Or, it was a bluff to see if she'd been exposed in some fashion. There was no way to know for sure, no test to employ. That's the problem with people. You can never really know. All I had to go on was my instincts about her. Instincts based on a ten minute conversation. If push came to shove, I could take the gun from her without moving from the chair. I just didn't know if I could do it before she got a shot off. My gut told me she was on the level, but I'd been wrong before. Everyone thought Endgame Smith was on the level, right up until he wasn't.

I rolled the dice. "I don't know much. Based on what I've gleaned, they're an organization. They have access to time travel, which means they're inside this unit or were at some point. They're executing a mission of some kind, messing around with history, but God knows why. Incidentally, that's what my day trip to New York City stopped. Unless I'm very, very far off, all those new faces out there are working, maybe directly, maybe unwittingly, for Red Cord."

"What else, Jones?"

"What do you mean, what else? I only heard that name for the first time a few weeks ago."

"I don't believe you."

I looked at her and shook my head. "I don't really care what you believe. For all I know, you're Red Cord. I told you what I know. So either shoot me and get it over with, or put that gun away."

4

Kane stood there for what felt like a very long time, just pointing the gun at me. I started prepping myself to do one of those seemingly impossible things I always left out of my reports. Then, she lowered the gun.

I took a deep breath. "So, how close a call was it?"

"Very damn."

"Thought so. What made it go my way?"

It was Kane's turn to give me an uncertain look. I had a feeling she wasn't as good a liar as I am.

She walked around her desk, sat down and put the gun away. "I've been at this even longer than you have Jones. I read your reports, what they say and the things they don't say. I can read between the lines a little. I also hear the stories about you."

"You can't put too much stock in rumors."

"There are stories and then there are *stories*. I'm talking about the ones the field Agents tell when they think no one is listening."

I wasn't sure how much I liked that idea. "What kinds of tales do they tell?"

"The kind that paint you as a madman, or a idiot, and always in a tone of hushed awe."

"We all exaggerate. I'm nothing special."

"You really don't get it, do you? You get called in when everything, *everything*, has gone to hell. They talk about it. They talk about you walking into some nightmare scenario and, when the dust settles, the problem is solved. Then you're gone. No post-game analysis, no after-crisis drink with the boys. The fact of the matter is that you scare the hell out of people."

"How did that work in my favor?"

"If you wanted to betray us, all you had to do was be less competent. You've had plenty of opportunities."

"That's it?"

"Well, that and the fact that I'm still alive."

I blinked at her. "Come again?"

"You compelled an arch-demon. You killed Archan, once and for all. If you could do that, I suspect you could have killed me without breaking a sweat."

"Now you really are exaggerating. I'd have given me even odds at best."

She gave me a little shrug. "Either way, I'm choosing to believe you, because I have to believe someone."

"So it's real then. A rogue organization really is mucking with history."

Kane closed her eyes and shuddered. Something peeked through her expression, a look of absolute exhaustion and fear. She nodded. "You had doubts."

"Hey, I got my information from a demon. You have to take that shit with a grain of salt. So you know what I know. What do you know?"

"Frustratingly little. I don't really know any more than you do. Of course, I've been working with shackles on. It's hard to investigate when you can't trust anyone."

"What about our illustrious leader, August Worth?"

She raised an eyebrow at me. "Did you report your suspicions to him?"

"Um, no, but I'm renowned for my utter contempt and distrust for authority figures. Plus, I didn't know who to trust, either."

"What about Clea? Can she be trusted?"

A dark, tangled knot of uncertainties pulled tight in my stomach. "I wish I knew. I want to trust her. In some situations, I have to trust her. Her actual allegiances, though, who can tell? She's said some things that give me pause."

"Such as?"

"Questions about the mission and our moral authority in carrying it out."

"Maybe I should pull her from the field."

"Don't. It'd be like setting yourself on fire. She's Worth's granddaughter."

Kane's mouth dropped open. "What? How the hell did that get missed in her background check?"

"I strongly suspect that Worth arranged for it to be missed. He's got the juice to delete that kind of information from every database in the world."

"Why would he do that?"

I shook my head. "I've got about 14 hypotheses on that, some of them are benign and some aren't. He's in a dangerous line of work. It might have been a protective measure to keep his family safe. Or…"

"Or, he might be running an agenda. Maybe he's using her to try to ferret out Red Cord."

"Or, he might be in charge of Red Cord."

"Or, he might be in the dark about it. This is a mess, Jones."

"Welcome to my world."

"What's your first instinct about Clea? Is she a mole?"

I let the question rest on the surface on my mind for a moment. My first instinct? "If she's there as part of an agenda, I don't think she's aware of it. Or she's a much better liar than I am, which is entirely possible."

"That's an unsettling thought."

"It's more unsettling for me. I sleep all of twenty feet from her."

"Fair point. I'd probably be drinking myself to sleep every night in your situation."

"Short-term solution to a long-term problem. Besides, she's got me on this cardio routine that would kill a gazelle. Can't do that and drink all the time."

Kane rubbed at her eyes. "I could use a drink right now. Want one?"

I gave her a half-smile. "I don't usually date in the workplace, but ask me when this is all over. I'll insist on dinner, as well."

I watched the gears come to a crashing halt in Kane's head as she tried to process both the topic change and the offer.

She gave me an uncomplicated smile that lit up her face. "I think dinner is entirely possible."

"Assuming we survive."

She sighed. "Yes, assuming we survive. So, the question becomes, what is our next step?"

5

"You're the Captain. I just follow orders."

"As if."

"My first step is to ask what the deal is with all the extra, civilian personnel out there." I hiked a thumb toward the door.

"Officially, it's civilian oversight. The Chancellor is of the opinion that what we're doing here is too dangerous to continue without it."

"To hell with operational security?"

"So it seems."

"You said officially. What about unofficially?"

"No one knows," said Kane. "Or, they aren't talking about it if they do know. That set off some warning bells for me."

"You're the political one, so I'll trust you on that. Anything we do needs to stay off their radar. What about the other field Agents? Any we can trust?"

"It's hard to know. They're insulated, in some respects, so they're less likely to be compromised. Then again, they're isolated, which makes them easier to get at if Red Cord has access to time travel. At the moment, I'm not ready to trust them. What about you? Anyone you'd be willing to vouch for?"

I shook my head. I believed, to my bones, that J'adoube could be trusted, but I wasn't about to out him to Kane without a conversation first. "Like you said, we're isolated. I almost never cross paths with other Agents unless you send me. Plus, after Endgame, well, I'm not terribly popular in the ranks. I'm pretty sure half of them believe I made the whole thing up."

"Everyone did, at first. It was hard to swallow."

I nodded. "I think my strategy would be to watch, gather intelligence, and try to get a read on the other field Agents. I might have a lead on something, but it could turn out to be shadows and fairy dust."

"You don't trust the source?"

"I don't trust anything right now."

"I've got some favors I can call in. I might be able to gather some information if I come at it from an oblique angle."

I lifted an eyebrow. "Oblique angle?"

"You *really* aren't political. You ask for information that covers a wide enough spectrum that it'll show what you want, without making it obvious what you're after. If the data set is big enough, it doesn't alarm the wrong people."

"Sounds complicated."

"More complicated that compelling an arch demon?"

"Profoundly."

"Sooner or later, we'll need to get a solid read on Worth and Clea. If they're not part of it, we'll need them. If they are, we'll need to deal with it."

I nodded and tried to ignore the sour taste in my mouth. I knew Kane was right. I'd already drawn a similar conclusion. I just didn't relish the idea of putting a bullet in Clea's brain.

Episode 7 - Small Mercies

1

I stood in the doorway and tried to make sense of what I saw. An old woman was in the bed, the covers thrown aside in some kind of fit. Her white hair was a tangled mess, and her face trapped in a rictus of pain or fear. Her graying pallor and the unpleasant odor of piss and shit told me she was dead. Clea stood next to the bed, swaying back and forth, muttering something I couldn't make out. An empty pill bottle sat on the floor, resting against the toe of Clea's boot. I stepped into the room and stopped, not sure what to do.

I took a few more steps and then stopped again. "Clea?"

Her head turned fractionally in my direction and her low muttering picked up in pace, if not volume.

"Clea, what happened?"

She looked in my direction, her eyes unfocused, and finally said something I could understand. "I murdered her."

I took a second to digest that while I looked from Clea to the pill bottle and then the old woman's body. The math was easy enough to do. Clea got there and force fed the old woman the pills. Problem solved. Only, the emotional math didn't add up. I'd seen Clea kill before and watched the fallout. While I still didn't entirely trust her, I didn't have Clea pegged as a cold blooded murderer. It takes a sociopath to dump a bottle of pills down someone's throat, make them swallow, and then hang around to watch.

Then again, the old woman *was* dead. Clea *was* standing over her body. If I was a cop, I'd take her into custody. I rubbed at the stab of pain that materialized in my left temple and wondered if all the other Agents had this much trouble with their trainees. I doubted it. Then again, all the other Agents weren't saddled with August Worth's granddaughter. There was nothing like a little potential career suicide and unspeakable vengeance to make a training officer go the extra mile. I glanced out the window. It was pitch black outside, except for the occasional flash of lighting that left an odd afterglow across my vision. We had time.

"Walk me through this, Clea. Tell me exactly what happened in this room."

"I told you. I murdered her."

I checked an annoyed noise and tried not to think about how my day off had been ruined by all of this.

2

(6 hours earlier)

I sat on the bench and, for once, thought about nothing. I just let the scene in front of me unfold, however it wanted, with no intervention on my part. Kids kicked a ball around in some kind of game I was sure they were making up as they went. There certainly didn't seem to be any hard and fast rules, except that whoever controlled the ball, controlled the microcosm of the park. Sort of like that old novel, *Dune*, but with lower stakes and fewer freaky eyes.

I glanced around and saw an ice cream truck. A young mother forked over some cash and the old guy in the truck passed her a small ice cream cone. She held the cone out to a little boy that was maybe three years old. He wore a bright yellow shirt and well-loved, not to mention very grass stained, overalls. The little boy took all of one lick off the cone before a passing pickup truck backfired. The little boy jumped and dropped the cone. I saw the dawning horror on his face before he started wailing. The mother tried to console the kid, to no avail. He just pointed at the cone on the sidewalk and cried even harder. This went on for a minute or so before the old guy in the truck pushed another cone out the side window. The mom saw the cone and stood up. I invented a conversation in my head.

She shook her head, aware that she didn't have any more spare cash. "No, I'm sorry, I can't."

The little boy was jumping up and down, pointing at the cone. "Eyescrean! Eyescrean!"

The ice cream man shook his head. "Don't worry about it. Kid shouldn't suffer 'cause some guy isn't taking care of his truck."

The mom looked down at the boy, who seemed to understand that the ice cream was no longer a certainty. He looked up at her with wide, pleading, little boy eyes. The mom folded.

"If you're sure," she said to Ice Cream Hero.

"I am."

The mom took the cone and handed it down to the boy. "You keep hold of this one."

The boy nodded enthusiastically, and nearly crushed the cone in a death grip, determined not to lose that one. Ice Cream Hero smiled, a little wistfully, as the mom and boy walked off together. I made my way over to the truck. Ice Cream Hero gave me a little nod.

"What can I get you, sir?"

"Ice cream sandwich."

He dug around for a second and came up with a plump rectangle covered in white paper. He passed it over to me. I handed him a ten, and he handed the change back. I dumped it all in the tip jar.

"Thanks! Not that I'm complaining, but what's that for?"

I pointed toward the mom and little boy. "It's for being a stand up guy."

I unwrapped the ice cream sandwich and took a bite. The chocolate cookie resisted momentarily, but ultimately succumbed to the irresistible force of my hunger. Clea would probably have had kittens if she knew that I was having ice cream at my "advanced age," but it was my day off. Something I only did about once every six months. I'd have ice cream if I bloody well pleased, and I bloody well pleased. I held the ice cream sandwich up to the Ice Cream Hero in a little salute and wandered away.

3

"Clea, pretend for a second that I'm your training officer and that I've got to write this up in a report. Pretend I need the details. Better yet, don't pretend and just start at what happened when you got to that door."

Clea shuddered and seemed to pull herself together a little bit. "God, it was such a mess, I couldn't tell what was real and what wasn't. I almost fell through the hole in the stairs."

"Yeah, me too."

I saw it on her face, the struggle to separate what had been real from the psychic projections. There was a lot of that in my near future, as well. She shook her head back and forth in a slow arc. She didn't want to remember.

"Please don't make me," she whispered.

I almost let it go. Something deep down told me that, if I did, it would be irrevocable and Clea would suffer for it.

"Take your time."

She bit her lip hard enough that I winced a little.

"I got to the top of the stairs. There were, I mean, I thought there were snakes everywhere. God, I hate snakes." She rubbed her arms, as if she was cold. "I stepped around them. Then, I opened the door. There was blood everywhere. She was floating in mid air. At least, I thought she was. Her hands, God, Contingency, she had human hearts in her hands. They were still beating and the blood was just…it was just…"

She took a couple of short, shuddering breaths through clenched teeth. I looked around the room. There was no blood anywhere. It had been an illusion, but so had everything else. I'd opened fire on lamp post that I thought was a crazed man with a machete. It had been insanity. Not mine and not Clea's, but that didn't make it feel any less real. Clea stared at something in her memory, her lips moving a little, slipping back into something that had never been, or maybe it had, but not the way she remembered it.

"Clea, what happened then?"

"Blood was spurting from the hearts. She was laughing, like a little girl, like it was all some kind of a game. She was laughing about it. I just stood there. I didn't know what to do. She had hearts in her hands and she was laughing. Who does that? Who does something like that and laughs about it?"

She fell silent again and I walked over to her. I reached out a hand and tried to put it on her shoulder. She slapped my hand away with a scream. Her eyes were wide and her lips drew back into a near-feral snarl. "Don't touch me. Don't you dare touch me!"

"Clea!"

"I see you Contingency Jones. I see what you've done. I see what you are!"

I shrank back from her. I didn't know what to do or think about that. "What are you talking about?"

"You think I don't know. You think I'm stupid. You think I don't see that you're biding your time. Watching me from the corner of your eye. Waiting for the right moment! I can smell the secrets and lies on you. Do you think I don't know what you're going to do?"

"What do you think I'm going to do?"

"It's written all over you. You're going to kill me. Sooner or later, you're going to kill me to protect your plans. You think you're so clever, with your secret meetings and your rendezvous and your coded messages. I know the truth!"

The hysteria in her voice was real. She thought she knew something about me, or my supposed plans, and maybe there even was a kernel of truth buried deep down inside of her paranoia. That didn't mean it was safe or sane to even hint at that.

"I'm not going to kill you, Clea. What possible reason could I have to do that?"

"You're a traitor. I can't prove it, but you are. So, why don't you just get it out of the way now? Go on, do it. Do it!"

"I'm not going to hurt you."

Clea pulled her 9mm and pointed it at my face. "I'm tired of waiting. I'm tired of being afraid of you!"

She clicked off the safety and, hysteria or no, the gun was steady in her hands. I raised my hands very slowly and took a step back. "Clea, you've got no reason to be afraid of me. You must know that."

She laughed then. It was a hollow, empty, inhuman parody of what a laugh should have been and it broke my heart.

"No reason? I've got no reason to be afraid of you? You summoned a damned angel. You compelled an arch-demon. You single-handedly laid waste to a half-dozen machine gun toting mercenaries. Only a moron wouldn't be afraid of you!"

I was loath to admit it, but she had a point.

4

(4 hours earlier)

I stood in front of the zoo exhibit and eyed a bird called a Bali Mynah. It was snow white, save for a touch of black at the tips of its wings and tail. A startling ring of leathery blue skin around its eyes that gave the bird a reptilian cast that unsettled me. There was no evidence that my intense scrutiny unsettled the bird. It chirped at other Mynahs from time to time and, eventually flew to the far side of the exhibit. I frowned after it and moved on.

I had mixed feelings about zoos. I knew that many participated in captive breeding programs that helped to preserve endangered species. The cages bothered me. Oh they called them exhibits and enclosures and other euphemisms, but I know a cage when I see one. There were zoos in my time, but they weren't like the zoos of the twenty-first century. In my time, the zoos were tightly controlled scientific facilities that the general public couldn't enter without nine kinds of special permissions. Those zoos were more like a combination of wildlife sanctuaries, ecological microcosms and state-of-the-art hospitals set on several square miles of land.

I wandered from exhibit to exhibit, rarely pausing for more than a moment. It was enough to simply be and see, to feel the telltale presence of the animals, and the obvious enthusiasm of most of the people there. It was real life, instead of the half-thing I lived. It reminded me why I stuck with the job, despite the costs and recent exposure of what seemed to be a full-on conspiracy.

The soccer mom being dragged from snake enclosure to snake enclosure didn't care about demons and necromancers. She just wanted her kid to do well in school, even if that meant enduring hours on end by all those creepy snakes. The young couple who were holding hands by the giraffe exhibit weren't concerned about temporal shockwaves. They were probably fretting about student loans and mortgage payments, in the spare moments around being in love. On some level, they were all dead already, and they were also painfully alive around me. Whichever they were, alive or dead, they soothed an ache in my soul.

I stopped in front of a lion enclosure and observed a lioness dozing on a rock. Unlike the bird, she noticed my scrutiny and stood. We watched each other and I felt something from the lioness, something more than the normal presence you expect from all living things. I wasn't quite sure what to make of it. The lioness watched me for a very long time and then her head dipped in a kind of nod. I smiled and returned the nod. We were predators, and we recognized our own. I turned away and headed for the entrance. I'd gone to the zoo for something. I'd received it. It didn't matter to me that I didn't know precisely what I'd gotten.

5

When enemies threatened you, pointed guns at you, hurled spells at you, it was easy to know what to do. You retaliated. You issued threats of your own. You shot back. You summoned primordial powers to fend off their primordial powers. It was Conflict 101. When someone you knew and nominally trusted threatened you, the rules went out the window. It shocked your sensibilities. Your normal strategies failed to account for the relationship and it left you blindly fumbling in the dark for a path. All you could do was your best and hope that it was enough.

"Okay, so maybe I was overstating it when I said you've got no reason to be afraid. But I'm not spending my time looking for reasons to hurt you, Clea. You've got to know that. I could have sent you packing any time I wanted with a bad report and a formal request. If I really wanted you gone, wouldn't that have been easier for me? It would damn sure be less difficult to explain than if you turned up dead."

I saw a touch of uncertainty creep into her eyes. The gun dropped a few inches. I let that idea steep for a few seconds.

"We're professional secret keepers, Clea. We keep secrets from our friends, our families, the public, even the people we're trying to help. It's second nature, but that doesn't make my secrets malicious. If you're really that concerned, just go. I won't stop you."

The gun dropped another inch or two as the uncertainty in her eyes grew. I paused to take a breath and that was my mistake. If I'd kept talking, it might have worked. The fear in her eyes crystallized and the gun snapped back up to my face.

"You're lying! I know you're lying! You lie about everything. You live in darkness. I know, Jones. I know about the gray dreamer, the bone wolves, the Spirit Isle. I know what you did there!"

Something was very wrong. There were a lot of things I left out of my reports and everything on Clea's impromptu list fell into that category. No one else had been with me in those times and places. For one person to know about one of them, through some supernatural means, fell into the category of possible. For someone to know about all of them fell into the category of nigh impossible. Either Clea had managed to fool me about her intentions and a hitherto unseen magical prowess that dwarfed my own, or something else was at work here.

I glanced at the dead woman on the bed. She was very dead. If I'd learned anything from Archan, though, it was that dead does not always mean gone. Angelica Lomas had been a first order psychic. Powerful enough that she'd blanketed most of a small city with projections of insanity as her mind collapsed in her final hours. Even with all my training and experience, I'd fallen prey to those projections. I'd just started to sort the real from the unreal when it all vanished like smoke. No doubt at the moment of Lomas' death.

Of course, I'd been outside when it happened. Clea was standing in the room, at the absolute epicenter of all that power, immersed in the unbound contents of someone else's psyche. When death came knocking, what could a psychic as powerful and confused as the dying Lomas to do someone standing that close? I shuddered at the idea. Then, it became obvious. I lowered my eyes for a moment and gathered the power I needed. I did it fast because I was pretty sure she was going to notice.

Clea took a step. "What are you doing, Jones?"

I looked up. "Clea, *Somnusarum*."

Power swept out from me and coalesced around Clea in a misty haze. It sank into her skin and Clea's eyes went out of focus. The hand holding the gun dropped to her side and the weapon slid from her fingers. I frowned at her and considered the idea that I'd been wrong. Clea's eyes drooped and her body started to go slack. I stepped forward to catch her and Clea's eyes snapped open. Her body straightened into a stiff, unyielding posture that was a million miles away from her normal relaxed stance. I looked away. I'd almost rather have been wrong. The sight of Clea's body supporting that alien posture turned my stomach. I marshaled my thoughts, pushed down my disgust and looked at her.

I shook my head. "Angelica Lomas, I presume."

6

(2 hours earlier)

The crucified Jesus loomed large behind the altar. I wasn't much for religion, but it seemed like good manners to make the occasional visit to a church. A tip of the hat to whatever power resided behind the religion and, I was quite certain, some power did. I'd seen too much and done too much to write it off as so much folklore. Still, I was forced to wonder why anyone would want to see their savior in so much agony. Why not in his ascent to heaven? Like so many things, I was sure there was a deeper lesson in human nature to be gleaned from that fixation on pain, but I lacked the insight to seize it. I turned and started down the aisle.

"Can I help you, son?"

I turned and saw a middle-aged man with a round face and an easy smile. The white square at his throat marked him as a member of the clergy. I hadn't wanted to talk to a priest, just pay my respects and be on my way.

I smiled. "No, Father, I'm fine. Thank you."

He walked over and took me in at a glance. "Is that so?"

"Of course."

He smiled the smile of someone who has heard the lie ten thousand times and gestured to a pew. I accepted the inevitable and sat. He sat next to me and seemed to ponder how best to crack open the nut of my, apparently, obvious problems.

"I enjoy this time of the day," he said. "The evening always seems hopeful to me."

That wasn't what I expected. "Why is that?"

"It reminds me that everything is mutable. The day gives way to night. Youth gives way to age. Ignorance gives way to wisdom, when we're lucky."

"Isn't God immutable?"

"His existence, certainly, but even God gave up vengeance and proffered us love. Seems like a fairly major change in the order of things."

"Fair point."

"Problems tend to be the same. They often look immutable and insurmountable when we first see them, but they give way too."

"Some more than others."

The priest chuckled. "That is also a fair point. Still, Christ tells us that if we have faith the size of a mustard seed, we can move mountains."

I smiled. "Not an exact translation."

The priest shrugged. "It's one of those rare instances when it's actually the thought that counts. Though, I get the feeling that too much thinking is the problem in your case."

"Why's that?"

"Son, sooner or later, every type comes through those doors. The kind, the terrible, the foolish, and the thinkers all come here. You're a thinker. It's easy to spot them, because they're always so burdened. It's been a great long while since I last saw someone as burdened as you. If I didn't know better, I'd think you really did have the weight of the world on your shoulders."

I sniffed. "You'd be surprised."

"I doubt it."

I looked hard at the priest and performed the sign of the cross. I knew the process. "Forgive me father for I have sinned. This is my first confession."

The priest gave me a patient nod. I unburdened myself on him. After the first two minutes, I could see how much he wished I hadn't. After five minutes, he looked ill. After ten minutes, he just looked shell shocked. I told him about my profession, the people I'd killed, the bargains I'd made, the powers I'd invoked and evoked, the threats that hung over me and, by proxy, all of human history. It took me about forty-five minutes. I wound down and gave him a few minutes to gather himself.

He crossed himself before he looked at me again. "You aren't insane, are you?"

"My life would be so much easier if I were."

"I don't even know if there is a penance I could give you, nor, for that matter, if one is called for. It's too fantastical to consider."

"Save your penance, Father. I don't require absolution, merely the silence mandated by the confessional seal."

I stood, slid past the priest, and walked toward the door. He called after me and I looked back. He stood and made his way toward me with grave steps.

"Son, the girl you spoke of, Clea?"

"Yes."

"If you won't take absolution, than perhaps you'll take some advice. You don't strike me as the sort of man who trusts anyone, but you want to trust her. Trust that intuition."

I looked away. "I don't think it's her I doubt. What I don't trust is the orders she might be under."

The priest raised a graying eyebrow. "Don't hate the player, hate the game?"

I winced. "Something like that."

The priest might have said something else, but one of the doors burst open and Clea came running the down the aisle. She had her work coat on and mine flapping under one arm. She all but flung it at me as she grabbed my arm.

"Contingency, we need to go! Sorry, Father. Right now, Contingency!

Forgive the ruckus, Father. Move, Contingency!"

Once I got my body and brain working together again, Clea let go of my arm as we ran out of the church into darkness of late evening.

"What the hell, Clea?"

"There's a psychic crisis in some little city called Manning. It's in South Carolina."

"What year?"

"This year. Right this second, it's happening."

"Holy shit."

7

Angelica Lomas glared at me through Clea's eyes. I saw Clea's arm twitch.

"What have you done?" She demanded with raspy words.

"Don't bother. I put Clea to sleep. I expect it's taking everything you've got just to keep her upright."

"Release your spell."

"This is wrong, Angelica. You have to know that. That isn't your body. You can't keep it."

"I will keep it. I earned it!"

The last came out as a full scream, but Clea's body started tipping to the side the second Lomas stopped focusing on keeping it body upright.

"Look at what's happening? Do you really think you can keep this up? Let her go."

"No."

"You had your life, Angelica Lomas. Well-spent or ill-spent, it's over. I won't let you steal my friend's life."

"Your *friend* is afraid of you," whispered Angelica. "But not half as afraid as she should be. I've seen you for what you are and what you can become. I've seen your true strength. If they knew, they would all hunt you down and kill you."

I clucked. "So that's why she wound up in this room, instead of me. You thought she'd be easier prey. How's that working out for you, toots? Was tender, sweet little Clea made of sterner stuff than you expected?"

Angelica made a strangled noise.

"I'm of half a mind to walk outside and wake her up. I give you ten minutes before she casts you out."

"Then do it," croaked Angelica. "We'll see who wins."

"And let you rake your nails all over her mind while you fight it out. Give you a chance to give her even more psychic scars? Fat chance of that. Idle curiosity, were the pills your idea? Let me guess, you hooked a compulsion onto her empathy to make her feed you those pills."

The errant mind of Angelica Lomas said nothing, just emoted hate at me.

"You're a piece of work, lady. It's really too bad I didn't meet you sooner. I'd have saved us all a lot of trouble."

"You have no idea what I've done. You think you've seen horror. I fought the darkness for ninety years!"

"Thank you," I said with all the sincerity I could muster. "Now you've had exactly and precisely the reward you earned for that. Move on."

"I won't. You'll have to make me." Angelica spat in my face then and nearly lost control of Clea's body.

I wiped the spittle off my face with my hand and rubbed it off on my jeans. I fought down the urge to deck her. It wouldn't hurt Angelica, just leave Clea with an aching jaw.

"I don't want to do that, but you know I can. You know I will. If you force my hand, you won't like where I send you."

"I'll drag your Clea's soul down with me. Maybe I can't keep her body, but I can do that. I think you know I can and that I will. Checkmate, Contingency Jones."

I looked out the window. She was probably right that she could, if I exorcised her. Lightning flashed outside window and thunder rattled the windows in their frames.

"You know," I said, "today was supposed to be my day off. It was a good day. I sat in the sun, had some ice cream."

Angelica gave me a confused look. "What are you talking about?"

I walked over to a table, picked up a glass and broke it against the table's edge. "I even went to church. I spoke to a priest. He reminded me of something I hadn't thought of in a long time."

I opened my left palm with the jagged edge of the glass. My blood welled up in my palm, a red reflecting pool.

"What is the meaning of this, Jones?"

"He reminded me that if we have faith the size of a mustard seed, we can move mountains. Faith, Angelica Lomas, is what you do not have. It's faith that sees us through. Maybe it's not faith in God, but faith that when we reach the end of our fight, we'll find a new life befitting our sacrifices. I have faith that when I call, the Lords of Order hear me. Faith that my sacrifices are not in vain. Faith that when I cry out in the darkness, the light will come forth. I summon that light. Lords of Order, I beseech thee…"

"Stop this!" Angelica tried to move at me, but her control failed and Clea's body fell.

"Lords of Order, I call for you aid…"

She manifested, before I could finish the summoning or the power could gather. She appeared before I could constrain her actions. The angel appeared and I felt her white hot fury.

8

(1 hour earlier)

I hadn't approved when Clea came home with it, but it wasn't strictly against regulations. The problem was that motorcycles are conspicuous. They're loud, flashy and, when Clea bought them, fast as hell. For once, I didn't mind. We raced through the streets and I was uncomfortably aware of her arms gripping my chest and her body pressed against mine. Mentally, there was no spark there beyond basic camaraderie in the face of danger. My body, on the other hand, was just very interested in the close proximity of gender woman. It had been a while. I thought about the last psychic crisis I'd been in and that did plenty to cool my body's jets.

I turned the bike into a light, sideways skid, laid on the gas and we shot down the alley. I dropped the bike right in front of the right brick. Clea leaned back from me and popped up her face shield. I popped my own and looked back at her.

"Okay. Okay," she said. "I admit it. You know how to ride a motorcycle."

"Damn skippy, I do. How close are we going to be to the epicenter of the event?"

"About four miles out," she said and started to get off the motorcycle.

"Where are you going?" I asked. "I'm not walking four miles before a fight."

I grabbed her arm and plopped her back down on the seat. I pulled my device from my coat pocket and pressed it against the brick. Me, Clea and the motorcycle took a ride through the ley lines. We rematerialized inside a barn. I put a leg down hard to keep us from toppling over. Even so, the disorientation was even worse than usual. Maybe it had something to do with all of the motorcycle's extra mass. I shook my head and looked back at Clea. She looked green around the gills, but she threw me a thumbs up and snapped down the face shield on her helmet.

    I checked the device. It gave me a detailed map of the local roadways and the best route to get where we needed to go. I dropped the bike into gear with my toe and we shot out of the barn, scaring the bejeezus out of a few chickens. The countryside whipped by in a blur and before long, all of the worst nightmares of a profoundly powerful psychic started to manifest around us. Clea's arms jerked extra tight around me as she caught sight of some tentacle-handed beast straight out of Lovecraft. Strangely enough, my body didn't find her hard squeezing at all arousing. Then again, maybe it was distracted by me swerving to avoid a spider the size of a car that wasn't actually there. Sometimes, I hate psychics.

    After another mile of pitiful screaming, all mine, and swerving around obstacles both real and imaginary, we arrived outside a house. At least, I assumed it was a house. There was no way to tell whether the gothic monstrosity we saw on the outside bore any relation to the inside. I parked the bike on the lawn next to a hissing, acid-spewing dragon I felt pretty confident wasn't really there. I hadn't warned Clea and she threw herself off to one side as the dragon swiped at us with huge, illusory claws. I swung off the bike and went over to help her up. Before I got to her, something very large and very real slammed into me.

    Right at first, it was just a tangled mess of rolling, punching and kicking. Eventually, I got loose. I backed off enough to see a mechanic's shirt worn by a big, bearded man. His nametag said Red, and his shirt told me to ask him about the tune-up special. What the hell, I decided. It was worth a shot.

"Hey Red, what's the tune up special?"

It was like a switch flipped in his head and the beard split open to reveal a row of straight white teeth that would, I was sure, have caused me to smile back on any other day.

"The tune up special is our pride and joy. We walk your vehicle through a 128 point inspection, change the oil, replace the air filters, top off the air in your tires, check your belts, your coolant, your…"

I walked away, and heard Red continue on with his spiel as though I was still there. Clea was nowhere to be seen. I started toward the house. An angry looking guy with a bloody machete in his hands rounded the corner of the house and sprinted at me. I wasn't taking any more chances. I pulled my Smith & Wesson, Model 27 and put a bullet straight through the illusion's head and into a lamppost.

"Damn psychics," I muttered.

Then, all the phantasms vanished and I heard someone in the house scream. I ran toward the house, which really was a gothic monstrosity, and bolted up the stairs. I almost dropped my leg through a hole in one of the steps. I got up to the second floor and looked around. There was light shining beneath one of the doors. I approached it cautiously and opened the door.

"What the hell?"

9

The angel's fury pounded against my skull, my body, my soul. It hurt and she wasn't even looking at me. She walked toward Clea's possessed body and stood over it like judgment incarnate.

"Angelica Lomas," whispered the angel.

Those six syllable felt like getting hit by six cars. I fell to the floor in physical agony. The noise seemed to jar the angel who looked over at me. Shame, actual, legitimate, honest-to-God shame crossed her face at the sight of me. If not for the feeling that all of my tendons and ligaments were about to rip free from my bones, I might have even enjoyed it. The pounding in my skull and the pain in my body vanished.

"Forgive me, Contingency Jones," she said, head bowed. "That voice was not meant for you."

"You showed up," I said, getting to my feet. "That's enough for me. You're forgiven."

She nodded to me and turned back to Clea's prone form. She used a foot to turn Clea's body face up. At the sight of the angel, Angelica squeezed shut Clea's eyes like a small child who imagines that, if she can't see you, you can't see her.

"Angelica Lomas, how dare you treat this child thus? How dare you use your gifts for such an abomination?"

Angelica turned her face to the side, refusing to look at her accuser. If there was any pity left in me for her, I would have felt it then. I didn't.

"You will answer me, Angelica Lomas."

Even shielded from her power, I felt the sheer weight of the angel's words. The finality of them left nothing to chance.

"I'm afraid," whimpered Angelica in Clea's voice. "I don't want to leave."

"And this gives you the right to defy the natural order? To cast aside laws that were ancient before the dust that made your world even existed? To displace the soul of an innocent so that you might have a grotesque mockery of life? I marvel that you can bear the shame of this."

Clea's body gave a convulsive twitch and a tear slipped from the corner of her eye. The thought of Angelica using Clea's stolen body to cry made me furious. I had to turn away and close my eyes.

"What will become of me?" Angelica asked.

"What becomes of all mortal kind," said the angel. "You will be given neither knowledge, nor comfort to ease your passage into the Mystery."

I heard the capital m on the word mystery and, I was shocked to discover, it didn't frighten me. It should have. Only a fool harbors no fear of death and what comes next, but, at that moment, I didn't. I chalked it up to faith and probably more than my fair share of knowledge. Maybe I didn't know what came next, but I was pretty sure that there at least was a next. If that came with some kind of judgment, I was prepared to account for my deeds.

"Your time here is over, Angelica Lomas. Leave her."

There an audible crack in the air, and I felt another presence. Angelica had either left or been driven out of Clea's body. Separated from a human body, I could finally sense her. The angel reached out a hand and touched something I couldn't see.

"Go now," said the angel, gently.

I thought I saw a glimmer of light in the air and then the presence of Angelica Lomas was gone.

"Good riddance, bitch," I muttered.

The angel gave me an icy look. "Such unkindness is unwarranted, Contingency Jones. She was alone and afraid. Her last years were spent bending a failing mind on the sole purpose of containing her powers. That was a battle she lost only at the very last. She stood against the darkness, bravely and selflessly, for longer than most of your kind lives. If you cannot forgive her transgression, you *will* apply yourself to comprehending it."

I felt myself blush in shame. It was obvious. Anyone with that kind of power who was actually evil would have shown up on my radar. I didn't always do something about them, for a lot of reasons, but I knew about them.

Still, she'd possessed my friend. Angelica had compelled Clea to murder her. I said as much.

"It was not murder," said the angel. "Angelica might have lived for days in that state. Imagine the damage that might have been done. Her death was a mercy granted to her. As it will be a mercy granted to everyone influenced this night when you remove their knowledge of it."

"What?"

"Things were seen and done this night by those who could not bear the knowledge of it," said the angel with a pointed glance at Clea. "You will spare them that knowledge."

"I've never done anything like that before, not on a scale like this. Where would I even get the power?"

Lightning flashed close enough that it hurt my eyes. The thunder that followed a fraction of a second later drowned out everything else. The angel lifted an eyebrow.

A thought occurred to me. "I can't remove my own knowledge of this night."

"Consider it penance for your unkindness. Perhaps it will serve to remind you in the future that your judgment should be informed."

I nodded. "Point taken."

I looked at Angelica Lomas' earthly remains and then to the pill bottle on the floor. I went over, picked up the bottle and put it in my pocket.

"Can you obscure how she died?" I asked the angel. "She didn't kill herself. People shouldn't think that she did."

The angel nodded and then gave me a smile. "Better."

I ducked my head and went outside to do something else that would never find its way into a report.

10

I closed the door to the little house Clea and I shared. I was tired. I'd done as the angel instructed and wiped all knowledge of the events of the night from Clea and several thousand other people. I wasn't sure I'd pulled it off completely. Some people might remember, but it'd become one more urban legend. Clea had seemed satisfied with the yarn I wove about what happened. I guess there was no reason why she wouldn't. It was all true, just minus some salient details. I sat down on the couch and gestured to the easy chair Clea seemed to prefer. The priest's words had been rolling around in my head on the ride home.

"There's a few things we should talk about, Clea."

She stifled a yawn. "Can it wait until morning?"

"I don't think it should. Before I start, you should know that this might change how you see some things. In all likelihood, it'll change how you see some things that matter a lot to you. If you've been thinking you should get clear of me and that I'm going to drag you down with me, say so right now. I'll have you reassigned tomorrow, because it's even odds that you're right."

Clea pulled her legs up and rested her chin on her knees. She was quiet for a long time and I could see from the look in her dark eyes that the gears in her head were spinning very fast. She gave me a sidelong glance.

"Contingency Jones, if I didn't know better, I'd say you were worried about me."

I cocked my head to one side. "I am worried about you. I always worry about my friends. Mostly, I worry because they are my friends."

She jerked a little at the word friends, but she smiled a little too. "So much for your infinite well of grumpiness."

"Do not doubt the infinity of my grump. It has been tested and verified. Really, though, if you want to go, I'm telling you that you should."

She shook her said. "Say your piece, Contingency."

So, I did. I laid it all out for her. I told her about what I knew for certain. I told her about my suspicions that I couldn't prove, but that seemed to hold with the circumstantial evidence. I told her about the conspiracy that I thought was in place and that I intended to do something about it, if I could. I also told her that there was a good chance that I'd die in the attempt, and anyone even remotely connected to me would suffer for that connection. I did leave out J'adoube and Captain Kane. If I was wrong about Clea, then I'd suffer for it. I wouldn't put their heads' in a noose with mine. I fell silent. Clea's eyes were huge in the dim light.

"Well," she said. "That clears some things up. Why tell me?"

"You have to trust someone. I trust you. So, that's it. That's what I've been keeping back from you. Now that you know, do you feel better?"

"Of course I don't feel better, you idiot," she said. "Well, no, I feel better about you, but worse about everything else. God, I need a drink. Beer?"

"Sure," I said.

She came back and handed me a beer. "How sure are you about this, Contingency? I mean, are you really, really sure or just getting a kinda, sorta hinky vibe?"

"'Kinda, sorta hinky vibe?'"

"You know what I mean."

I shrugged. "I'm as sure as you can be without little things like hard evidence and a data trail. It's not like people in conspiracies advertise it."

"What a mess."

I nodded and took a long pull off the beer.

"Totally off subject, but do you have any idea what a gray dreamer is? That phrase has been stuck in my head."

I stopped myself from spraying beer all over the coffee table, barely. Some secrets needed to stay secrets, even from friends.

"Doesn't ring a bell," I lied.

Episode 8 - The Man in the Grey Fedora

1

"Why are you so sure this will work?"

I lowered the small pair of binoculars and glanced at Clea. She looked at me with her big, dark eyes and, if there was reproach in her voice or expression, I couldn't find it. I supposed that the question was driven by real curiosity and, quite probably, a little too much reliance on technology. The notion of taking out personal ads in a newspaper to communicate just wasn't part of the standard issue Agent's playbook. Then again, I wasn't the standard issue Agent. So maybe Clea's question should have surprised me more than it did. As a rule, Agents communicated with our devices, using encryptions that would give God fits. Newspapers were too public and primitive to make sense to an Agent raised on the mother's milk of protocol. As with so many other things, I bemoaned Clea's lack of familiarity with early twentieth century spy fiction.

"I'm not sure," I admitted, but without conviction. "Still, if gray fedora man could have communicated with me using more sophisticated methods, do you really think he would have taped a handwritten letter to our door?"

Clea opened her mouth, stopped, closed her mouth and then

frowned. "I guess not. All of this just seems, I don't know, unnecessarily complicated."

I smiled a little, on the inside. "That depends on how high you think the stakes are. If you were wandering around with knowledge of time travelers who have access to terrifying technology, how paranoid would you be? If you also knew that some of those time travelers were running a not so warm and cuddly agenda, you'd want to take precautions too."

"Precautions like showing up early to check out the meeting place with binoculars?"

"I'd have used a telescope if the damn things weren't so cumbersome."

The truth was that the personal ads play had been a wild, Hail Mary, stab-in-the-dark guess. I'd agonized over the content of that first message for the better part of a week, writing it and then rewriting it. I made it vaguer, and then clearer, and then vague again. It had to be specific enough that he'd understand it, but vague enough not to attract unwanted attention. For example, I very much wanted to avoid the attention of my superiors and, for that matter, the attention of the nebulous Red Cord. The untimely arrival of either, assuming they even were separate entities, would be bad for me and for Clea. I suspected it would turn out to be fatal for the man in the gray fedora, regardless of who showed up. I wanted to talk to him and discover how he came by his rather unlikely knowledge of me. In an ideal world, that conversation would not take place while we were under fire, friendly or otherwise. In the end, I settled on something simple and hoped for the best.

Gray Fedora,

Your NY tip was on the nose. Would like a meeting to discuss.

C.J.

I had them run the same ad every day for a week. Then, I waited. It turned out that waiting wasn't my forte. I haunted news stands in the early morning, waiting for the new papers to come out. I paced the house and scrutinized every ad with something that I refused to call obsession. Clea, on the other hand, had no such compunctions.

"Contingency," she all but screamed on the fourth day of my paper fixation. "You *must* go out and do something else. Go see a movie. Go get drunk. Find a prostitute. Anything to distract you. You're driving me to the brink of insanity with this obsession. Look at this place!"

She swept her arm around the living room. I came out of my analysis haze and looked around. I looked around again. Newspaper pages were strewn everywhere. They covered every flat surface. The floor and the tables, not to mention the couch and even Clea's chair, looked like the beginnings of the world biggest paper mache project. All of that had eluded my notice.

"Wow," I murmured. "I didn't even realize."

"I found a page in the shower, Contingency."

She held up the soggy evidence of her statement. I stared at the soggy newsprint in disbelief. Then, I narrowed my eyes at her. She held my gaze for a five count before her cheeks went red and she looked away.

"You just ran that under some water a minute ago, didn't you?"

"Yes," she admitted, "but it could have been true. You didn't know. Ob. Sess. Sion."

I heaved a sigh. "Alright, I've got one page left. If it's not in there, I'll lay off for a couple days."

I watched the pent-up tension in Clea's body drain away.

"Thank you," she said.

There was no reply on the last page, so I did what I said I would and laid off for a couple days. I still bought the papers. I folded them neatly and left them on the coffee table. Then, I moved them to the kitchen counter. Then, I wrapped them in plastic and put them under several bags of frozen vegetables in the freezer. Out of sight is out of mind, after all. After two days, and a lot of cleaning, I went out and bought that day's papers. I found my answer.

C.J.

I agree. A meeting could be beneficial.

Gray Fedora

A day later, a new letter was taped to my door with a date, time and location. I made sure Clea read it.

2

I scanned the park bench and the surrounding areas for the umpteenth time. I didn't see anything I didn't like, which made me paranoid in its own right. I need something else to occupy the time. I looked over at Clea, who appeared to be playing a game on her device.

"So what did you tell your grandfather?"

She didn't look up, but there was a forced casualness to her response. "What do you mean?"

"I mean what did you tell your grandfather about my conspiracy theory, the man in the gray fedora and this meeting?"

She let the question hang for a minute without answering. I frowned at her.

"Clea, that wasn't a cryptic question that required deep consideration. If you have to think that long to answer, it generally means you're deciding how much lying to do."

She closed her eyes and took a deep breath. "I told him all of it."

"Well, glad that's cleared up. I'll arrange for your transfer as soon as we get back."

She stood straight up and grabbed my arm. "What?"

"What part of all that's going on sounded like information I was interested in sending up the food chain? If I wanted your grandfather to know, I could have told him. I told you all of that in confidence, Clea. I trusted you. You betrayed that trust."

"I *had* to tell him."

"No, you chose to tell him. Now, I choose to send you away."

I saw anger and frustration and guilt flicker across her face. "He's my grandfather. He's our commanding officer. I had a duty."

I leaned in close, way inside her personal space. "Did you ever really consider, for one second, that he might be behind all of it? You damn well should have, since I told you he might be."

"But he's…"

"Did you consider that you might be sentencing me to torture and death?"

"He would never do that," she said, low and dangerous, and desperate to believe her own words.

"That's probably true," I agreed. "I doubt he'd do it himself. He'd send someone to do it. Or, for me, probably several people. I do have that reputation and all."

There was a rustle behind me. "The actual number would be eight, Jones. If August Worth wanted you taken alive, the team would consist of eight people. We did the math."

I turned and looked at the source of the voice. He was a medium built man, with coal black eyes and black hair cut almost down to his scalp. He was dangerous. He moved with liquid grace and his gaze wandered constantly in the way of people who are always aware of their surroundings. I'd met a few like him along the way. I was not in a hurry to fight that man, unless it could not, under any circumstance, be avoided. He gave me his undivided attention for a moment. I was pleased to discover cautious wariness in his gaze. I seemed he wasn't in a hurry to fight me either.

"Uncle John," said Clea, her gaze still on the side of my head.

He smiled at her and an actual emotion showed through. He was pleased to see her. "Clea."

"Uncle John, is it?" I asked.

"Merely an honorific. I'm close with her parents."

"Well, Uncle John, just to settle my curiosity, how many would Worth send if he just wanted me dead?"

"Contingency," said Clea, horrified, "how can you…"

I held up a hand and Clea went silent. That got Uncle John's attention.

"He would send one person," offered Uncle John.

"He'd send you."

"As you say, you have a certain reputation. After reviewing the footage from your, hmmm, let us say, impromptu demonstration in the unarmed combat class, along with new information about your other skills, it was determined that a traditional strike team would prove ineffective."

"You did the math?"

"Indeed."

I raised my eyebrows at him. "Care to share?"

"The probability of a normal strike team achieving its objective in your case was placed at 5.3%, with an 87.6% chance that the entire strike team would die in the attempt."

I snorted. "I think that's got less to do with my skills than it does with their crappy training. Clea could take most of them at this point."

Once she got my cardiovascular health where she thought it should be, the tables turned and I started getting Clea's hand-to-hand where I thought it should be. I pity the next person to pick a fight with her. I was still sporting half a dozen bruises from the last time we sparred. Uncle John raised an eyebrow at Clea. She shrugged and muttered something about gym time.

"He's exaggerating," she said, almost selling it.

"He's not," I corrected. "I can't help but notice a distinct lack of 7 other people."

Clea's head jerked and she looked around. "Uncle John, you can't be here for that."

He raised his hands. "Jones posed a hypothetical, I answered it. However, that isn't why I am here."

"You're here for gray fedora man," I said.

"To speak with him, at least. When is he due to arrive?"

"Any time now," answered Clea.

I put the binoculars up to my eyes and scanned the park again. I saw him or his fedora at any rate. He was sitting on the appointed bench.

I pointed. "There."

3

I walked up to the man in the gray fedora and sat down next to him on the bench. Clea and Uncle John stood a few paces away. The gray fedora man looked at me first, and then at them. He raised an eyebrow.

"C.J.?" He asked.

"That would be me," I said.

Gray fedora man reached into a pocket and removed an envelope. He handed it to me. *C.J.* was scrawled on the outside. The man nodded to me and stood up.

"I was told to tell you and any companions that the park is lovely this time of year and that you should take advantage of it."

"I'll take that under advisement. Thank you," I said.

The man dropped his fedora onto the bench and walked away. Uncle John started to walk after him.

"Don't bother," I said. "It's not him. Just a messenger."

I ripped open the envelope and pulled out a sheet of paper. It read:

Dear Contingency,

I fear I have been unavoidably detained by pressing matters, of which I am sure you will become aware before too long. I am, however, committed to our meeting. When present concerns resolves themselves, I will contact you again with a new time and place to meet.

Sincerely,

Your Friend

"I guess no one gets to talk to him today," I said.

I held the paper out in the general direction of Clea and Uncle John. Clea snatched paper from my hand, read it, and then handed it to my potential, would-be assassin. His eyes flicked over it and narrowed. Clea was glaring at me. If pure anger could be fired like a gun, I'd have been riddled with holes.

"Most convenient timing for pressing matters to arise," said Uncle John, sparing me a look of mild annoyance.

"You did this," said Clea. "You set this whole thing up, didn't you?"

I stood and raised an eyebrow. "Me? How could I possibly have set this up? You've been with me almost non-stop the last month. When could I have secretly sent a message to gray fedora man? More importantly, where would I have sent it? It's not like I know where he lives."

Clea's mouth hung open. She knew I was lying. When John looked back down at the paper, I gave her a little smile. That is how you lie in answer to a question, I thought. I never saw it coming when she punched me in the face. That girl was scary fast. When the bright lights cleared, Uncle John had dragged her away from me. She was screaming at me.

"You set this up. You set me up! All of this was just to make me look stupid!"

I said nothing. Uncle John noticed me neither confirming nor denying anything.

I gave him a long look. "So, are you supposed to kill me now?"

He waited a beat, probably to scare me, which it did, before he answered. "No."

Clea had stopped struggling and was watching me with spooky, empty eyes. "I won't forget this, Jones."

"Try not to forget why it happened, either. You hung me out to dry."

"I take it," said Uncle John, "that you will no longer be sharing information with Clea."

"No. I was going to send her back later, but she may as well go with you. Should I be expecting that team soon?"

"Director Worth informed me that you, and Clea, were she to stay, are to continue your investigation. You will carry on alone until another Agent can be sent to replace Clea."

"No."

Uncle John wasn't prepared for that answer. "No to what?"

"No, there will be no more partners. I work alone. I always have. The whole reason Worth sent her was to make sure I'm not a traitor. That question has been answered. The next partner could give it away or be Red Cord. I don't care how Worth fixes it, but no more partners."

"I don't suppose assurances of fidelity regarding prospective partners, provided by myself or Director Worth, will change your thinking."

"With all due respect, or none whatsoever, I have no more reason to trust you now than I did ten minutes ago."

"You are neither dead, nor in custody. A little good faith on your part seems to be in order."

I shook my head. "Doesn't prove anything. You could just be biding your time. Or he could. Trusting you would be stupid."

A touch of frosty anger peeked through Uncle John's calm. "Take care when you question a man's honor."

"It's not your honor I question, merely your allegiance. Honor doesn't preclude you being my enemy."

Uncle John's expression turned thoughtful and he inclined his head. "Perhaps not. There is a practical matter to discuss. I need your recommendation regarding Clea's future service."

Clea spun on him. "What? He gets to decide what happens to me?"

Uncle John gave her an understanding, but firm look. "As you yourself said, on numerous occasions, he is eminently competent and not a traitor. He is your training officer. Who else are we to ask to assess your field performance?"

"But, but," Clea stuttered, "but *him?*"

I didn't look at Clea. "Keep her at home base for six months. Run her through some of the advanced training courses. She definitely needs the advanced work in magic and psychic defense."

"What advanced courses?" Clea asked. "There are advanced courses?"

It was my turn to spare Uncle John a mildly annoyed look. "Since when did those become secret?"

He shrugged, "A few years ago. Didn't you get the memo?"

"Probably. I delete most of what you people send me."

"Ah," he said, unsurprised.

"Anyway, her empathy is way too open, and I'm seeing a lot more active magic recently. Magical basics aren't going to cut it anymore. After that, she'll probably be as ready as anyone ever is to go back into the field."

"Interesting," said Uncle John.

"What is?" I asked.

"You. I expected more vitriol, and perhaps talk of an oubliette."

Clea was looking at me like I might have gone mad or grown a third arm.

I shrugged. "I don't trust her to be here. I certainly don't want to be spied on in my own house. I trust her to do the job, though, you know, somewhere else."

"I don't suppose there is any point in asking you to keep us in the loop regarding your ongoing investigation."

"There really wouldn't be."

"Very well, Jones. Clea, do you need a moment?"

She shot me a dirty look. "I don't have anything to say to him."

Uncle John nodded. "As you wish. Jones, good luck and Godspeed. Come along Clea."

4

I watched the two of them leave and then sat on the park bench for two hours. Watching a man do nothing for two hours makes surveillance people bored and careless. I didn't believe for one minute that Uncle John just left. I don't think in straight lines. I do unpredictable things. The idea that I sabotaged a meeting just to tweak the nose of command fit neatly into what my performance reviews referred to as my "reckless" and "anarchist" behavior pattern. Dusk had settled by the time my two hours of non-performance art ended. In grabbed the fedora, stood and did a full-throttle sprint for a wooded area about a hundred yards to my right. If there was surveillance, they probably weren't prepared for a full-on pursuit.

I hoped I wouldn't break an ankle in the woods while I made my mad dash through them. I had to slow down a little, just to avoid tripping over fallen limbs, but I made it through without too much trouble. I vaulted over a low-fence that separated the park from the sidewalk. A man was waiting next to a motorcycle. He handed me a helmet and a backpack. I shoved the fedora into the backpack, slid my arms through the straps and plunked the helmet over my head. I hopped onto the motorcycle and zoomed off into the light, evening traffic. I drove aimlessly, made random turns, and took shortcuts that would not accommodate cars for the better part of an hour. When I was certain I wasn't being followed, I turned into a small parking lot behind a bookstore. A dark sedan with tinted windows sat in one of the parking spaces. I looked at it again, thinking I hadn't seen it properly. The proportions looked wrong, probably because it was a stretched sedan, almost a limo. Whatever, I thought. I took off my helmet and a window rolled down. A plump, middle-aged man peered at me from inside the vehicle and then waved me over.

I got into the backseat of the sedan and was surprised to see that the front and back seats were separated by thick glass. I opened the backpack and handed the fedora to its rightful owner. He smiled at it and set the hat down on the seat. I leaned my head back and waited. When gray fedora man was ready to talk, we would talk. I'd had a stressful day and done no small amount of lying. Say what you want, but I find lying psychologically taxing. The sedan pulled out of the parking lot and the driver appeared to do exactly what I had done. He drove at random. He didn't speed or draw attention to himself, but he clearly had no specific destination in mind.

"You weren't followed," said gray fedora man.

I couldn't tell if it was a question or a statement, so I shook my head. "No, I wasn't. At least, I wasn't as far as I could tell."

"You're surprisingly trusting, all things considered. How do you know this isn't a trap?"

"I don't know that this isn't a trap. That's why I brought this."

I slid my Smith & Wesson, Model 27 out of my coat pocket, cocked it and pointed it at the gray fedora man. The man eyed the revolver with curiosity, but not discernible fear. He looked up at me.

"What if the rounds in the cylinder aren't enough?"

I gave him a cold smile. "I have other skills."

"So you do. Very well. I assume you have any number of questions, but let me see I can answer the most likely up front. First and foremost, I expect you're wondering just how it is that I know about your existence and, as it were, profession."

"You could say that it's been on my mind."

"My grandmother told me about you," he said. "She created a foundation, of sorts, with a singular purpose. We exist to assist you."

I struggled to figure out which of the several dozen questions that occurred to me to ask first. I settled on what I thought would be the easiest. "Who is your grandmother?"

The man looked down, a touch sad, but it was old sadness. "Was, I'm afraid. She passed on about ten years ago. Her name was Abigail Esterbrook. You knew her as Abigail Mercer."

The man might as well have punched me in the throat. My vision went dark around the edges and it felt like I was staring at him down a long, dark tunnel. I forced myself to slow my breathing, to calm down, before I passed out. No one had spoken that name aloud to me in a very long time. When the initial shock passed, bloodthirsty anger replaced it.

"Abigail Mercer has been dead for more than seventy years. She died in 1939, in London, during a Luftwaffe airstrike," I said.

Granted, it probably sounded more like choked growling and the revolver trembled as my hands shook in fury. He looked at me with sympathy and compassion.

"The name Abigail Mercer died in 1939. The woman did not. She escaped the destruction or, more specifically, she was saved. By you."

"I didn't save her," I screamed, in rage, in guilt, in despair. "I left her there to die! I didn't save her."

He didn't break eye contact. "You will."

"What?"

His words stunned me. Somewhere in the back of my head, something was bellowing a warning, but I wasn't hearing it.

"You saved her. You went back and got her out. You took her to the country, where she'd be safe. You gave her a new identity, a new life."

The bellowing warning was getting louder, distracting, but the words were meaningless. "You can't possibly know that's true."

"I do know it's true. I know, because this isn't the first time I've met you. Though, I suppose it is the first time you've met me."

The bellowing voice, one that was equal parts me and one of the instructors at the academy, intruded on my active consciousness. I realized what was happening and the danger it posed.

"Stop! Jesus Christ, stop talking! You can't tell me anything else."

"Oh?"

"You can't tell me about my future actions. If we really had met before, I'd have told you as much. My God, do you realize the kind of damage that can do?"

"I do. You explained it to me in excruciating detail. That was right before you told me to tell you, and I quote, 'to stop being such an orthodox priss with suicidal levels of self-reliance,' and to 'take a helping hand when you offer it to yourself.'"

5

I frowned at him. "I really said to tell me to stop being an orthodox priss?"

"You did."

"I guess I'm cranky when I'm older."

"Actually, you weren't much older," he started.

"Stop! Don't tell me."

He sighed. "I'm not telling you anything that unnecessarily pollutes the timeline or endangers, and I'm quoting again, 'the delicate fucking equilibrium of future events, the galaxy, the universe or cranberry sauce production.' I'm only to tell you the things you need to know in order to survive what's coming. As you put it, "tell me what I need to survive the whirlwind and maybe we'll all survive the hurricane." The instructions were actually quite specific, both from you and from my grandmother."

"Do I really talk like that in the future, or past, or my future, I guess?"

Gray fedora man gave me a bemused look. "You talk like that now Jones. I spent some time observing you before I made contact."

I hadn't known. I hadn't even suspected I was being watched. I wondered if it was because I was fixated on figuring out where Clea stood or if he was just that good. I hoped it was the former. If it was the later, I was losing my edge.

"So, I assume you're here to tell me about Red Cord?"

"No. You have larger problems. Wait, that's inaccurate, you have more immediate problems to deal with than Red Cord."

"More immediate? They feel pretty immediate to me."

Gray fedora spread his hands wide. "I'm just telling you what I was told to tell you. Something big is coming, very soon, for you. If you don't act to stop it, your future, as you know it, will die. I was told to tell you that you'll need the gray dreamer. Do you understand what that means?"

I turned my face away and looked out the window. "Yes."

I understood what that meant and it also gave me a vague sense of what was coming. The gray dreamer was, in all likelihood, the most dangerous thing I'd ever stood face-to-face with in my life. It was dangerous the way nuclear reactor meltdowns or pandemics were dangerous. Even in the best case scenario, people almost always die. I'd rather have fought Archan fifty times than ever gotten near the gray dreamer again. If I was going to need that thing, it meant something unspeakably evil was on its way. Apparently, it was coming for me. Then again, if I was to believe fedora man, I'd already survived the encounter. All I needed to do was figure out how I did it. Easy as differential equations, right?

"Is there anything else you're supposed to tell me?"

"That was all."

I looked over at him. He looked pale and afraid.

"If I asked your name, would you give it to me?"

He blinked, as if I was throwing something into the recipe he hadn't expected. "Ryan."

"It's nice to meet you, Ryan."

He gave me a bloodless smile. "It was nice to see you again."

I couldn't tell you how I knew it, or why I knew it, or why I reacted the way I did, but I grabbed Ryan by the shirt and half-dragged, half-shoved him toward the floor. It would have been impossible in a normal sized car, but the stretched sedan had a lot of leg room. The window on his side of the car shattered inward and the rear window spiderwebbed as a bullet passed through them. Ryan tried to put his head up to see and I almost punched him.

"Keep your God damn head down."

"You don't understand," he shouted.

The window between the front seat and the back seat rolled down. I hollered, "Drive! Drive!"

The driver turned back and I saw the gun in his hand. I don't think he knew that I'd had a cocked revolver in my hand the entire drive. If he had, he might have been more subtle. Maybe he'll know better in the next life, I thought, right around the time I shot him. I opened my door and gave it a three count before I slid out of the car. The first shot had probably come from a rooftop on Ryan's side of the car. I reached into the car and hauled him toward me by the collar, like a squirming, writhing dog.

"Stop fighting me," I snarled at him. "I'm not trying to kill you."

"That's what I'm trying to tell you. I'm supposed…"

Automatic gunfire drowned out his words and pelted my open door. I hazarded a peek around my makeshift shield. Two men in very nice suits were advancing on the car in a leapfrog pattern, providing each other cover and keeping me pinned down with short, professional bursts of fire. Something inside me snapped. I'd been playing things subtle all day and I was sick of it. If those assholes wanted a firefight, I'd give them one.

"Cover your eyes," I barked at Ryan.

Then I did something that, under normal circumstance, would probably have been stupid. I stood up and stepped into the open. I had the feeling that I wasn't the target. More to the point, a guy striding into the open wearing a long, black coat draws attention. It makes people stop and stare for a second. I slid the revolver back into my pocket. I pointed one hand down the street toward the men with the automatics and the other straight up into the air. There is power in the world. Spells, incantations, sacred relics, talismans and rituals all provided practitioners with access to that power. They were, so to speak, keys that opened locks. Put someone in the right frame of mind, though, and the keys become unnecessary. Until that moment, I never believed I'd be one of the people to achieve that frame of mind. I reached into the world, into the bones of creation, into the sky and stars and moon. I reached beyond the gates and I seized power.

An orange-red fireball the approximate temperature of the molten core of the earth and the size of a step van shot down the street. The men with the automatics dove for cover. I closed my eyes. Lighting crackled up from my hand and shot skyward in a blinding, blue-white web that would destroy the night vision, not to mention terrify, anyone up on a rooftop with a sniper rifle. Thunder detonated at street level and windows exploded from the concussive force, showering the street in glass fragments. The noise was unbelievable, beyond deafening, and it stopped my heart for a few seconds. When my heart lurched back into action, I turned to the car. I stumbled toward it, half-blinded and mostly deaf, yanked Ryan free and shoved him toward the nearest corner. He was screaming something at me, but I couldn't understand the words.

I pointed down the street and said, or yelled, or minimally made noises at some volume, to the effect of, "Run!"

He ran and I followed, checking behind us every once in a while for pursuit. There wasn't any, but I kept checking. We ran until Ryan was a huffing, red-faced heart attack waiting to happen. I tapped him on the shoulder and pointed to an empty bus bench. We sat and I was surprised by how little a toll the run had taken on me. Clea would have been proud. The deafness started to fade a little and sounds were bleeding through in a distorted warble. After a few minutes, Ryan grabbed my shirt and turned me to him.

"Why did you do that?" He shouted.

I mostly lip read it.

"Because they were trying to kill us," I mouthed back.

He shook his head, his face was going a terrifying shade of white, and he mouthed back.

"No. Me." He pointed at himself.

"Same difference," I mouthed.

He shook his head so hard it bordered on violence. He looked at me with tears in his eyes.

"Don't understand. I was supposed to die. It. Was. My. Time."

I sat in stunned silence for a second before I mouthed the first thing that came into my head.

"Well, that's not good."

Episode 9 - Witching Hour

1

"I received your message, Jones," said J'adoube Green.

I looked at him and my overtired brain very nearly cheered in relief. "J'adoube. Thanks for coming. Come inside."

I stepped aside to let J'adoube into our, I corrected myself, my little house. I'd sent Clea away, back to the oh-so-loving embrace of command. I wondered, not for the first time, if I'd made the right choice. I thought I had, but doubt was a tireless taskmaster and he'd been working double time on me the last two days. J'adoube strode past me.

I blinked in surprise. I'd forgotten how tall the man was. He was so lean that that was all I ever remembered about him. Every time we crossed paths, my psyche did a double-take when it registered that he towered over me by a good six inches. I wasn't a particularly short man at six foot, one inch. If he'd been born in the twenty-first century, college basketball scouts would probably have hounded him mercilessly. As it was, I was just relieved that some kind of support was there. I had a problem.

I heard J'adoube draw in a sharp breath. "What in the name of God?"

I closed the door and turned. J'adoube stood stock still, staring at my problem. Ryan was tied to a chair in nothing but his pants. I'd gagged him to stop the yelling and shouting. People get so worked up sometimes over the little things. I mean, yeah, he was supposed to be dead. I'd intervened all full of self-righteous fury and total ignorance. Saving his ass had seemed like the right move at the time. Of course, I'd done it using magic. After I'd done that, though, things got complicated. I mean, if he was supposed to be dead, I'd done the exact thing I was in the past to prevent. I'd used magic to change history.

"J'adoube, meet problem. Problem, this is J'adoube."

Both men gave me a look that suggested someone in the room had lost complete touch with reality and that the person was me. I suppose it might have looked that way from their perspectives. I was too tired to really care. I'd been keeping Ryan under an involuntary suicide watch for the last forty-eight hours.

"Jones, would you care to explain this, this, whatever this is?"

I rubbed a hand over my face and tried to organize a coherent answer. The futility of that became apparent inside five seconds. I tried again, forgot about coherence and aimed for accurate. That proved a much easier row to hoe.

"Ryan here is possessed of foreknowledge about me and my actions. He told me some of it. Then someone tried to kill him. I stopped them from killing him."

J'adoube's eyes darted between me and Ryan. I could see him doing what I had done. He was weighing the implications, weighing the potential damage, trying to decide what, if anything, he dared to know. I'd put him in a hell of a situation and, to be fair, I felt bad about it. On the other hand, I needed some kind of assistance and, God help me, someone with a clearer head. I trusted J'adoube. He was on a very short list. He was the only person on that list that could conceivable come to my place without raising way, way too many eyebrows. Necessity and kindness rarely held hands in my experience.

"Jones," started J'adoube with warning in his voice.

"There's one other thing."

"Yes?"

"According to Ryan, he was supposed to die when I saved him."

J'adoube's eyes went very wide and he looked hard at Ryan. Ryan nodded his head vigorously. J'adoube raised his very dark hands to his temples and rubbed at them firmly. Let it never be said I don't know how to share. J'adoube was sharing my pain. I started to feel better immediately.

"Why is he bound, Jones? And, for God's sake, why is he half naked?"

"He tried to hang himself with his tie. That," I said, waving a hand in Ryan's direction, "seemed like the best solution to the problem."

"The best solution," repeated J'adoube in disbelief. "Jones, have you taken leave of your senses? You allowed him to give you foreknowledge. You prevented his appointed death. When he tried, as any sane person would do, to correct that horrendous error, you stopped him again. Why?"

"Mostly, I did it because I sent him."

2

J'adoube returned to rubbing his temples. Given how hard he was pressing his fingertips into his skin, I doubted he was getting much therapeutic value from the action.

"You sent him? Explain."

"Well, not me. Not me from now. Some future version of me sent him."

J'adoube peered down at me from his great height like someone examining a new and somewhat disquieting new species of insect.

"So," he said, "not only have you meddled with history as we know it. You have meddled with your own past. I think you've lost your mind."

"Whoa there, big guy. First of all, *I* didn't do anything. Second of all, before you go having me committed, hear me out. I've got a theory about this."

J'adoube spoke slowly. "You have a theory. You think there is theory that makes any of this comprehensible?"

"I do. I think future me is playing a long game. If saving Ryan over there wasn't supposed to happen and would create irrevocable damage to the future, wouldn't it have happened by now? I mean, no one would know what specific damage was done, but the existence of some kind of damage to time and space would have been registered and logged, correct?"

J'adoube didn't say anything at first, but he tilted his head to one side and seemed to ponder something. "Go on."

"I think future me sent Ryan knowing full well that I wouldn't just sit idly by and let someone kill the guy. Future me is still me, after a fashion, and he'd know I wouldn't just let somebody off Ryan right in front of me. I think future me sent Ryan knowing I'd save him, because future me already had saved him. I think that was the point, or part of the point anyway."

I glanced at Ryan. He looked like he was thinking very hard. He was probably trying to decide whether he bought my explanation. He might have prepared himself to die, but that didn't mean he wasn't ready to grab whatever slender hope of survival I offered.

"If that was the case, hypothetically speaking, why not inform your," J'adoube looked at Ryan, "friend there?"

"Probably to keep things clean. Tell Ryan he isn't actually going to his death and he might act differently, do something that would throw off the equilibrium. In order to save him, things needed to go down exactly the way future me remembered them. Change something and the whole situation becomes a temporal free for all."

J'adoube nodded, slowly, cautiously. "It is plausible. I'll grant you that much. Yet, you also said that Ryan provided you with foreknowledge. Does that not inextricable pollute the timeline? Does that not inherently change your behavior?"

"I guess not, or not enough to be dangerous. At least, future me didn't think so. This is new ground for me and I'm playing it as it lays, so to speak."

J'adoube stood there in silence, lost in deep thought, so I walked over to Ryan. He stared up with his intelligent eyes. I couldn't read anything in them.

"If I take your gag out, are you going to start screaming and yelling?" I asked.

Ryan shook his head and I removed the makeshift gag.

"Can I get some water?" Ryan croaked.

I got him a glass of water and helped him sip it. He looked up at me.

"It'd be easier if you let me hold the glass," he said.

"Yeah, it'd also be easy for you to smash the glass and cut your wrists or your own throat," I said. "I went through some serious trouble to save your ass. I'm not going to let you off yourself until I'm sure it's the right decision."

He gave me a thoughtful, serious look. "Do you really think future you sent me knowing that you'd save me?"

I shrugged.

J'adoube chimed in. "It would be consistent with Jones' character. He has always had a," J'adoube smirked, "tenuous relationship with rules."

"Even I respect the rules of time travel," I said. "Still, this all makes a lot less sense if I sent you knowing you would die. *That* isn't consistent with my character."

I'd knowingly put my own life in danger to try to make sure Clea didn't die on more than one occasion. It was true that I didn't really know Ryan, but he didn't strike me as someone evil or deserving of death. Unless I'd completely lost my conscience sometime in the future, it just didn't compute. Me trying doing an end run around "fate" sounded a lot more like my modus operandi.

"The question remains," said J'adoube, "what now?"

3

I rolled my head and tried to figure out an answer to that question. I'd been trying to figure it out for two days. I looked at J'adoube and then at Ryan.

"Assuming I can convince Ryan not to step into traffic or something else calamitous, there's still a problem. Someone did try to kill him. I'm assuming they don't know about me or they would probably have stormed the house by now. Someone needs to keep an eye on him until we can get him back to his people. I assume they can protect you?"

Ryan was quiet for a long moment. "Yes, I expect they could. Assuming they didn't simply kill me. I'm not the only one who knew I was supposed to die."

I waved that off. "If I'm right, I'd have told everyone the real score right after you left. I wouldn't go through the trouble of having me save you only to let your own people kill you."

"Jones, if someone tried to kill him, why do you assume they don't know about you? The only purpose in killing him would have been to prevent you from getting the information he had to provide," said J'adoube.

I blinked. That made sense. If that was true…

"Then where are they? If they knew about him, then they'd know about me. This house isn't a fortress. It would only take a few men to get in here."

The tall man gave me a strange look. "Perhaps you underestimate the shadow you cast."

I rubbed my eyes. I was tired and Ryan wasn't my only problem. What had Uncle John said? Eight men to bring me in alive? Hell, maybe I was underestimating the length of my own shadow, but maybe that was because I knew me. I could probably take four guys, if I knew they were coming and I was rested up. But how often were things going to be that convenient? I looked at Ryan. I looked at J'adoube. I shrugged.

"Could be. Ryan, if I untie you, do you think you can refrain from self-murder long enough to at least call your people?"

"No need to be an ass about it," said Ryan. "This is serious shit we're talking about."

"Yeah, I am aware of that. So can you?"

Ryan rolled his eyes, but he nodded. I untied him and he made a beeline for the bathroom. Oops. I forgot about that.

"You realize he may be in there cutting his wrists right now," said J'adoube.

"Yeah, I know, but I can't watch him forever. If he's really determined, nothing is going to prevent it."

J'adoube ran a hand over his bald scalp. "If I assist you in this, we're taking a terrible risk. A risk based on your predictions of what a future version of you might do or think. By rights, I should kill both of you."

I walked over and sat down on the couch. "I know. I didn't call you here for permission. I called you here as a sanity test. If you think that's what needs to happen, I won't try to stop you. The dangers aren't lost on me."

"Do you think he's telling the truth?"

"I can't see what he'd possibly gain by lying about it. If he's lying, there's no danger and nothing changes. If he's telling the truth, something bad is coming our way. Well, my way, specifically, and I need to deal with it. Assuming you don't kill me."

"I find your calm regarding your own death a matter of concern."

I shrugged. "I'm not happy about the prospect, but you know what the life expectancy is in this job. Statistically, I should be dead already. I came to grips with the idea that I'd die on the job a long time ago."

J'adoube nodded. "I think we should allow him to contact his people. If they confirm your theory, I will help you. If not," he gave me a significant look.

"If not, do what you need to do."

Ryan came out of the bathroom. He looked like he intuited what the conversation had been about, but he didn't say anything about it.

"Where's your phone?" He asked.

"Oh," I said, with a blink. "I don't have one."

"For God's sake, Jones," said J'adoube, drawing his device from his work coat. He held it up and said, "Phone mode, United States, early twenty-first century."

The device made a short series of noises and J'adoube handed the device to a wide-eyed Ryan. Ryan eyed us and then dialed in a number. He held the device up to the side of his head and I heard a telltale ringing sound. Someone picked up and I heard a voice that I couldn't make out.

"It's Ryan."

There was a moment of chatter from the other side and Ryan shot me a look.

"What?" I said.

He shook his head and listened. He nodded and asked me for the address. I gave it to him and he relayed the information to the speaker. He hung up and, with another wide-eyed look at J'adoube's device, he handed it back.

"Well?" I demanded.

"They're sending a car, on your orders."

I nodded and then frowned. "Shit."

J'adoube raised an eyebrow at me.

I shook my head. "I just realized that I'm going to have to remember all of this, in detail."

Ryan piped up. "You could write it down."

J'adoube and I gave the man identical, disbelieving stares. Ryan stared at us, looking confused.

"What?" He said, then he squinted, and his cheeks went pink. "Oh, right, probably not a safe thing to do."

I looked at J'adoube. "Satisfied?"

"Not even slightly, but it seems your hypothesis was correct. What do you propose to do next?"

"I need you to stay with Ryan until his people get here. I have to go," I sighed, "run an errand."

"Technically," said Ryan, "they're your people."

"God, don't remind me. Leadership. Shudder."

"Errand," prompted J'adoube. "What sort of errand?"

"The less you know about it, the better," I muttered. "Let's just say that I need to fetch something unpleasant."

4

I disliked leaving J'adoube alone to manage Ryan's transit back into the loving arms of his people. Unfortunately, if I knew me, and I did, I wouldn't have sent Ryan until the last possible minute. If for no other reason than to make sure I didn't leave myself room to screw everything up. I also wouldn't have left me much time to overthink retrieving the gray dreamer. As it was, I still second-guessed the decision for two important reasons. Reason one: it was an incredible pain in the ass to get to the Spirit Isle. At least it was for living, breathing type people. Dead things, undead things, divine and demonic things didn't seem to have any trouble with it. They could just scuttle their sorry asses right on in to the place. No, I don't know why. It's just one of those things.

Reason two: it was the damned gray dreamer. I'd gone to an awful lot of trouble to get the stupid, terrible thing to the Spirit Isle in the first place, and then gone to even more trouble to trap it there. I wasn't inclined to let it out. All of which future you would know, I reasoned with myself. Therefore, whatever was coming must have paled in comparison. Or, I was getting played somehow. It happened sometimes. Clea had pulled it off, briefly. If I was getting played, though, the con was absurdly complicated and unlikely. There was too much information in play that just wasn't available outside my head. Barring something new to work with, I had to take it at face value. I sent Ryan. I would need the gray dreamer. What could be so ghastly that the gray dreamer would make a viable ally?

I pulled my car up outside an antique shop. It was an out of the way, tiny shop run by an odd woman who seemed wholly indifferent as to why her customers wanted particular items. She was also an insomniac, based on the fact that the place was always open, regardless of the hour I showed up. I opened the door and a bell dinged. A moment later, a painfully thin woman with thick glasses and a wild shock of hair appeared through a curtained door. She peered at me and her eyes looked enormous through the lenses of her glasses.

"Mr. Smith," she said. "What can I do for your pseudonymous self today?"

"Miss Quince," I said with a smile. "Antique bottle, pre-nineteen hundred if you have one. Smaller is better and color isn't important. Antique quill pen, metal tipped, as old as you have."

Her brows furrowed slightly and she shook her head. "You and your lot always have the strangest requests."

I frowned at her, as concern bloomed in my chest. "My lot."

"Yes," she said, waving a hand in my general direction, "yuppies. No sense of order in your purchases."

I did my best to keep a straight face. "Well, you know us. Slaves to fads."

I was quite certain that she would be horrified if she knew what I did with the things I got from her. Very few of them survived my ownership for long. I waited while she rummaged around in the back room. I glanced around the shop in curiosity. Clea would have loved the place, though I never did get around to showing it to her. There was an old writing desk that I'd thought about buying a few times, but I decided it was a bad idea. Attachments were dangerous. My brain was fixating on the spells I'd need to cast on the bottle when she came back out and set the items on the counter.

There were a handful of small bottles in a variety of clear, amber and cobalt blue colors. I picked a few of them up and ultimately settled on an amber one that had some old cork in it. The cork would help. The bottle itself was mostly smooth glass, so scratching what I needed into it would be easier. I picked up the one quill she had set out on the counter. It looked rough, like it'd had belonged to someone with no time to fret about the state of their quill. It was perfect. My brain registered that she was talking to me. It was something about liking Chinese food. She must have been asking if I liked it.

"Sure," I said absently.

"Really?"

A warning bell went off in the back of my head. I'd missed something. I looked at her. She was beaming at me in stunned disbelief. I'd definitely missed something. Dammit, I thought. I must have agreed to something.

I shrugged, "Why not?"

"I just," she stammered.

She looked down at the counter, grabbed a pen and scribbled on a small sheet of paper. She held it out. I glanced down at it. It was a telephone number scratched under the name Ruth.

"Friday, seven?" She asked. "I know a good place."

Understanding finally dawned. I'd agreed to a date. If the stupid gray dreamer hadn't had me so distracted, I'd never have agreed. Still, she looked so pleased in a huge-eyed kind of way. What could it hurt to let her think it would happen? Hell, now that I knew the device functioned as a phone, I could call her up and cancel later, family emergency or some such thing. Or I could just relocate to another decade. I'd done it before. The nineteen-thirties weren't so bad. She was still smiling at me, but it looked a little forced. She was fidgeting in nervous agitation. My conscience gut-checked me. Or, I could just go have dinner with her. For all I knew, the gray dreamer was going to kill me in an hour or two anyway. It might not be an issue.

"Friday at seven will be fine," I said.

She smiled even wider and, apparently uncertain what else to do, she held her hand out to shake. I grinned at her and shook her hand. She turned and started toward the back room. I shook my head.

"Ruth," I said.

She froze in place and I could almost feel her apprehension.

"I still need to pay for these," I said, holding up the quill and a bottle.

5

The fire crackled in front of me. I'd driven out of the city to a campground I knew didn't get much use. I needed more privacy than I could reasonably get at home or anywhere else inside the city. Even knowing what I needed to do, and the likely limited time I had, I procrastinated. I took my time building the campfire. I took my time pulling out the bottle and the quill. I just took my time. The gray dreamer scared me more than I liked to admit to myself. The idea of confronting it again filled me with a shapeless dread. When I'd imprisoned it, I assumed I was leaving it there forever. I might have taunted it a little before I left. I pushed those thoughts away and set to work on the bottle.

It took almost an hour to scratch a couple dozen containment spells and symbols into the glass with the quill. I supposed I could have used any bottle and sharp implement, but old things held a gravity that made the spells stick better. I needed every advantage I could get with the gray dreamer. It wouldn't be happy with me. I sighed and slid the bottle into the big pocket of my work coat. The easy part of the day was over. I sat by the fire and tried to prepare myself mentally for getting to the Spirit Isle. The place, if it could properly be called a *place*, was considered pure fiction even by the knowledgeable. I'd gone looking for it out of pure boredom a handful of years back. It had taken months, even with my many advantages. The trick to getting there was realizing that it didn't exist on this plane of existence.

In some ways, that simplified getting there. You didn't need to go a special geographic location to access it the way you did with so many other things. Of course, simple didn't make it easy. Leveling a mountain was simple.

You just applied enough high explosives. Dealing with the explosives, on the other hand, wasn't easy at all. A lot of things could go wrong. If they did go wrong, you wound up a mangled, screaming mess. Getting to the Spirit Isle was a lot like that. I started a low chant that I'd learned from an unbelievably ancient Romani I found outside of Madrid. I didn't really know what the chant meant, aside from a poor explanation given to me in broken English. I spoke several languages, but Romani wasn't one of them.

As I chanted, I felt power gathering around me. It was strange power, very different from the kinds I normally used, slippery and light. The magic I used always felt like a heavy wave that gathered and fell with crushing force. The magic called by the chant reminded me of wind. Not that wind was harmless, but it was dangerous in a different way. The chant took on a life of its own, building speed and volume. The air around me thrummed with the accumulating power, like a drumbeat against my skin. The campfire grew dimmer, smaller, until it was barely a flicker. Without the aid of the fire, it was dark around me. I heard things in that darkness, laughing voices, ponderous steps, and I checked a shudder. The fire was reduced to glowing embers as the power damped it down even more.

My chanting grew more fervent and faster, no longer distinct words, but a string of syllables forming one long word, over and over again. The drumbeat on my skin felt like a relentless staccato hammering. The coals dimmed down to a barely discernible red glow. The gathered power rushed inward toward the glowing coals and there was an audible crack. A swirling vortex of blue and green flames that stretched three feet across shot into the air. There was no heat or sound from those flames, just their swirling, visual presence. A wave of otherness rolled through me. The Spirit Isle was not the mortal plane. I always had the disquieting feeling that staying there for any length of time would prove catastrophic for my long-term health prospects.

I stood and faced that vortex of alien flames. I knew what came next would hurt. I clenched my jaw to keep from screaming and stepped into that gate of fire. There was a moment of displacement and a breakdown of linear time that reminded me of traveling in the ley lines. Then the displacement was replaced by a sensation that all the skin on my body was being peeled back by blades of ice. I pushed forward, keeping my mind fixed on the destination. Fire came next and it felt like it seared the exposed flesh down to my bones. I did scream that time. It struck me that I would look a lot like the grim reaper as a skeleton in my big, black work coat. I pushed forward. An avalanche of force slammed against my skeleton, shattering it to powder, leaving nothing but my exposed consciousness. I pushed forward, a fragile flame of life in a dead eternity. Then the whispers started.

"It comes again."

"It thinks it is alive."

"It thinks it is worthy."

"Turn back tiny false mind."

"Turn back or we will eat your memories."

"Turn back or we will consume your soul."

"Leave the tiny thing to wander the endless empty."

"Leave it to wander forever."

"Let us peel it like fruit."

It went on and on and on. I ignored the whispers, driving my consciousness through the empty netherspace, never faltering, never wavering. I didn't know if the things whispering could make good on their threats, but I believed hesitation would prove disastrous. With magic, commitment meant everything. If you didn't commit, without reservation, the gathered forces would turn on you like a rabid animal. I figured the same thing applied to wandering the vastness of whatever the hell the in-between spaces were. There was no time in the in-between, just the struggle forward through the whispers and the emptiness. Just like the last time, there was a break in the whispers.

"It is worthy," said a vaguely feminine voice that filled the vast emptiness.

I was dropped, face first and unceremoniously, onto a hard, flat surface.

"Ow," I muttered.

6

I lay there for a minute as my body tried to figure out that it was not in fact skinless, fleshless and boneless. It was no wonder that more people didn't try to get to the Spirit Isle. Who would go through that more than once, except under duress? My limbs stopped twitching and my nervous system stopped screaming that I was hurting. I pushed myself up and managed to stand. I looked around. The place always looked the same. Behind me was a hazy blankness that was my portal back to the real world. Beyond that was a set of stone steps that led down to a shallow beach. There were a few feet of visible water that lapped up against the beach. Beyond that was nothing but impenetrable mist. I'd walked the shoreline on one of my earlier visits and the patch of land was tiny. It reminded me of the small islands I'd seen from time to time in the middle of lakes.

In the middle of the island was a squat, deceptive, rectangular building. It was made of huge slabs of moss covered granite. There were no windows and one open space that served as a door. From the outside, it looked like the interior might be all of ten feet by twenty feet. I walked toward the door, my steps more of drunken lurch before my body remembered I wasn't actually in pain. I stepped through the open space in the weathered granite, went down half a dozen steps and entered the building.

The interior bore no resemblance to the exterior. There was an open hallway that stretched out so far that the perspective got screwy and it vanished into a dot. The floor of the hallway was covered in a mosaic made of what appeared to be precious gems.

The gems were arranged into hall-spanning runes I didn't recognize. I didn't think that runes were active, but I could still feel the power in them. The rune I stood on held enough passive power to level a skyscraper. The runes appeared every ten feet for as far as my eye could make out. They had made me shudder the previous times I'd seen them. The implied threat of all that power lost none of it potency on a fresh viewing. I tried to imagine who or what could have made such a thing. It was either the work of generations or something that had once been nigh omnipotent. On either side of the hall were doors every twenty feet. I'd spent some time exploring those rooms. They were vast and contained miracles, terrors, treasures and power. I'd taken nothing from the place. I knew they weren't meant for me.

Not for the first time, I wondered if a serious search would reveal King Arthur held in suspended animation until the moment Excalibur was needed again. The Spirit Isle seemed like a plausible location for Avalon. There was certainly enough protection in place to make sure Arthur wouldn't be disturbed. If Geoffrey of Monmouth had it right, though, Avalon was populated. I probably didn't want to run into Morgan le Fay or any of her family. Last thing I needed was a throw down with a clan of powerful, experienced sorceresses. I dismissed the idea. If the place was populated, they'd had plenty of opportunity to tell me to step off.

I walked down the hall, ignoring the many doors. I knew which room I needed. Of all the rooms I'd explored, it was the only one that hadn't left me feeling like a barely tolerated intruder. It was as if it had been constructed for my use, and *that* idea unsettled me. There were already too many people playing with my life. The idea that some ancient sect or deity had foreseen me, my discovery of the Isle, my needs, and then constructed a room to meet those needs stank of destiny. In my experience, people with destinies met bad, ugly ends. Still, the room had existed, and I had used it to good effect. I'd scratched out a warning on the door in every language I knew that the room contained evil and danger. It also made the room easy to find. I unlatched the door, pushed it open and stepped inside.

It was a small room, compared to some of the others, a mere twenty feet by twenty feet. Every square inch of the walls were covered in mirrors. It was anyone's guess how the mirrors were fastened to the walls, but they were very firmly stuck to the walls. I'd checked. For the first few moments, I just saw myself, reflected over and over again. Then, I saw something moving in the mirrors, a figure wrapped from head to foot in tattered gray scraps. It flew toward me from the inside of mirror and right before it would have passed out of the mirror and into the room, the spells I'd scratched into the mirrors flared to life. The gray figure bounced off the mirror and I heard it howling. I stepped into the center of the room.

"Jones," it wailed in a voice made of brittle corn husks rubbing together.

"Dreamer," I said, as nonchalant as I could manage. "It's been a while. How's the vacation treating you?"

I pounded its rag encased fists against the mirror. No one knew what the grey dreamer looked like, or what its actual name was, or even where it had come from. It just was, and it was terrible. It consumed consciousness, leaving the spirit trapped in a body lost to a vegetative state. I'd found one of its victims, a young man, and taken him to the future for examination. The examination revealed that the man's brain tissue, although alive, was stripped. There were only enough synaptic connections left to keep the body alive. Anything that related to personality, memory, or experience was simply dead. There would be no recovery. We performed a mercy killing and put the body somewhere it would be found. The cause of death would remain unknown.

"Release me," it bellowed, well, rasped loudly.

"I will, if we can come to an understanding."

The foul creature went absolutely still, staring at me from the other side of the mirror. It was silent for a very long while. Then it spoke with as much incredulity as something talking in that weird husk rubbing on husk voice could.

"What?"

It was one of the most gratifying things I'd ever heard.

7

"Short version. You want out. I need you to do something. If we can make that happen, we part ways and do our level best to avoid each other. I won't hunt you down, and you leave me and mine alone."

"Why should I believe you?" It asked.

"Maybe you shouldn't, but I lead a dangerous life. Pretty good chance I'll get killed soon. You might have noticed there aren't many tourists here. The odds that someone will find you before you starve to death aren't great. The odds that they'll be able to disarm my spells are downright infinitesimal. I built a lot of failsafes into this. I'm rather proud of it. Someone does it wrong, you get a one way trip into oblivion."

The gray dreamer screamed in rage and slammed a fist against the enchanted glass hard enough that the spells flared visibly. It screamed again, in pain, and jerked its fist back. The rags were scorched and smoking. It bellowed something in a language that never originated in a human tongue, but the meaning was pretty clear. Go fuck yourself was said in the same tone everywhere in the universe, it seemed. I rolled my eyes at it. I hoped I was putting on a good show. Even with it trapped on the other side of that mirror, the creepy thing still terrified me. I'd kept my hands in my coat pockets. I didn't want that inhuman thing to see them shaking. The gray dreamer railed and raged in that other language for a while before it finally lost steam.

"Well?" I asked.

"What do you want me to do?"

"There's something big and bad coming for me. Something big enough and bad enough that it might even sate your hunger. I want you to eat it."

There was another one of those protracted pauses. "What comes for you?"

I shrugged. "Not sure. I know that it's coming, but not what it is."

Another pause. "How do you know?"

I sighed. I'd hoped to entice it with the promise of a big meal and lies about safe passage afterwards. I guess it wasn't as stupid and hungry as I'd hoped it would be. I contemplated lying to it. It was a thing, not a human being, and I didn't feel any moral obligation to play it straight. On the other hand, it ate minds and memories. I was willing to bet it understood human psychology pretty well and could spot a lie a mile away. I rolled it over in my head for a moment.

"I sent myself a message from the future."

The gray dreamer recoiled from the other side of the mirror. "Fool! Madman! Foreknowledge! You'll destroy us all!"

"Oh, for God's sake. Take the twist out of your tattered gray thong, you big crybaby. It's got to be better than starving death in that mirror."

That gave the thing pause. I waited it out. I could imagine its internal debate. If the fool was playing with foreknowledge, it could mean temporal disintegration and dimensional entropy cascades. If that happened, it would mean certain destruction for all in his proximity when it happened. Of course, if the fool managed to pull off his mad gambit, it would mean freedom. It would mean food. Food, I thought, it was such a powerful motivator. The gray dreamer wasn't human, but it understood hunger and it hadn't eaten in a long time.

"Name your terms," it said.

"Simple. You accompany me. You eat what I tell you to eat and nothing else. When it's dead, you're free to go. We leave each other alone."

It hovered on the other side of the mirror and watched me, probably wondering how good I would taste, before it bowed its head.

"Agreed," it said.

I nodded. "Agreed."

I went to work. The spellwork I'd etched into the mirrors was exceedingly fine, done with a tiny diamond, and all but invisible more than an inch or two away. I worked mirror by mirror, adding the symbols, the words, the equations that would nullify the magic. Then I broke each mirror. When I removed the final spell, I only wanted gray dreamer to have one place to come out. Not that I didn't trust the ghastly creature, but I didn't trust it. I did not want it reentering the world from behind me. I got to the last mirror and slid one hand into my left pocket, grabbing the bottle. I reached out with the tiny diamond, made a handful of adjustments, and I felt the magic fail. I threw myself to one side and the gray dreamer exploded into the world. It flew into the center of the room and whirled toward me.

I could feel its malevolence from across the room, its hatred for life in general and me in particular. Yet, for all that, it malevolence and hate just weren't that scary. I'd squared off against things that were more malevolent and harboring much more hatred. No, what made the gray dreamer scary was the real possibility of having everything that made me who I was sucked out of my skull. Oh, sure, there would still be a soul in there somewhere, but I suspected that the soul wasn't the root of personality. It was a thread that connected you to the Immanent, rooted you inside the universe or the Samsaric cycle of rebirth, but it wasn't personality. You built that, brick by dysfunctional brick, over time. When it was gone, you were gone.

"You should have left me trapped," it rasped. "By what means to you imagine you will compel me now."

I'd expected the betrayal and prepared for it.

"I was younger the last we met," I said, turning to face it. "I've learned one or two things since then."

My adventure with Ryan had taught me one thing I hadn't known before. It taught me how to access power directly. It wasn't much use for containing something long term, since you'd have to keep up constant pressure and concentration. I'd made the bottle for precisely that purpose. What it was good for was laying a mighty hurting on something in a hurry. The gray dreamer laughed at me.

"You don't have time to set up your parlor tricks this time," it jeered. "I'll eat you very, very slowly. I'm told it's agonizing."

While the creature monologued like he was giving a master class at Bad Guy University – there had to be a handbook out there that they got after their first dozen murders or something – I took stock of the room. How smart of me to leave all of those big chunks of broken mirror on the floor. I reached deep and took hold of power. I spread the power out across the floor, seizing about a dozen large pieces of sharp glass.

"The better to shred your gray rags with, my dear," I said.

The gray dreamer cocked its head in confusion. I shrugged and sent the mirror pieces hurtling into the ragged form hovering in the center of the room. Gray cloth shredded and flew as razor edges cut through the figure. The gray dreamer howled in fury or pain. Either was good by me. I pulled the bottle out and popped the cork out. Streams of brackish liquid sprayed from the body. I gritted my teeth, picked up a few more pieces and used those to slash at the gray dreamer's face. More cloth and brackish liquid, it had to be the creature's version of blood, flew into the room. It started to bat wildly at the pieces. Some shattered and I replaced them with new pieces. Others embedded themselves into the gray dreamer's hands. It collapsed to the floor and I kept up the barrage of flying, mirrored agony.

I didn't stop until the damn was half the size it had been and couldn't much more than wave a limp hand at the glass. I kept the pieces hovering mere inches away as walked toward the downed body of the gray dreamer. The tattered rags that swathed its body were soaked in the thing's blood. What must have passed for the gray dreamer's body was tiny, no bigger than a child of five or six. It was sobbing and coughing, its face still hidden by the gray cloth.

"You're coming with me, dreamer. You are going to do what I tell you to do. Afterwards, if I'm feeling forgetful about this, I might even let you go. In the meantime," I said, "You travel like this."

I shoved the open mouth of the bottle into the mass of wet, stinking material and said a word under my breath. The spells on the bottle burst into iridescent white, blues and purples. The gray dreamer screamed in pain and fear, before its mass was sucked into the interior of the bottle. I shoved the cork into the bottle, activating another layer of magic that should keep the damn creature locked inside. I released the power holding the pieces of mirror in the air and they dropped to floor, splintering into fragments. A wave of tiredness rolled over me and I sank down onto one knee. I'd done it. I'd contained the gray dreamer not once, but twice. Granted, I'd tricked it both times, used its hubris against it, but no one else had done it.

"Well played, shaper," said a voice from the doorway. "I was right about you, but you must hurry now. Time grows short."

8

I had my Smith & Wesson, Model 27 out and pointed at the figure before I really processed the words. The reaction had become an instinct. I wasn't sure how I felt about that, but better safe than sorry, I guess. I stopped to take in the person I was pointing a gun at and frowned. He was tall, not J'adoube tall, but taller than me. He had the look of an academic, pale, thin, with wire rimmed glasses and disheveled, dark hair threaded with silver. He wore a plain brown robe that reminded me of a monk, but a pair of modern leather shoes poked out from beneath the robe. He looked at the weapon, then me, and shook his head in annoyance.

"Your toy won't be necessary. If I wanted to harm you, I could have simply unmade the room and left you trapped in solid rock."

That was a chilling idea. It would probably have hurt a lot too, at least for a few seconds. I put the gun away. "Who are you?"

The man shrugged. "A caretaker of this place. We have watched you."

I struggled to my feet as the fatigue faded. "And?"

"We find you inoffensive. You do not loot, you do no harm, you bind the mind eater. We will not bar you from this place. But, you must hurry now. Events transpire to which you must attend. Come."

The man vanished into the hall and I followed him. I closed the door to the room and, I blinked, the door vanished and was replaced by smooth, granite wall. Weird. I hurried after the man and fell into step beside him. I didn't know what to think.

"So, you watched me?"

"We watch all who come here. Rare though such things are now. In your case, however, we were expecting you."

"How's that work?"

"Instructions were provided regarding your arrival. There were several forked paths that you might have taken prior to coming here. We were told what to expect from you on each path. On this fork, we were not to hinder you, so we did not."

"On the other forks?"

"Be glad you came on this fork. You are formidable, but that strength would not have saved you here."

"Bad things, got it."

As we approached the steps that would take me outside, back to the portal, I stopped and pointed at the rune we were on.

"Idle curiosity," I said, "what are these? I don't recognize them and I was pretty sure I knew all the extant runic systems."

The thin man regarded me with a veiled expression. "If you survive what is to come and you follow the correct forks, you will return here one day. I will teach you then, if you wish it."

"Why not now?"

"Because the temptation to use what you learned would be too great in the conflict ahead of you. It would destroy you and all you love."

Gulp. "Oh, that's a good reason."

"Travel safely, shaper. The whisperers in the dark will no longer trouble you."

"Thanks," I said.

The trip home was both whisper and pain free. That was a pleasant first. Until then, the trip was excruciating in both directions. I stepped out of the weird blue and green flames and into predawn light. There was a mild pop and the portal vanished. The morning light was startling. How long had I been in there? I glanced down at where the fire had been. It had burned down to heatless ash hours before. I pulled the bottle out of my pocket. The clear glass was filled with swirling gray mist. One wholly unpredictable weapon in hand, check. I emptied a large bottle of water on the cold ashes just to be safe and headed home.

I knew something was wrong before I even got to my street. There were too many flickering, flashing lights around. I drove through the intersection, parked a half a block up and walked back to get a look. I stared in stunned horror. I hadn't been the only one playing with fire the night before. Where my little rented house had been was nothing but a blackened pile of rubble. I saw two body bags being carted away and felt a little nauseous. I turned away from the little house and headed back to my car. I felt the presence of the other person before I heard their footsteps. I drew the revolver out of my pocket, turned, raised it and very nearly shot J'adoube in the head.

"Oh, thank God," I said.

"Jones," gurgled J'adoube.

I could see his teeth were bloody and he was holding a hand to his stomach. He lurched and I caught him. I managed to wrangle the back door open and get him inside. I kept looking around, waiting for a cop or a neighbor to raise a fuss, but I got lucky. I started driving.

"Where are we going," wheezed J'adoube.

"Home," I said. "To get you help. I'm clearly burned in this decade."

"Can't go home."

"What?

"Ryan," said J'adoube, "got away. His people got him out."

I winced at J'adoube's words. He was clearly in a lot of pain.

"We can talk about this later," I said.

"No," growled the injured man.

His bloody hand clamped down on my shoulder hard enough to make me glad I'd never had to fight him.

"Can't go home. Strike team. It was," J'adoube took a shuddering breath, "don't know how. It was Endgame Smith."

"What?" I screamed.

Or, I started to scream it, before an explosion rocked the front end of the car. As the back end of the car lurched into the air and I realized we were, without doubt, going to flip, I had a moment of clarity. If Endgame Smith was alive, somehow, that meant that some faction in the future had made it happen. Despite what he had done, they'd resurrected that evil bastard. I had another moment of clarity. If I survived the next few minutes, I was going to murder the shit out of an awful lot of people.

Episode 10 - Godshead Revisited

1

I'd already had a long day. In fact, I'd had several long days. Between managing Clea's betrayal, Ryan's insistence on telling me about my personal future, traveling to the Spirit Isle, and securing the gray dreamer's "assistance," it'd been something of a busy week. So, coming back to find my home burned to the ground and J'adoube bleeding to death had already left me in a foul mood. Finding out that Endgame Smith was somehow still alive, no doubt through technology only available in the future, would have been enough to send a lesser man into an apoplectic fit. I *had* shot him in the head. You expected someone you shot in the head to stay dead. It was the polite thing to do. I might have even managed to cope with that new information. Then some bastard tried to blow my car up with me and J'adoube inside of it.

As the front of the car was shattered by the explosive force of what, I assumed, was a rocket propelled grenade, the back of the car tried to follow physics. Objects in motion stayed in motion. The rear end of the Beige Beast lifted into the air and swung forward like a pendulum. The vehicle was going to flip. The impact would probably kill J'adoube. If I was lucky, it'd just cripple me. The clarity you only experienced when your life was on the line and you needed to do something immediately took over. I did the math.

Someone in the future had decided to save Endgame Smith's life, against all reason. Then they'd sent him to kill Ryan, J'adoube and me. If I survived the next few minutes, I was going to murder the shit out of a whole lot of people and do it so hard that their parent's would bleed. Those thoughts took me a full quarter of a second to complete.

With that decision made, I needed to actually survive the next few minutes. That way I could get on with all the stabbing, shooting, and blowing up my decision demanded. I hadn't buckled up and J'adoube was just sprawled in the back seat. We'd get tossed around like blood filled bags inside the car on impact. That wouldn't do. Concussions, broken backs and massive internal bleeding tended to put a damper on a killing spree. There was only one available option, so I took it. I turned inward and reached out for magic. The process was still uncertain, strange and new. I'd always had the buffer of ritual and incantation. Working without them felt like working without a net. Still, it beat the hell out of dying from internal injuries. Another fraction of a second was gone and the car was already perpendicular to the road. I decided it was too late to stop the impact, so I needed to cushion me and J'adoube against the crash.

Working directly with magic took a lot more imagination that I was used to using. Rituals and incantations guided and shaped the magic, gave it function and form. Direct evocation demanded visualizing what you wanted to have happen, pouring as much juice as you could into the idea and hoping it was enough to get the job done. At least, that was my operational hypothesis. Direct workings were not standard operating procedure, so it was given short shrift in training. We got a smattering of practical theory, a dash of conjecture, and a dollop of confusion. Come to think of it, our training in direct workings had been a lot like a firefight, only in very slow motion. You knew just enough to know you were in over your head and not much more. For example, I had no idea if there were physical limits to the amount of magic I could use in an hour or a day. I didn't know if I could use too much and, if I could, what that might do to me. I didn't even know if what I was doing was white magic or black magic. I didn't think it was black magic, but it wasn't like there was ever signage that said Black Magic Thataway.

I concentrated. I imagined me and J'adoude wrapped in layers and layers of spongy, protective material. The magic poured into the idea like molten glass and it felt like the heat of it poured out of my chest and into the car. I felt something soft and warm curl around my body like an invisible blanket. Time took up its normal pace again and the car slammed against the pavement with a skull rattling noise, but it didn't toss me around. The invisible cushion compressed around me and I felt the magic disperse and redirect the killing force away from my body. I let the magic go slowly and my body settled onto the roof. The windows were all blown out and safety glass was scattered in every direction. I was looking out the spot where the windshield used to protect my face from bugs. I heard shouting, but didn't see anyone. I snuck a glance over my shoulder. J'adoube was face down on the roof.

"J'adoube," I said, reaching out to grab his shoulder.

"What did you do?" He asked.

J'adoube sounded weak, but he was alive. Chalk up one victory for Team Jones.

"I'll explain later."

I looked over his body and out the empty space where the rear window used to be. I saw a pair of military style boots making their way toward the car. I looked back out the front window. I saw three pairs of feet moving toward the car. I slid my hand into my coat pocket. By some miracle, the Smith & Wesson, Model 27 was still there. Four targets against me, my revolver and an injured J'adoube. I didn't like those odds. I drew out the sturdy gun and looked at J'adoube. He couldn't have survived as long as he had without coloring outside the lines a little. He was too practical.

"Are you armed?" I asked.

J'adoube moaned.

"Dammit, J'adoube, are you armed!"

There was an agonizing second before he pushed a blood covered hand into his own pocket and came up with sleek HK P9. The German semi-automatic wasn't to my taste, but beggars did not get to be choosers. I grabbed the gun with my left hand, flicked the safety off, and pointed it out toward the three people approaching the front of the car. I kept my revolver in my right hand and pointed it at the right knee of the person approaching the rear of the car. My heart pounded in my ears and my hands trembled a little, adrenaline and fear making me shaky. I forced myself to calm down as much as possible, falling back on years of practice firing rounds down dozens of ranges. The end of the revolver steadied. I breathed in slowly, and then fired the revolver. The person's knee disappeared in an explosion of red. I glanced to out the front, took half aim and popped off two rounds in their general direction. I missed with one, but heard a cry of pain when the second bullet hit someone.

I looked back out the rear, there was a woman on the ground, face contorted in pain, trying to drag herself out of harm's way. There was a small submachine gun hanging from her tactical harness. I didn't hesitate. Hesitation in that situation was death. She wasn't a woman, or a person, or anything for which I might have empathy. She was an enemy who would have participated in my cold-blooded execution, given the opportunity. I shot again and the back of her head erupted in a shower of bone, blood and brain tissue. My brain screamed at me to get the hell out of the car. It was a tactical nightmare. I'd caught them off guard, but they would shower the car with bullets the second they got to cover. I looked at J'adoube. I couldn't carry him and fight. There wasn't time to debate with myself about it. If I left him there and drew attention to myself, they might think he was already dead. I crawled over J'adoube toward the back window. He groaned in pain. I ignored the squelch of blood under my hand.

"Stay here, don't move. I'll draw them away," I told him in a harsh whisper.

I didn't know if he was still coherent enough to understand me, but there wasn't time to be sure. I crawled out the back and took a few precious seconds to close my coat and draw up the hood. The coat was functionally bulletproof, but I had a feeling that Endgame Smith had been a lot better at magic than he ever let on. With any luck, the coat would shed his magic the way it shed every other kind of magic that got directed at me. Unless, that was, he'd figured out a workaround. I shrugged that thought off. If he had, I was fucked no matter what. I popped up over the rear bumper, glanced around, and dropped down again. I heard shots. I replayed the look I'd just taken in my head and did my best to position where the shots had come from in that mental scene. Off to left, I thought. There had been some kind of truck or SUV over there. I looked at the memory again. It was the only decent cover in easy reach. I took another deep breath, stood and put a round from the revolver through the rear passenger window of a yellow SUV. I didn't know if it would penetrate through the back window with enough force to kill, but it would probably shatter that window and scare the hell out of them.

I turned and zigzagged toward the dead woman. A few shots whizzed by me like hyperthyroid bees and one clipped my head. The coat stopped the bullet from tearing out the side of my skull, but it hurt like hell, knocked me off balance and sent me down. I hit the road hard and the Smith and Wesson slid away. I also peeled a few layers of skin off my hand. It hurt. Since I was seeing double, though, I figured it was a low priority. I'd been close to the dead woman. I scrambled toward her body and the better offense offered by her submachine gun. Used properly, you could damn near cut a man in half with one of those. I heard a triumphant cry from behind me, followed by a sharp word spoken in a tone of command. There was a moment of silence. I got to her body and my vision started to clear up. Even as I unclipped the gun from her tactical harness, my mind insisted on noticing details. She'd had pretty blue eyes that still held a remnant look of surprise. There was a pale scar along her right cheekbone. Her fingernails were painted pink. I blinked at that. What kind of person painted her fingernails pink before going out as part of an execution squad?

I shook that thought off. The blow to my head was throwing off my focus. I set the submachine gun aside and rifled the woman's tactical harness. I pilfered a second magazine and a couple of flashbang grenades. That made me smile. Those were a lot more effective in an enclosed space, but they could still disorient people outside if you got the grenades close enough. I shoved the magazine into one coat pocket, forcing it in around the device, and put the flashbangs into the other pocket, along with J'adoube's HK. I glanced around and saw my Smith & Wesson nearly ten feet away. The overturned car was still giving me a little cover, but I'd have to run into the open to retrieve my revolver. I ground my teeth and left it where it was. I popped the magazine out of the submachine gun, still full, slid it back in and then really looked at the weapon. It resembled a KRISS Vector, but with a collapsible stock and downward cocking handle. I shrugged. It seemed simple enough. I flicked the selector up to the two-round burst, rather than full auto. I knew enough to know that anything more than the two-round burst would end with me raining bullets into some bystander's house. I didn't want that on my head.

Someone bellowed. "Jones!"

I flicked the safety off and crouch-walked my way to the rear of the overturned car. I hoped J'adoube hadn't bled out on me. I risked a glance over the back of the car. I saw three men, two dressed like the woman I'd killed, probably mercenaries from the relative present, and someone dressed in a coat like mine. One of the mercenaries was wiping blood out of his eyes every few seconds, courtesy of a nasty gash in his forehead. I expected that was my handiwork from shooting at the SUV. I didn't recognize the man in the coat, but that didn't mean anything. There were plenty of other active Agents I hadn't met. Of course, the coat didn't necessarily make him an Agent. Time travel technology was in the open, why not the technology to make to the coats too. I dipped my head behind the car, just in case one of the mercenaries tried to take a shot at me.

"You have the advantage on me," I shouted back. "Who the hell are you?"

"Where's Green, Jones?"

"Dead. He bled out. I have you assholes to thank for that?"

I crossed my fingers and hoped that I was lying, rather than reporting. If they thought he was dead, though, they had no reason to firebomb the car with him still inside it. I took another peek over the back of the car. The two mercenaries were creeping forward. I shook my head. They had the numerical advantage, but had to move over open ground to get to my comparatively concealed position. I slid sideways, still crouched, brought the submachine gun to bear on center mass of the closer mercenary, and opened fire. The gun wasn't sighted in for me, which was unfortunate for the mercenary. The first shot caught him in the ribcage, but the recoil on the gun carried it up and to the right. The mercenary's throat burst into a scarlet fountain with the second shot. I rolled right as the second mercenary fired reflexively in my general direction. I heard the bullets hit the pavement and ricochet to who knew where.

Someone bellowed. "Fall back!"

"So," I said, yelling through the ringing in my ears, "I was expecting Endgame. Who are you?"

"Misinformed, it seems," the man yelled back. "You're tougher than I was led to believe."

"Oh, you know how it is. Me and the cockroaches."

The device in my pocket started making noises. The extra magazine made it tough, but with a little application of brute force the device popped free. I entered an access code and did a double take. Staring at me through the screen was a battered Captain Kane. As if things weren't complicated enough.

"Not a good time," I growled.

"What?" She barked at me.

I shook my head and turned the devise toward the dead woman's body. Then I turned it back so she could see me. She looked grim.

"Like I said, not a good time."

"Jones, you should just come out. I am going to kill you. One way or the other."

"Who's that?" Kane sounded nonchalant, like we were just chatting about the weather.

"I don't know him. He's got a nice coat, though. It looks a lot like mine."

"Shit," said Kane, then she gave me nonplussed look. "Are you in real trouble?"

I thought it through and shook my head. "No, not really. I figured I'd try to pump the guy for information, but he's being uncooperative. I'll have to kill him soon. The cops must be on their way by now."

"Things have gone to hell here. Get your ass back as soon as you can. We're holding the transit room, at least for the moment."

Apparently, my would-be assassin felt he wasn't getting enough attention. "Who are you talking to Jones?"

"A hot chic. I figure after I brutally murder you, I'll be peckish. Just setting up a lunch date."

"Jones," chided Kane.

"What? This is how I roll. I'll get back as soon as I can."

I cut Kane off before she could object and shoved the device back in my pocket. I sighed. Whoever the guy in the coat like mine actually was, he wasn't going to tell me anything. J'adoube certainly didn't have any more time to waste. I needed to get serious.

I thought for a second. The hit team and I shared a quandary. To get to them, I needed to cross too much open ground. I didn't have any practice throwing grenades, so it would only be sheer dumb luck if I got one close to them. I needed more cover. The mental rolodex of spells I knew whirred into motion. Exploding shells had the same problem as the grenades. Sleep spell required me to get too close. Flip. Flip. Flip. No. No. No. Fire and flood were too destructive for a residential neighborhood. Come on, brain, give me something, I demanded. Flip. Flip. Flip. No. No. *Yes!* I crouch-walked back to the dead woman and gave her an apologetic look as I dipped a finger into the pool of blood around her obliterated knee.

"Sorry lady, but I need this more than you do right now."

I used her blood to scrawl an incantation onto the pavement. It took longer than I would have liked, because I sensed a presence closing in on me from behind. I dove over the woman's corpse, rolled and threw a hand back in the direction of the incantation.

I growled, "Nebol!"

The last mercenary was bringing his assault rifle to bear on me when fog billowed out of the bloody incantation I'd laid on the pavement. The sight was sufficiently bizarre that he paused in confusion. I didn't waste the opportunity. I jerked the almost-KRISS up and sent four rounds at the man. I was rewarded with a red spray before the fog bank washed over us all. I didn't know where their leader had gotten off to and it seemed like an extraordinarily bad idea to stay in one place. For all I knew, they'd been flanking me. I stood and started walking as slowly and quietly as I could toward where I thought the yellow SUV was parked. I couldn't be absolutely certain. The fog was so thick it acted like a visual and auditory blanket, obscuring and muffling all sight and sound. It would hinder me as much as it would hinder the other man, but at least it was a level playing field.

"What are you playing at, Jones?"

I stopped in my tracks, trying desperately to pinpoint the source of the voice. I'd done too good of a job on the fog. His voice sounded like a transmission from Pluto. Of course, that meant my voice would probably be the same to him. It could be an opportunity.

"What are you playing at? Unless you stole that coat, we're supposed to be on the same team," I said.

There was a long pause. "You aren't a team player Jones. Never have been. That's a problem that needs to be fixed."

"You really must have stolen that coat. Not a team player is in our job description."

"Treason isn't."

He was closer now. I turned to my right and took a few steps. "I'm no traitor. You're the one trying to execute colleagues."

There was another long pause before he spoke again. "I'm following my orders. Can you say that?"

He'd done what I'd done. Used my voice to try to get closer to me, but he'd gotten too close. I closed the distance and I saw his general shape. I pulled J'adoube's HK from my pocket and took careful aim at his head. I took a slow step, then a second, and finally a third. His back was to me and his hood was up. I frowned and then picked a new target that wasn't protected by the bullet-shedding coat. I pulled the trigger. The human ankle is a surprisingly simple thing, comprised of just three bones: the tibia, the fibula and the talus. There are also several rather important tendons in there. None of those things respond well to a bullet passing through them. The mist-shrouded figure screamed and fell, hands instinctively clamping down on the wounded ankle. I put another round through the same ankle and, incidentally, through the hands holding it. There were more screams, agonized shouting, you get the idea. I walked over and calmly kicked the man in the face. His nose broke and I heard teeth crack. I leveled J'adoube's gun at the man's face.

"Who are you?"

I'd kicked him too hard, because he just stared at me blankly. Then again, that might have been all the pain. I gave it a few seconds to see if he was going to rally. He did.

"Go to hell," he groaned.

I sighed, shook my head, and then kicked him in the ribs. The coat would probably protect him enough to avoid broken ribs, but it would still hurt.

"I've got a very small reservoir of patience. You've used it up already. Who are you?"

"We're not like you. We don't make up stupid names. I'm just Four."

"Four? Yeah, that's so much less stupid than a name. Who do you answer to? Where is Endgame Smith?"

He said nothing, just glared at me. I rolled my eyes, shook my head, and shot his other ankle. There was more screaming.

"One! I answer to One!"

"Names, moron! Tell me their names!"

"I don't know! I never knew!"

"Smith?"

"You killed him."

I didn't have time to play ten thousand questions with "Four." I'd probably already wasted more time than J'adoube had to give.

"Where's your car?"

He stared up at me without understanding.

"You're vehicle. How did you get here?"

"It's a black, um, sports umbilical thing?"

"Rock solid training they gave you there. Where is it?"

"Around the corner," he gasped.

I knelt down by the guy, rifled through his pockets and came up with the keys. I cocked my head at that. Dude must have been a serious control freak. I shrugged, unfastened the front of his coat and flipped it open to reveal a plain, gray shirt. I started jerking him out of the coat in a bevy of more pained screams.

He gasped out a question. "What are you doing?"

"Can't leave future technology sitting around where authorities can find it," I said.

He got a look of dawning comprehension. "You can't. Not like this."

"You just tried to execute me."

He grimaced and looked away. "Make it quick."

"By the way," I said, "if you're going to shoot someone, finish the job. You don't leave someone alive with a bullet in their stomach. Gut shots are a horrible way to go."

Then I shot him in the stomach. I walked away. I got about five steps before I went back. Gut shots really *are* a horrible way to go, so I shot him in the head three times. Apparently once was enough anymore.

2

By the time J'adoube regained consciousness, we were safely ensconced in a storage unit that I called Armory Ten. It had taken some effort to get J'adoube into the "sports umbilical thing." He weighs more than one would expect for such a thin man. I managed it, though, and even managed to avoid high-speed or low-speed pursuit. I'd taken to renting storage units in every decade I covered, paying ridiculously far in advance, and storing things I thought I might need, like clothes and cash. Mostly, though, I used them to store period appropriate weapons and a few of the medical patches. I suspected Command believed I got injured on every mission given how many of the things I've requisitioned over the years. I'd slapped two of them onto J'adoube. They're freaky devices. I actually watched the bullet slowly get pressed out of J'adoube's stomach. I guess it was better than me digging around in there with needle nose pliers. He blinked a few times as he tried to sort out where he was, or maybe it was just all the guns.

"Jones," he said.

"Green."

"I'm not dead. I'm a little surprised."

I snorted. "Me too, honestly. I couldn't take you to a hospital. I didn't dare send you home. You were pretty shocky by the time I got you here."

J'adoube looked around again and lifted an eyebrow at me. He looked amused. "Where exactly is here? A museum?"

"Think of it as an insurance policy."

"A well-armed insurance policy."

"I like to keep my options open."

"Why couldn't you send me home?"

"What? Oh, right, you weren't conscious for that. Kane called. Apparently I'm not the only one having a bad day. Looked like there was some kind of coup or insurrection going on at headquarters."

J'adoube's eyes bugged out. "Why are you still here?"

"Take it easy. I thought about rushing in, but it seemed prudent to wait until I knew if you were going to die."

J'adoube opened his mouth, probably to yell at me again, but then he thought it through. His process was probably a lot like mine. There was an adverse situation going on at Command. Unknown enemies in unknown numbers were carrying out an unknown goal. You've got a wounded friend right there in immediate danger. If you leave the friend, you go into combat without backup and possibly leave them to die. Odds of survival improve significantly if you can help the friend and take them with you when you drop into an ongoing firefight at Command. At the moment of choice, you wait and hope the folks at Command can do without you for a while. It was ultimately better if two trained Agents showed up, a little later, but ready to fight, than just one Agent. It was harsh math. It was a day for harsh math. J'adoube nodded.

"Backup," he said.

"Backup," I agreed. "Of course, there is a good chance we'll arrive and be shot on sight by bad guys. I may not have done you any favors."

"You've save my life twice now. Least I can do is go with you for the ride."

J'adoube tried to sit up and had to brace himself against a shelf. I thought that might happen. I waited until he seemed to have his balance before I slid him some beef jerky and a bottle of water. He eyed the jerky and started to push it away. I shook my head.

"You lost an unwholesome amount of blood. Even with the nanites supporting your system, you need the protein. You're no good to anyone if you pass out."

J'adoube heaved an enormous sigh, but he opened the jerky and started chewing on a piece. You'd have thought it was solid toxic waste from the expression on his face. He stopped chewing, seemed to make a mental effort, and swallowed the jerky. He actually shuddered.

"Do you know anything else about the situation at home?" He asked.

I shook my head. "Just that, as of an hour ago, Kane's people still controlled the transit room. No way to know if that's still the case. I think it's safe to assume Endgame is there, lurking like some kind of undead thing."

"I don't relish the idea of confronting an Agent of Smith's skill," said J'adoube around another hateful bite of jerky.

I shrugged. "He's not so tough. I beat him."

J'adoube shook his head. "No, you didn't. He underestimated you and died for that misjudgment. Do you honestly believe he'll make that mistake a second time?"

I thought about the *thing* I'd caged in an enchanted bottle. I gave J'adoube a humorless smile. "Yes. I fully expect him to make exactly the same mistake. It's his character. Character is destiny."

"Plato?"

"Heraclitus."

"Ah. Still, it won't do for you to underestimate Smith. Do you have a plan? He'll know you're coming."

"A plan? Not as such. There's just too much we won't know until we're on site. I do have a general strategy."

"Which is?"

I spread my arms wide at all the shelves filled with weapons and ammunition. J'adoube really looked around for the first time and his eyes went a little wide. Then his face went a little dark. He'd finally tripped to my intentions. He chewed sullenly on the jerky for a while without saying anything. He sipped at the water and seemed to come to some kind of a conclusion.

"I can't countenance wholesale slaughter, Jones."

I frowned at him. "Don't be naïve."

Anger twisted his face. "I'm not an assassin!"

I mulled that for a moment. I supposed it was possible. Floaters got different training than the rest of us. I didn't have any illusions about my job description. I was an assassin, more often than not. J'adoube's statement seemed off somehow, like he didn't quite mean it or believe it. Maybe it was self-delusion or indoctrination, but that didn't seem right either. He wasn't stupid enough to blindly accept indoctrination. Self-delusion felt out of character for the man. He was still giving me a hard look. I took a shot in the dark.

"You don't like the idea of killing friendlies?"

The anger bled out of his expression and was replaced with one equal parts fatigue and judgment. "You do?"

I stood, took a few steps, picked up the coat I'd taken from the self-styled Four and showed it J'adoube. His forehead crinkled as he took in the coat. He lifted his eyes to meet mine.

"I don't understand."

"Smith isn't the only person from home gunning for us. I took this off one of the team who tried to blow us up in the car."

He stared at the coat in my hands for a very long time. It was a hell of a thing. There would be no efficient way to tell friend from foe if everyone was wearing coats like that. It'd be even more difficult with random staff. Turning our backs on anyone was a possibly suicidal move. He closed his eyes and nodded. He got it. We wouldn't have the luxury of doubt or hesitation.

I gave him a sympathetic look. "If you're not up for this, I understand."

"How can *you* be up for it? God, Jones, we're talking about killing our own."

I shrugged. "Someone has to be up for it. Isn't this why you brought me in to begin with? Unconventional solutions?"

"I," J'adoube hesitated. "Yes, I suppose so. I just never imagined this.

Is life really so meaningless to you?"

That one hurt. I looked away and dropped the coat back onto a crate of .40 caliber incendiary rounds. The crate was probably overkill, but I got a good deal when I bought it. Incendiary rounds weren't nearly as dangerous as people imagined, but they would be scary as hell if used in the right situation. I'd loaded a couple throwaway pistols with them while J'adoube was unconscious. The weight of his gaze on my back was heavier than I expected. What could a person say to a question like that? "It's complicated" sure wasn't going to cut it. I faced him.

"That sentiment will get you shot in the head," I said. "I'm not a psychopath, but these people tried to murder us. Right now, they're trying to murder our allies in the future. This isn't a family squabble, J'adoube. This is a war. I intend to survive it. Now eat your jerky, we leave in ten minutes."

While J'adoube choked down some more jerky, I started the process of strapping a ridiculous number of weapons to my person. I stuck mostly with small arms. In all likelihood, we'd face close quarters fighting. I made sure to grab a few fragmentation grenades. I looked at the shelves and pulled down one last weapon. A magazine snapped into the top of the weapon. I managed to find room for an extra magazine or two. I turned and found J'adoube doing his own version of the load for bear dance. He glanced over at me as he grabbed magazines I'd preloaded a while back. He eyed the compact submachine gun in my hand.

"What's that?" He asked.

"It's called a P90. Meant for close quarters combat."

He raised an eyebrow at me. "I don't suppose you have another one?"

"In point of fact, I do have another one."

I made sure to grab the extra coat on our way out of the storage unit. There was no guarantee I'd ever get back there. The guns would raise eyebrows if someone eventually opened it up, but none of it was future tech. We made our way back down to the stolen SUV. I felt slow with all the extra weight strapped to my body, but I'd rather go in over-armed than under-armed. J'adoube was quiet as I drove us across the city toward a particular alley. He seemed to be watching the people on the sidewalks.

"I don't know how you can live here," said J'adoube.

I glanced at him. "It's not that bad. It's a little primitive, but I've lived worse places."

He shook his head. "That's not what I meant. I don't know how you, any of you, can live among all these people without getting involved."

"Oh. It's the job. They screen us all pretty rigorously beforehand, tests and psychological profiling," I snickered to myself at that. "It's not for everyone."

"I would imagine it's not. Is that what happened to Clea? Not cut out for the work?"

I rolled a shoulder. "She's cut out for it, maybe even better than I am. I just took issue with Command planting a full-time spy in my house. I sent her home."

"What?"

"Oh, right, I didn't have time to get you up to speed on everything. Our esteemed leader, August Worth, planted her with me."

J'adoube blinked rapidly a few times at the mention of the secretive director's name. "Worth planted her with you. He did it personally?"

"Yep."

"You know this how?"

"He told me so. Well, he implied the hell out of it anyway."

"There are times when I'm profoundly glad I'm not you, Jones."

"Times? Such as?"

J'adoube gave me a bemused smile. "When I'm awake."

"Thanks."

J'adoube got down to business. "What's the first order of business when we get back?"

"Assuming we aren't gunned down in the first three seconds, we need to find Captain Kane."

"Kane? Why her?"

"I trust her. She'll have access to the most information. And why the hell am I making all the decisions? You're the senior Agent here."

"I follow a somewhat different command structure. Operate out of a different facility. You know the ground. Besides, this sort of operation isn't my strong suit."

"Really? I'd have thought you'd be trained for this kind of thing."

J'adoube shrugged. "My training wasn't built around large scale conflict. If it were half a dozen people, that would be different. Hundreds of people spread across a huge complex is a bit outside my experience."

"You think that's inside my experience?"

"I read your file, Jones. The real one."

I didn't say anything.

"You're good at downplaying your capacities," he continued. "We both know this isn't the first time you've faced something like this."

I shuddered. "That was different."

"How so?"

I fell silent and did my best to shove the memories away. It had been a bloodbath and, in retrospect, I didn't think I was meant to survive the experience. "It just was."

"Of course," said J'adoube.

We passed the rest of the ride in silence. J'adoube closed his eyes and appeared to nap. It was a good idea. He was probably still fatigued. I made a mental note to find a place to stash him once it was nominally safe. The poor bastard always seemed to wind up on the cusp of death whenever he spent more than a few hours in proximity to me. It was a damn miracle he didn't just spontaneously combust right then and there at the rate we were going. I shamelessly double parked the SUV and we got out. There was too much foot traffic for two men in huge black coats, one of them tall enough to be an NBA forward, to be discreet. We got some looks. I did my best to let it roll off my back as we walked down the alley. I kept my back to the mouth of the alley, pulled the P90 loose and clipped it to the tactical harness that was housing a lot of my gear. J'adoube followed suit, minus the harness. I'd never gotten around to buying a second harness and would have had to special order one for a man J'adoube's size.

I pulled the device free from my coat pocket and held it against the right brick. J'adoube shifted his P90 to his left hand and touched my shoulder with his right. There was an interminable wait as the device connected with command. It made a quiet noise to indicate the connection was established.

"Be ready," I said.

J'adoube nodded and then linear time evaporated.

3

Those first few seconds after we arrived were some of the most nerve wracking of my life. The disorientation from being transported through the ley lines across space and time only lasts a few seconds, but it was immutable. No matter how tough minded or physically fit you were, you always experienced that moment or two of mental incoherence. Most days, it wasn't an issue. Arriving when you didn't know what to expect, with a high probability that the enemy would be waiting, made it terrifying. Two or three seconds was an eternity in a combat scenario. I did the only thing I could do on arrival. I let my body falls sideways. It wasn't a great move, but it might buy a few fractions of second to get my head together enough to defend myself. When my vision cleared and reality started ordering itself in familiar ways again, J'adoube and I were in the transit room. The room was silent and empty. It was creepy. I glanced at J'adoube. He raised an eyebrow at me.

"Not what I was expecting," I muttered, getting to my feet.

"No. If not the enemy, then an ally ought to be here waiting for us."

The weird curvature of the walls gave me a touch of phantom vertigo. I sighed and gestured toward the door. "I guess there's nothing to do but check things out."

J'adoube nodded at me. We took two steps toward the door before gunfire erupted in the hallway outside. I darted to one side of the door and J'adoube took up position on the other. He held up three fingers and did a slow countdown. I waved a hand in front of the door when he dropped the last finger. The door slid open and I took an angled peek down the hallway. There was nothing but bodies and the smell of fresh cordite in the air. J'adoube tilted his head out just enough to glance in the other direction. He frowned and shook his head. I went out first, sweeping the P90 in one direction and then the other. Nothing moved. J'adoube came into the hall and we waited for a moment.

"Well," I said. "This is a touch unnerving, if anticlimactic."

J'adoube nodded. "Agreed."

A man in a loose-fitting set of pants and shirt charged into the hallway. He leveled something at us that vaguely resembled a rifle, if you could grow rifles out of organic material. I brought my P90 up and saw J'adoube doing the same, even as we both moved toward the walls. It wasn't necessary. The man made it all of three steps before someone melted out of a shadow I hadn't even noticed, seized the man by the chin and the back of his head, and twisted hard. There was a dull pop. The man with the almost-rifle convulsed and then dropped to the floor. I eyed our would-be savior for a long beat before I recognized him.

"Lester?"

"Jones," said Lester.

His hair was partially matted with dried blood and he stood a little crooked, like his right side was giving him pain. It might have been the pain dulling his senses, because he jerked a little when he saw J'adoube and I were still pointing guns at him.

"Kane sent me," he muttered, "to hold the transit room until you arrived."

I glanced at all the bodies on the ground. "How many men did you lose?"

He blinked at me. "None."

I blinked at him. "You did all this?"

He shrugged. "She said to hold the room."

"Impressive," said J'adoube.

"No kidding. Hang on a second, Lester, I need to grab something."

I went back into the transit room and grabbed the other coat I'd brought back with us from the past. I took it into the hall and walked up to Lester. I held out the coat. He stared at it.

"Put it on," I said. "It's a field promotion, Agent."

Lester took the coat and put it on. "Agent Lester Gibbons."

"I don't know who that is," I said. "J'adoube, you know somebody named Lester Gibbons?"

"I don't believe any such person exists," said J'adoube, with a little twitch at the corner of his mouth.

I glanced around the hallway. "I think Chokepoint Williams here is talking about some kind of cover identity."

Lester gave me a look. "Chokepoint Williams?"

"You don't think my name is actually Contingency Jones, do you?"

Lester snorted. "Fair point."

J'adoube coughed gently. "Jones, time might be an issue here."

I sighed. "Yeah. Chokepoint, do you know where Kane is?"

The newly minted Chokepoint adjusted his new work coat and stepped over to a wall. He pressed his hand against it and a panel slid open. I traded a look with J'adoube. He shrugged. Command sure loved its secrets. Chokepoint punched in a code and then issued a muffled voice recognition passphrase. There was a long pause and a screen came to life. Kane's face appeared as a holographic projection.

"Lester, what are you, no, never mind. Update."

"Jones has arrived with," Lester turned to J'adoube, "who are you again?"

"J'adoube Green."

"Green," said Kane through the holograph. "What are you doing here?"

"Assisting Jones, apparently."

"Aren't we all," muttered Kane. "The training wing is compromised. We've regrouped in the Administration wing. You should be able to get there through sublevel 3 without too much resistance."

I looked at the projection. "Where's Smith?"

"Dammit, Jones, can't you just follow orders once in your life?"

"This doesn't stop until Smith is put down. Where is he?"

Kane rubbed a hand across her face. "This is a lot bigger than Smith. We've got a full-on hostile takeover going on here."

I stared at her for a moment. "Why do I have to keep explaining this to people? This is war. Smith and his backers declared war on us. It's time for the gloves to come off, Captain."

Something in Kane's eyes, hope maybe, died right there. Maybe she hadn't wanted to admit to herself what was going on. Maybe she just wanted to keep the casualty count down. She nodded to me.

"Probably, but I still need all of you to regroup with us. We need to coordinate this before," she closed her eyes, "before we take the gloves off. Lester, you know how to access sublevel 3."

"Yes, ma'am."

"Get them here."

The projection vanished. Chokepoint pressed a button and the panel slid closed. I eyed it. Then I thought about Kane's orders. Then I gave J'adoube a look. His lips were pressed into a tight line. I could see he was a few ounces of pressure on the trigger away from shooting the young man. I put a hand on J'adoube's arm. He gave me a questioning look, but eased off the trigger. It was only then that Chokepoint realized how much danger he'd been in a moment before.

"The two of you don't trust anyone, do you?"

J'adoube tilted his head to one side. "Can you give us a reason we should trust you, all things considered?"

The kid opened his mouth, seemed to think briefly, and then frowned. "I guess not."

"Damn," I said. "I guess he's on the up and up."

"Why do you say that?" J'adoube asked.

"If he was colluding with the enemy, he'd have had an answer to that question ready to go. Allies don't spend their time thinking up reasons why you should believe them."

"True," said J'adoube and he appeared to relax.

"We should get moving," said Chokepoint.

"Yeah," I murmured, stepping past him, "we should do that."

I walked over to the body of the last man Lester killed. The odd, rifle-shaped object lay on the floor next to him. Up close, it looked less organic. I started to reach for it.

"Don't!"

I looked up at Chokepoint. "Why? What is this thing?"

"Rail gun. It's genetically coded. It'll explode if anyone but him touches it."

"Rail gun? We finally cracked the energy and material problems?"

"We didn't, but someone did. It seems like they were designed specifically to kill Agents. Cut right through these," he tugged at the coat.

I shuddered at that thought. I'd gotten very comfortable with the idea that the coats would stop projectiles. I pulled my hand back from the rail gun. I didn't want to accidentally kill us all. I found myself thinking that even with all the guns strapped to me, I still hadn't been paranoid enough. They hadn't declared war on us. They'd declared genocide. Whoever they were. I stood and shook my head. I turned to Chokepoint.

"Are you armed?"

He shook his head. "Ran out of ammo a while back."

"You have a preferred caliber?"

"Today, the bigger, the better."

I slid a pair of 40 caliber Glocks out and handed them over. He inspected the weapons for a moment, pocketed one and flicked the safety off with a thumb on the other. He gave me half a smile.

"These are ancient," he said, without criticism.

"Still get the job done," I said, handing over a couple of extra magazines.

He took them with a nod and then headed down the hall. J'adoube followed and I took up the rear, keeping a close eye behind us. I really didn't want to find out what it felt like to have a rail gun projectile tear through me. We didn't see anyone, which made me both nervous and a little relieved. I had some business to finish with Smith and I didn't want to get sidetracked any longer than necessary. On the other hand, if the bad guys weren't bothering us, who were they bothering? Chokepoint drew up short and leaned out a little to get a look around the curved corner of another hallway. He jerked his head back and a split-second later a chunk of wall exploded. I felt oddly better at that turn of event. I pulled out one of the fragmentation grenades.

"Chokepoint," I said, then sighed when he didn't look. "Lester."

His head whipped toward me. I tossed him the grenade. He caught it and then looked at in confusion.

"Give me that," said J'adoube.

J'adoube pulled the pin and waited a hair-raising two count. In a deft motion, he whipped the grenade around the corner and then dragged Chokepoint back a couple of steps. I covered my ears. The concussion from the explosion, not to mention the noise, rattled my jaw. Damn things were noisy. If people didn't know we were here before, they did now. I was in motion first, rounding the corner with the P90 at my shoulder. There was still a cloud of dust and debris in the air, so I wasn't an obvious target. I moved down the hallway, shoulder sliding along one wall. The smell of blood and the stink of shit from shredded intestines made me want to gag. I choked the impulse down and kept moving. If anyone survived that little surprise, I didn't want to give them a chance to recover. A figure staggered forward through the dust cloud.

"Wait," a woman shouted.

I didn't. Unlike the Vector I'd been shooting earlier, the P90 was sighted in for me. The bullet snapped her head back as it passed through her skull. I moved forward and was surprised to see it was Janet, an evaluator who had once called me a soul-less hell-spawn. I was less surprised to see the gun in her hand. I shook my head. This whole thing was going to be a nightmare. I'd known some of the staff might be playing for the other side, but it wasn't always going to be so obvious. I cleared the rest of the hall and then circled back to Janet, mostly because J'adoube and Chokepoint were standing next to her. J'adoube looked a little grim, but Chokepoint looked ill.

"You okay, kid?" I asked.

"Janet?" He asked, incredulous. "I mean, how could she be part of this?"

"We may never know," said J'adoube, giving the kid a compassionate look.

"How did you know she wasn't trying to help?" Chokepoint asked as he gave me a hard look.

"I didn't know, not absolutely."

"You didn't know!"

I closed my eyes and took a breath, trying to remind myself that I was probably one of the only people in the building to ever face a scenario even remotely like the one in front of us. "We're going to have to make a lot of educated guesses in the next couple hours. We aren't going to have time to vet everyone we run across. Odds are, if we run into someone familiar immediately after we just killed obvious bad guys, that person isn't a friend."

"God," said Chokepoint. "You're a piece of work, Jones."

"He's also right," said J'adoube, who looked deeply uncomfortable with that admission. "We can't take the chance that we might be wrong. There's too much at stake here. We cannot allow this facility to fall into the hands of those who would misuse it."

A thought occurred to me. "Jesus, the transit room. We left it unguarded."

Chokepoint made an obvious effort to push his anger aside. "It's not an issue. The whole system locked down the minute you got here, Kane's orders. No one is traveling from that room for forty-eight hours without her explicit say-so."

"That's something anyway," I said.

J'adoube cocked his head and he listened for a moment. "We need to move, others are coming."

I was stunned he could hear anything farther away than a few feet after that grenade. My ears were still ringing from the explosion. We followed Chokepoint through a series of hallways before he stopped in front of another blank patch of wall. He repeated the process of opening secret panels, entering and verbalizing codes and then a doorway slid open to reveal a cramped elevator car. We stuffed ourselves into the tiny car and the wall sealed itself before the elevator doors slid shut. A woman's voice piped in from an anonymous speaker.

"Greetings Agent Jones, Agent Green, and Agent Williams. What is your destination?"

"Sublevel three," said Chokepoint.

"Security clearance access required. Please hold."

J'adoube gave me a stunned look. "That field commission was real? What's your rank?"

"I don't know," I whispered. "It's not like promotions would have changed anything for me. The bigger question is how the hell the computer knew about that little field commission."

The voice chimed in again. "Security clearance access granted, Agent Williams. Security clearance access granted, Major Green. Security clearance access granted, Commander Jones."

All three of us jerked at that last. Commander? When in the hell did I become a Commander? J'adoube shook his head at me. Chokepoint turned and gave me a confused look.

"You're a Commander? Why the hell are you still operating in the field? Do the regs even permit that?"

"Those are great questions you should definitely ask someone else."

The elevator started dropping at a somewhat alarming speed, so Chokepoint didn't follow up on his questions. It was for the best. I had no answers for him. The elevator slowed to a stop fast enough that it made me a little queasy.

"Sublevel three. Enjoy your day," said the voice.

The door slid open and we stepped out into something that belonged in one of my nightmares.

4

As someone versed in arcane principles, I knew that magic could have devastating effects on reality. Understanding that as theory just couldn't prepare me for confronting it as fact. What should have been a hallway with curving walls made of a smooth composite material had been transformed into a throbbing, undulating cave of diseased flesh shot through with black veins and tumorous protuberances. Even as I watched, one of the masses split open and yellow pus sprayed out. The part of my mind that wasn't sobbing uncontrollably and asking to be let back into the elevator noted that Chokepoint was retching with violent, body-jerking motions. J'adoube spoke under his breath in a language I didn't recognize. I couldn't say how long I stood transfixed by the horror, but at some point I noticed I'd lifted a hand. That seemed odd, as I couldn't remember telling my arm to do that. Then I slapped myself in the face very, very hard. The pain snapped me out of my stupor.

I grabbed the back of Chokepoint's coat and jerked him upright. "Which way?"

He looked at me in absolute terror. "What?"

"Which way, dammit?"

Chokepoint closed his eyes, shuddered hard, and pointed left. I watched another of the protuberances split open and spew yellow pus. Maybe it was an intuition, or the voice of long experience, or just a keen familiarity with Murphy's Law, but I was willing to bet that it would be very bad if that pus came into contact with bare skin. In point of fact, I was pretty confident that any kind of extended exposure to that altered environment would probably kill us. I looked at the other two. J'adoube's face was fixed in revulsion. Chokepoint just looked afraid. Chokepoint was probably smarter than me and J'adoube, or maybe just less desensitized.

"Hoods up," I said, and followed my own advice. "Keep your hands in your sleeves or pockets. I don't know what that yellow shit is, but you probably want it to land on your coats first."

J'adoube just nodded and pulled up his hood. Chokepoint took a second and seemed to steel himself to the abomination around us. He reached back and jerked the hood up harder than necessary. For my part, I found myself wishing we had gas masks or rebreathers. Once the shock of what I was seeing wore off, the smell hit me. The actual smell wasn't something I could identify. It was too big, too solid, a veritable wall of olfactory corruption that threatened to embed itself into my sinuses forever. I tried to take shallow breaths.

"I'll take lead," I said. "J'adoube, cover the rear. Chokepoint, in the middle."

I set off down the hallway in the direction Chokepoint indicated and did my best to ignore the squelching noises my boots made as I walked. Every once in a while, I noticed extremely large protuberances and hurried past them, even as suspicions formed in the back of my mind. I hoped I was wrong. If I was right, there was nothing to be done. We covered maybe a hundred squelching, nauseating yards when Chokepoint put a hand on my shoulder. I looked back.

"We need to hang a right up ahead," he said.

I looked up the hallway. I didn't see a place to take a right. I moved forward again, maybe five or ten feet, and I was sure. Wherever the branch in the hallway was supposed to be, the rotting flesh had covered it over. I looked back to Chokepoint again.

"I don't suppose you know precisely where that hallway is?"

He frowned at the wall in consternation. "Your Quirt should be able to tell you."

"Really?" I asked.

He blinked at me. "Why not? You're a commander. You should have full access to the building schematics."

I shook my head. "I really need to start reading my mail."

I pulled the device out of my pocket and punched in a code to unlock it. Then I just sort of stared at it. Use it to hack into computer systems? Sure. Data mine? You betcha. Access files for which I was apparently authorized? Um. It had literally been so long since I had accessed Command's computer system, hell, since I'd done anything even remotely licit with the device, I wasn't sure how to do it anymore. A long minute passed with me staring down at the device before J'adoube realized what was happening. I heard him heave an annoyed sigh.

"Help him," said J'adoube.

Chokepoint turned to look at J'adoube. "Help him with what?"

"He doesn't remember how to interface his device with the computers here."

Chokepoint turned to look at me. "Seriously? You're a *Commander* for God's sake."

"Yeah, yeah, yeah, and how much *Commander*-ing have you seen me doing since ever?"

"Give it," said Chokepoint, shaking his head and holding out his

I forked over the device. A solid five, maybe even seven, whole seconds passed before he handed it back. Showoff. The schematic on the screen showed a little blue dot that, I assumed, represented me. It took a second to orient before I started stepping slowly down the hall. I stopped, pointed and looked up, directly at a sizeable protuberance that looked ready to spew several gallons of pure poison onto us. As if it wasn't going to be problematic enough to get through the squelchy, sickening flesh wall. Screw it, I decided.

"We should probably all move back a ways," I said, shooing the other two back down the hallway.

"Why?" Chokepoint asked.

I opened my coat for moment. After digging around, I came up with one of the revolvers loaded with the incendiary rounds. It followed that super-icky, magically-conjured flesh was probably still prone to the many weaknesses of regular flesh. I gave him a big grin. Then I turned and fired an incendiary round directly in the protuberance. The strategy worked, after a fashion. The incendiary round hit the protuberance and the goop inside proved to be explosive when it came in contact with fire. The noise was profound. It also made me start worrying about my hearing. I'd been exposed to an unusual number of sonic traumas in the last, how many hours *had* it been? I tried to do the math and couldn't even remember how long I'd been awake. I settled on the vacuous term of "recently." Whatever the timeframe, all those concussive impacts on the sensitive interior mechanics of my ears could not be good things. Come to think of it, all those explosions probably weren't good for my soft tissues or more important things, like internal organs. Oh the stuff they left out of training.

I gave Chokepoint a look. "That's why."

I walked over and saw a great gaping hole in the flesh mass. That was good. What was not good was the way the diseased meat was already starting to seal up again. What kind of magic made this kind of nightmare, I wondered.

"Let's go," I shouted over the ringing in my ears and stepped through the hole.

The new hall was just as covered in the pestilential meat, but with more of the protuberances. I shook my head. The tactic was starting to become obvious. The coats might protect us from a few splashes of the goo inside the protuberances, but it seemed unlikely they could withstand a sustained barrage of the stuff. J'adoube and Chokepoint flanked me to either side and surveyed the obstacle course ahead of us.

"That isn't good," said J'adoube.

"No, not so much," I agreed.

"What?" Chokepoint asked.

J'adoube and I shared a look. Rookies.

I glanced over to Chokepoint. "You notice anything about those things filled with exploding foulness?"

He seemed to focus in a little. "Oh. Quite a few more of them. Bigger too."

"We're going to need to start moving a lot faster," said J'adoube.

I saw the worry on J'adoube's face. Even with the nanites in his system, the trauma of the gunshot wound wasn't something he could just shrug off. Any kind of sustained cardiovascular effort might overtax his system. He wouldn't die from that, but he might pass out. We couldn't leave him to recover in these halls, since that meant almost certain death. Yet, trying to drag his unconscious body with us could mean certain death for all three of us. I looked back and the hole had already sealed itself over, without a convenient explosive protuberance to blow it back open. Going back wasn't an easy option.

Chokepoint did the math a little faster that time. "How far do we got to go?"

I consulted the device and turned it so Chokepoint could get a look. "You tell me."

He frowned at the screen. "Maybe 200 meters."

"I can make it," said J'adoube.

"You sure?" I asked.

"Does it really matter?"

"I guess not."

J'adoube gave me a significant look. "You do seem to have another option."

"I don't have a good frame of reference to understand it. I could kill us all with the best of intentions. If I have to, I will, but only as a last resort."

Chokepoint looked at us, mystified. "What are you two talking about?"

"Nothing you need to worry about," I said. "Not yet, at any rate. If things get hairy and I tell you to get behind me, though, don't hesitate."

"That's pretty cryptic. Let's get this over with if we're doing it," muttered Chokepoint.

"Where's the next turn?" I asked.

"30 meters and we go left," said Chokepoint. "Assuming there's actually a way to go left."

After checking that we were all ready, we moved down the hall at a fast jog. The squelching beneath our feet and the smell started to work on my stomach again. It was a running fight to keep myself from vomiting. I noticed that the protuberances were growing in size and number the farther we got down the hall. A few were huge, three feet across and seven feet high. If one of those burst when we were passing, there would be no way to avoid coming into contact with the inevitably toxic crud inside. We'd made it about twenty meters and I could see there was another protuberance where we needed to turn. It was big and even more deformed than the rest. Another meter or two and I could see why.

"Oh Christ," I said.

I stopped moving and just stared. There was a human arm, shoulder and head stuck on the outside of the protuberance. The head hung down, as did the arm. I shuddered to imagine what kind hell that poor bastard suffered with most of his body inside that cesspit. I made myself move forward, but held a hand out to stop J'adoube and Chokepoint. I was about two meters away when the head jerked a little. I didn't scream. I wanted to scream, but the signal to do it just never seemed to cross from my brain to my mouth. The head turned toward me. The bones of the man's face pushed hard against his skin, as though he'd been starved for months. His eyes wandered for a several seconds before they seemed to find me. The scleras were a putrid yellow green. A shriveled tongue worked itself over the man's nearly non-existent lips.

"Kill me," he rasped. "Please, God, kill me."

I nodded. There was nothing else to do for him. I turned and walked back to J'adoube and Chokepoint. J'adoube's gaze was fixed in the far distance, his lips pressed into a grim line. Chokepoint looked aghast at what lay before us. I grabbed his jacket and pulled him close enough that all he could see was my very angry, very unforgiving face.

"That," I said, "is why we exist. We're supposed to prevent things exactly like that from ever happening. The people who set that horror in motion are what we're up against. The next time you think I should stop to have people fill out a fucking good or evil questionnaire, you remember that man down the hall."

I just stood there, shaking, glaring at the kid. For his part, Chokepoint looked like he didn't know whether to puke, cry or punch me in nestly, I don't know if I'd have blamed him for any of those

"Jones," said J'adoube, quiet and steady.

I let the kid go and stared down the hall. "Brace yourselves. This isn't going to be pretty."

I lifted the P-90 and sent a short burst down the hall. I spun and crouched, expecting a huge explosion to rock the building. Nothing happened. I waited a few second and snuck a peek. Nothing continued to happen. J'adoube and the kid were crouched with their backs to the huge protuberance. I frowned, contemplated standing up, and decided that Murphy was waiting in the wings somewhere to slap me down with his Law. I kept waiting. Chokepoint started to turn.

"Stay where you are," I bellowed.

The explosion was beyond huge. It was monstrous, world-eclipsing, and flung us all back down the hall. That probably saved our lives. The initial explosion set off several of the smaller protuberances, forever after referred to by my brain as the damn bomb nodules. I blacked out for a minute or two in the cascade of destruction. I suspected that was for the best. The next thing I knew, Chokepoint was dragging me in a half-stumble through another hallway. Unlike the last hallway, this one was lined from one end to the other with the enormous damn bomb modules. I had a moment of blissful ignorance before I remembered that there were probably people inside of those hellish cocoons.

"I'm okay," I mumbled.

I pushed away from Chokepoint and immediately fell down. J'adoube reached down and pulled me up, facing the wrong way down the hall. That was why I got to see one of the damn bomb nodules split open and something stepped out. It might have been human once. It had the right general shape and number of limbs, but the resemblances stopped there. It was hairless and the visible skin was nearly translucent, which provided a dandy view of its veins, arteries and the black sludge they were circulating. I didn't think. Thinking wouldn't have served me well at that moment. I lifted the P90 and pulled the trigger. The first couple shots missed. They also got the attention of the creature. It turned to look at me. Its eyes caught the light like a cat or dog and glowed. I was nominally aware that J'adoube and Chokepoint were shouting something, but the cacophony of the earlier explosions left me all but deaf. I adjusted my aim and put about a dozen rounds through the creature's chest. Other than driving it back a couple steps and sending a spray of black vileness down the hall, there was no visible response.

"You've got to be kidding me," I whined.

The thing fixated on me again and started bounding down the hall in an awful, skeletal loping motion that was far, far too graceful. It opened its mouth and let out a noise that pierced even my temporary deafness. Thanks to my deafness, however, it didn't incapacitate me the way it was no doubt intended to do. Instead, I got a very good look at its teeth, which looked like they belonged in the mouth of a shark. I was shocked into stillness by how much ground it had covered in a few seconds. Chokepoint recovered first and put several rounds through the thing's head. That seemed to kill it. Hanging around didn't seem like a good idea, so I turned and ran. We got all of a dozen steps before I heard a series of those weird shrieks. I risked a look behind us and saw a half-dozen of the things stepping out of the damn bomb nodules. We got to the far end of the hall and met another solid wall of meat. I turned and looked at J'adoube and Chokepoint. Then I looked at the creatures closing in on us. Some bit of rationality gave way in my head.

"Get behind me!"

I don't know if either of them actually heard the words, but J'adoube and Chokepoint both seemed to get the gist and positioned themselves d like to pretend there was some kind of deep process to what I .e method to the madness, but that wasn't how it went down. I just .ted to kill those creatures and obliterate whatever dark magic had turned human beings into monsters. I flung my hands out in the general direction of the things closing in on us and I reached for power. I took a half-second to imagine what I wanted and then…

Whump!

Flames so bright they hurt my eyes burst into life. They stretched from floor to ceiling and the smell, the unholy stench of that foul meat being seared by magical flames, there simply were no words in any language to describe it. It wasn't an odor, or a stink, or anything short of a total war blitzkrieg against the nose. It was olfactory napalm. It was Hiroshima for the sense of smell. With a mental effort, I sent the flames hurtling down the hallway, my own personal scorched earth answer to the olfactory napalm. Let there be light? Fuck that. Let there be cleansing fire. The remaining damn bomb nodules went off, but the force of the explosions was carried away from us. Whatever the creatures were, nothing survived the unforgiving wrath of that fire. I went deeper into the moment, into the magic itself. I sent the flames back the way we came, obliterating all the diseased flesh as it went.

The building shook that time. It was a deep trembling that knocked me off my feet. The structure screamed in agony under the assault. No, said some fragment of my mind that was still observing my surroundings. It wasn't the building shaking that knocked you off your feet or that made that noise. I swung my head around. The seared end of the meat hallway had jerked itself out from beneath us and was retreating. It had sealed itself around both of Chokepoint's legs and one of J'adoube's legs. They were both screaming in anger or terror, I couldn't tell. Chokepoint unloaded into the sickening flesh with his P90 before vanishing into darkness. I stumbled to my feet, still half-lost in the magic and I called the fire back to me. I heard it coming, felt the heat of it as it grew nearer, but I knew that I had nothing to fear from it this time. This fire wasn't some out of control thing like my earlier forays into direct wielding had been. *This time*, I was in control. The flames reared up behind me like the outstretched wings of a phoenix and I sprinted after Chokepoint and J'adoube.

More of the skeletal monstrosities were waiting, only to be vaporized by columns of fire that swept around me defensively. I kept waiting to run out of steam, to lose contact with the magic, but it didn't happen. I knew there had to be a limit, but I hadn't reached it yet and I couldn't afford to worry about it at that moment. I dropped deeper into the magical haze and got to where I wasn't sure if I was using the magic or it was using me. Maybe it was both, some kind of symbiotic relationship. Was the magic sentient? Conscious? Did it have a will of its own? If so, it had cheerfully sublimated its will to mine for the moment. I wished that my education in direct magical manipulation had been a lot less haphazard and wasn't driven by half-baked hypotheses I made up on the spot. I rounded a corner and only raw momentum kept me in motion.

Perhaps twenty meters away there was an open maw. It wasn't a mouth. A mouth speaks, sings, smiles and kisses. That gaping thing at the end of the hall had no purpose but to kill. It was a fleshy mass that barely squeezed into the hallway and was filled with row on row of razor teeth. What had clamped down around Chokepoint and J'adoube's legs appeared to be some kind of tongue. It was dragging them straight into that open maw and its waiting teeth. I gritted my teeth and concentrated. Fire swirled past me in blistering corkscrew, the flames compressing as they went until the tip was no bigger around than a pencil and so intensely white I didn't dare look directly at it. The pencil-wide tip of fire swept across the diseased flesh of the tongue with sizzling, popping noise and severed it cleanly. The severed end thrashed wildly, and slammed J'adoube and Chokepoint against the floor, the walls and, in one particularly intense seizure, the ceiling. The creature, whatever it was, let loose with a noise so loud and high pitched that white hot pain in one of my ears sent me sprawling to the floor as an eardrum ruptured. My connection to the magic wavered momentarily and I nearly panicked. I intuitively knew that if I lost control of the flames it would be beyond bad. I clamped down hard on the pain and the magic.

The maw was staring to close and whatever it was attached to was trying to retreat. Hell no, I thought. I wasn't going to chase that thing down. I focused as much as I could and sent the fire hurtling into the half-closed maw. I didn't know how big or resilient it was, so I encouraged the flames to do their worst. I worried that the building might actually come down around our heads the thing thrashed and banged around so much. It didn't let let loose with another of those horrendous, ear-splitting screeches again. Maybe the flames had burned what passed for its vocal cords. Maybe it was just in too much pain to bother. I didn't let up, even when the stench rose to hitherto unimaginable levels of awfulness that made me yearn for the comparatively light hell-stink I'd previously imagined as olfactory napalm. I didn't let up when noxious smoke started to fill the hallway. I diverted just a little of the magic to raising a wind that blew the smoke back toward the burning, thrashing monster. I didn't let up until there was nothing left of it but ashes. I pushed myself up to my feet and walked toward the semi-conscious J'adoube and Chokepoint. The magical flames swept out of the smoke and swirled around me. If I hadn't wanted to think in those terms, I'd have said the flames were downright giddy.

Chokepoint and J'adoube looked up at me with mixed expressions of wild fear, gratitude and incomprehension. I stared up at the blackened ceiling toward where I imagined Endgame Smith was realizing that his pet was dead. It had to have been his work. No one else would have been reckless enough to unleash a thing like that. I raised a fist and shook it at that imagined spot where Endgame stood.

"My house, motherfucker!" I screamed.

Then, an exhaustion so pure it resembled divine retribution sucker punched me in the face.

5

I was awake before I realized I was awake. The transition was so smooth that it wasn't until pain started to register that it hit me I'd been unconscious. The next thing that oozed into my groggy consciousness was the sound of voices. I was still too out of it to actually bother to open my eyes. I just lay there in a limp heap and listened while other people talked about me.

"He did?" asked Captain Kane.

J'adoube offered his thoughts in the tones of a bored academic. "It was impressive."

"Impressive," parroted Chokepoint. "That's how you want to describe it?"

"How would you describe it?" J'adoube asked.

"I don't know. The phrase, fucking terrifying, springs to mind. You saw what he did. He burned a damn Linton Worm to ashes with nothing but magic and his will. Did you have any idea he had that kind of power, Green? How about you, Captain?"

A Linton Worm, so that's what that thing was, I thought. I clearly needed to bone up on my mythological creatures. Then again, I'd always imagined Linton Worms looking more like snakes and less like a hollow meat tube with several thousand razor sharp teeth. My mistake.

"He is Contingency Jones," said J'adoube, as if my name alone were the answer to some age old question.

"No," said Kane, her voice soft. "I had no idea. I wonder if he even knew."

"With all due respect, Captain, he's dangerous."

"Every Agent is dangerous," said J'adoube. "Why should Jones be the exception?"

Chokepoint answered in an eerily calm voice. "There's dangerous, and then there's unacceptably dangerous. That kind of power in the hands of a man with so little regard for life is unacceptably dangerous."

A woman whose voice I didn't recognize chimed in. "Agreed. He cannot be trusted. Frankly, he should be put down immediately, for the safety of us all."

That got my attention in a hurry. I needed to put a stop to that kind of talk in a big damn hurry. I opened my eyes and saw a small knot of people off to my right. They'd laid me out on top of a desk and there was a flurry of activity around me. People slipped into something that I assumed was body armor. People checked weapons. People were doing things to computers at a pace I would normally have described as panicked. No one was paying attention to me, which was perfect for my purposes. I slipped off the desk with as little noise as I could manage. I was gratified to see that the paranoia hadn't ratcheted up far enough for them to disarm me. I slid my Model 27 out in one hand, a forty-five in the other, and ghosted toward the group. I assumed the woman with the blonde ponytail was the one advocating for my summary execution.

"I won't sanction Jones just because he scares you," I heard Kane say.

"Captain, it needs to be done," said Chokepoint.

"We knew this was a possibility since they day he entered the program," said the blonde woman. "Despite out best efforts, he's worked out direct manipulation of magic. He's on a forked variant that could end with him destroying everything. If you won't sanction him, I will."

That was the moment I chose to alert them all to the fact that I had joined the conversation. I did so by levering back the hammer on my revolver and pressing the barrel against the back of the blonde woman's skull. She went very still. J'adoube raised an eyebrow at me. Chokepoint went for a weapon, but I leveled the forty-five at his face. Kane stood up from behind a desk and gave me a hard look over the top of the blonde woman's head.

"Jones," said Kane, her voice soothing.

I gave the back of the blonde woman's head a little nudge with the barrel. "You do realize that I have to splatter your gray matter all over Captain Kane now, don't you? I certainly can't turn my back on you. Still, I'm a sporting man. You want to kill me? Try."

"Don't move!" Kane ordered, pointing her finger at the blonde woman.

"Jones, you son of bitch, put down that gun," barked Chokepoint.

"I heard the part where you insisted on shuffling me off the mortal coil. If I were you, ingrate, I'd work very hard to make me forget you exist."

Chokepoint managed to look a little ashamed of himself. It would have to do for now. I'd deal with him later. The blonde woman was a different matter. She'd clearly meant it when she said she'd sanction me if Kane wouldn't. I had no doubt that, given any opportunity, she'd carry through on that intention. Worse still, it'd be damned near impossible not to give her that opportunity. There was too much going on, and I couldn't be wasting my time looking over my shoulder every few seconds. I also couldn't trust that she wasn't working for the other side. Being in the room didn't make her trustworthy. She had to go.

"Sorry, Captain," I said. "It's her or me, and I vote me."

"Jones, don't," said Kane.

"How do you know she isn't working for the other side?"

"Because she isn't capable of it," said a familiar voice.

I didn't turn to look, but I did acknowledge him. "Hello, Uncle John. You here alone?"

It was a much more loaded question than anyone else standing there might have thought. Uncle John and I had had a conversation a while back. The gist of that conversation was that if August Worth wanted me dead, he'd send Uncle John to do the deed. More to the point, John would be sent alone.

"I am, but not for that. Please lower your weapons, Jones."

"Uncle John, I'm pretty sure that neither of us is in a mighty big hurry to fight the other."

Uncle John was quiet for a moment. "True."

"That being said, I'm not throwing my life away. She plans to kill me."

"What about the several dozen weapons being pointed at you right now?"

I sighed. "I don't want to kill all of these people, but I've already killed a lot of people today who didn't really deserve it. If they make me, I'll kill them too."

"Are you willing to bet your life that you're that skilled, Jones?"

I felt tired and numb. Washed out. I hadn't been lying. I'd killed the mercenaries and "Four," whoever he really was in real life. I'd also killed all the people that had been trapped in the damn bomb modules. Sure, it was probably a mercy, but those weren't the people I'd set out to kill. I was still in a murderous frame of mind, but people I didn't have a real problem with kept making me to waste those feelings on them.

"It's not a bet," I said, looking Kane in the eye when I did.

The blood drained from her face.

"Jones," said Uncle John, "I will personally guarantee your safety."

Lower your weapons and I'll order her to stand down."

The blonde woman jerked. "No! You can't!"

That was interesting. It sounded like she couldn't refuse the order. I guessed it was some kind of behavioral programming. Cool, problem solved.

"Okay," I said, and lowered my guns.

"Thank you, Jones. Jessica, I'm ordering you to," Uncle John started.

"No!" Jessica screamed.

She whirled toward me with synthetic speed. My brain idly noted that she must have been an A.I., while my body tried to lift the revolver in a vain attempt at self-defense. Based on the way her fingers were curled and the trajectory of her swing, I was pretty sure she planned to rip my throat out. My hand continued to lift the revolver at a snail's pace compared to Jessica's inhuman speed.

"Stand down," said Uncle John, calm and composed.

The robot froze in place. Unlike the robot, my body doesn't respond immediately to changes in external stimulus, which is why I wound up shooting her point blank in the chest. I might have fired twice before I managed to command my body to stand down. There was a strange look on the robot's face and a few ominous sounds from inside the robot's body.

"Agent Jones," said Jessica the murderous A.I., "please refrain from discharging your firearm at me."

"Oh," I said. "Um, okay. Sorry."

"Your apology has been duly noted and registered. Thank you."

I was getting a headache.

"Contingency Jones, I am taking you into custody," said Chokepoint.

He grabbed my wrist. As an object lesson, I broke his arm.

I let them dose him with some painkillers to get him more or less coherent again before I spoke.

"That was your friendly warning. Next time, it'll be your neck," I said and then turned to the room. "I didn't come here to fight friendlies and allies. So let's get it out of the way. Anyone else here in a mood to make me hurt them? Anyone else want to make it that much harder to fight the actual enemy? If so, step up now. Otherwise, keep your opinions to yourselves and get with the fucking program. Because, so help me, I am fresh out of patience and pity. Well? Any takers?"

I glared my way from one set of eyes to the next. Some of them look confused. Some of them looked pissed. Most of them just looked frightened. All of them kept their opinions to themselves. I was smart enough to know I'd just made a few enemies for life. Since I wasn't even close to confident I was going to survive for more than an hour or so, though, I figured that was probably an issue I didn't need to worry about. The message from my future self felt very distant and abstract as I stood in that room. I was an alien there. Oh, I wore the right coat and knew the right words, but I didn't belong. I had never belonged. It was a big part of the reason I wound up an Agent. Agents don't fit. Some fake it better than I do, but it's always a mirage to cover the fact that we're damaged. Maybe we're damaged from birth, but we're certainly broken from something. You just can't live our lives if your psyche is healthy. It's like asking someone with late stage lung cancer to run a marathon. Disaster will ensue.

"Jones. A word," said Kane without her teeth ever coming apart.

She stalked toward an empty corner. It wasn't exactly like she grabbed my ear and hauled me with her, but I had the impression we weren't very far off from that. I weighed my options, and then followed in the wake of her obvious anger. She stood with her back to me and, I wasn't sure, maybe she was counting breaths or something. I waited with patience. That was followed by waiting in impatience. That was when I started getting bored.

"Captain," I said.

She whirled on me with eyes so hard you could have struck sparks off them. I considered that maybe I should have waited in patience a bit longer than I had.

"What the hell were you thinking?"

I blinked a few times. I'd done an awful lot that day. I wasn't sure which particular thing she was mad about. I opened my mouth to ask, but she cut me off.

"Promoting Lester to Agent status?"

"Okay," I said, "in my defense, I didn't think that was for real. I just figured it was going to get ugly, and I wanted him in a cooperative frame of mind. Plus, he deserved it."

"You didn't think it was real? Why wouldn't you think it was real?"

"Why would I think it was real? That whole commander rank thing came out of left field."

She just stared at me for a long beat. "Do you ever read messages not marked orders or critical?"

I threw my hands up in exasperation. "No! You've met me. Why is that such a shock to everyone?"

She seemed to do some more counting in her head. "And breaking Lester's arm?"

I folded my arms over my chest. "He deserved that too."

"I'd have told him to stand down if you'd given me another second."

"We both know that's not why I broke his arm."

She looked away when she said it. "Have you considered the possibility that he's right?"

It was my turn to count in my head. The explosion of red-tinged anger that clouded my vision almost overwhelmed what passed as my better judgment. I counted slowly down from twenty before I answered. "No."

"I didn't see what happened down there, but the display of power Lester and Green described to me," she paused. "Can you blame him for being afraid?"

I let out a breath, my anger deflating. "I don't blame him for being afraid at the time. I blame him for being stupidly afraid after the fact. I'm probably one of the very few people in this building that has a ghost of a chance at taking down Endgame Smith and Chokepoint wanted to off me. If I didn't know any better, I'd say he'd been turned."

Kane arched an eyebrow at me. "One of the only people? Pretty high opinion of yourself, don't you think?"

"No. I just expect that I'm one of the very few people in the building who thinks that Smith *can* be beaten. He was a legend even before he came back from the dead. You should have heard the way Clea talked about the guy. Even knowing what he did at the end, she still talked in hushed whispers of awe. Which reminds me, where is Clea? No way she'd end up on the wrong side of this fight."

Kane face went still for a moment and then she shot a look past me. I looked over my shoulder to see Uncle John walking our way. I frowned at him and then at Kane. She didn't say anything until Uncle John was standing there. She clenched her jaw for a second and I watched her steeling herself for something. There was a cold spot in my stomach.

"Regarding Clea," said Kane. "Smith grabbed her in the initial assault. I'm not sure why he didn't just kill her."

Uncle John and I spoke in unison. "I know why."

6

"Yes, yes, she's the director's granddaughter, so there's the leverage angle," said Kane with a dismissive wave of the hand. "Smith is smart enough to realize that won't work."

Uncle John raised an eyebrow at Kane before he looked at me. "You told her."

It took a second for me to catch up. Kane and Uncle John were apparently on a very different wavelength than the one I was on. I shrugged. "She was bound to figure it out eventually."

"A questionable assumption, but the point is moot. Why wouldn't Smith assume she could be used as leverage?"

"We don't negotiate. Ever. Smith knows that," said Kane.

"He also knows that no one has ever had one of the director's family members to use as a chip in the game. Does this not change the balances."

Kane shook her head. "Even the director answers to someone. No one would ever let us negotiate, even under these circumstances."

Uncle John was very quiet. So quiet, in fact, that I got a nasty feeling in the pit of my stomach. "Uncle John, the director does answer to someone, doesn't he?"

Uncle John waggled a hand in a so-so gesture. "He is obligated to report to the Premiere, but saying that he answers to anyone probably stretches the reality."

"Shit," said Kane. "Like we didn't have enough problems."

Kane and Uncle John talked to each other for a moment while I pursued an entirely different line of possibility. I conceded that it was possible Smith intended to use Clea as a bargaining chip with the director, but it didn't feel right. What if he took her to get at me? My sending her away was, on paper, a matter of propriety. I didn't want Command embedding a spy in my home. I made sure that got into the report. That was a far cry from wanting to see the girl dead. I'd trained her and you couldn't do that without forming some kind of a bond. Killing her right in front of me would be just Endgame's speed. My imagination coughed up an even more unpleasant idea. What if he planned to sacrifice her? He'd been trying to raise a god the last time we crossed paths. Blood sacrifices were a time-honored method of making that happen. It'd be a way to revenge himself on me, the director, and he'd have himself a god to smash the rest of the organization into powder.

"Where is Smith? Right now, where is he?" I demanded.

Kane and Uncle John both turned toward me.

Kane tilted her head a little to one side as she looked at me. "Why?"

"I've got a bad feeling that I know what he's really planning here. Now, where is he in the facility?"

"Jones," said Uncle John, "explain yourself."

"Where?" I bellowed.

Kane took a quick step back and even imperturbable Uncle John visibly started at the sheer volume and ferocity of my voice.

Kane straightened her shirt, squared her shoulders and glowered at me. "As near as we can tell, he's holed up in Magical Practices. Now tell me what the hell…"

I didn't hear the rest of it. I jumped up onto a desk and started shouting.

"We move out in exactly five minutes! Every damn one of you, grab anything you can use as a weapon! Everyone with combat training, front and center!"

There was a moment of hesitation as everyone stared at me in bewilderment. Kane, god bless her, clued in that things were about to get very, terribly, horribly bad. She walked up next to the desk. "What the hell are you waiting for? You heard the man!"

Within 30 seconds, about two dozen people wearing the stuff I'd taken for body armor were standing in front of me. The non-combat trained or at least non-combat experienced people in the room were shuffling around, holding weapons uncertainly or hefting whatever heavy objects came to hand. It would have to do. I looked over the combat-ready men and women.

"You aren't going to like this, and I don't care. You won't want to do it, and I still don't care. We're storming Magical Practices because, unless I'm very wrong, Endgame Smith is about drop a pissed off Egyptian god of evil on top of all of us."

Kane's eyes went wide, but she didn't say anything. Not everyone was so accommodating.

One of the men in the back of the crowd piped up. "Spare us your bullshit, Jones. We all know Smith is dead and that you killed him."

I was about to answer, when J'adoube strolled over and pointed a gun at the man's temple. "Endgame Smith shot me earlier today. Interrupt again, I'll assume you're one of his and act accordingly."

There were no more interruptions.

"The long and short of it is this, we can't play favorites or second guess ourselves. If you see someone that's armed, you order them to stand down. If they comply, fine, if not, you kill them."

That generated some dark looks and even Kane looked like she wanted to object. Of everyone there, only J'adoube and Uncle John took that order in stride. In fact, Uncle John was studying me with an intensity that unsettled me. All it took to get J'adoube on board was him getting gut shot and then almost eaten by a living nightmare. I guess those are the kinds of things that clarify a situation for a person. It was clear that there had been some kind of fighting before I arrived, but it was just as clear that it had been a confused mess of a fight. No one really knew who the enemy was and, frankly, if anyone survived what was coming, I pitied the poor bastard who got the job of figuring out who was loyal and who was a traitor. Another thought occurred to me then, but I'd have to deal with it after.

"I know this is new territory for you. None of you were trained for this situation. We're all going to see people we know, friends and acquaintances, but those relationships mean nothing now. We can't know who to trust. We can't take the time to find out. If they'll stand down, we'll secure them and deal with it after. If they won't, it's you or them. Don't hesitate.

"I want four man teams. Two experienced and two to three inexperienced per team. You lot," I said, pointing at the experienced people, "you're job is clear the corners and do any necessary room entries. Inexperienced people, your job is to make sure these people don't get shot in the back. Radio check ins every five minutes. If you get separated from your team, hunker down and barricade yourself in a room. No unnecessary heroics. Get organized into teams. Two minutes people!"

There were more dark looks thrown my way as I climbed down off the desk. Screw it. I'd be the bastard if that's what they needed. Kane gave me a pained look. I held up a hand.

"I know, I know. It's harsh, but it's how it has to be," I said.

Kane was very quiet for a moment. "Can Smith really do it? Could he really raise a god?"

"Yes. He almost did it in a warehouse with no gear. They've got a dedicated circle down in Magical Practices. I'm surprised he hasn't done it already."

"You didn't offer much in the way of a strategy."

It was my turn to give her a pained look. "There's not much strategy to something like this other than clearing corners, moving in teams and shooting everything that breathes."

"This will be a bloodbath, Jones," said Uncle John, his forehead creasing.

I nodded. "It will, but it will be regardless of anything I do or say. There isn't a good solution here. Just the one that gives us the best shot of survival. If we do nothing, we'll all die and die badly."

"Victory or death?" Asked Kane.

"Victory and death is more likely," I said. "Uncle John, where is Director Worth?"

Uncle John's face was an opaque mask. "He is pursuing other avenues of inquiry."

I hoped that meant what I thought it meant. If it did, it was one less thing I'd need to worry about after the fact. I glanced around the room. The combat vets had divvied up the non-combat personnel into something resembling teams. I just watched them for a minute. The ones with combat experience looked as grim as I felt. They were aware of the tactical realities in front of us and the toll in blood it would take. The ones without combat experience looked afraid. I picked out the team with the hardest looking combat vets on it and walked over.

"You four stick with me," I said.

A tall woman with a dark olive complexion took a step forward and gave me a look somewhere between a sneer and utter loathing. "And where will that be, sir? Here?"

I met her eyes. She held my gaze for about three seconds before she looked away. She shivered at whatever she saw on my face. I didn't blame her. It couldn't have been pretty.

"We're the tip of the spear. I don't lead from behind." I looked around again and pointed at the other group I'd considered. "You four stick with Captain Kane. If she gets killed during this, I'm going to be annoyed."

The group I'd pointed to walked over to Kane without a word. Hating me was one thing. Kane was a different story. They might not like her, but I was willing to bet they all respected her. I tried not to imagine how many people in the room wouldn't see the next day. It was a struggle to remind myself that I hadn't brought this down on their heads. Smith had gone bad long before I found him in that warehouse. Something like this was bound to happen. I coughed loudly to get everyone's attention.

"The primary object is to get to Magical Practices. Once we're there, you need to secure the corridors and hold them."

There was a low murmur in the room.

Kane shot me a look. "Then what?"

"Then I go in and finish this once and for all."

"By yourself?" Asked the olive-complected woman.

I nodded. "If we storm the room en masse, Smith will start executing everyone in range. If I go in alone, he'll want to gloat."

"Absolutely not," said Kane.

She opened her mouth to tell me all the reasons why it was stupid and suicidal, but Uncle John put a hand on her arm.

"He's right. This is what Jones does," explained Uncle John. "If he fails, we can always storm the room."

Kane glowered at Uncle John and then turned the same look on me. "Damn it, Jones, how sure are you that you can beat him?"

I smiled at her. "He won't see what I've got in mind coming. That's why it needs to be me."

"That's not an answer," she said.

I shrugged. "I can do this."

She looked around at everyone in the room, doing the same math I'd done. It had to be worse for her. She'd need to answer for all of this, but she also knew that not acting was as good as signing everyone's death warrant. She looked at me again, her eyes going cool and distant. "You better be right about that. Let's move."

7

The trip from Administration to Magical Practices didn't take as long as I'd expected, but it was just as bloody as my worst fears. All of the extra staff members that I'd seen on my last visit were waiting in the halls and it was pretty clear they'd been trained for this exact scenario. Well, they'd been trained for *almost* this exact scenario. I had a suspicion that they weren't prepared for squaring off against Captain Kane and J'adoube Green. I only saw them in action early on, before teams started fanning out into branching hallways. Magical Practices was very nearly a building in and of itself. What I did see of J'adoube and Kane in action was impressive as hell. Agents usually worked alone, but hand them a support team to cover their backs and they became veritable war machines.

At one point, I saw J'adoube calmly step out of a shadow, pick a man up and throw him into two more guys who were firing on one of my teams. Then his guns came out and things got loud. Kane didn't have J'adoube's unexpected, and frankly shocking, strength. What she did have was speed and some hardcore training that she clearly hadn't gotten from our halfass, hand-to-hand combat instructor. She sprinted into the middle of a group and went to work with a wicked knife. In a blur of motion, she hamstrung one guy and damn near decapitated another. She pulled some kind of weird move that reminded me of aikido to get a third guy to shoot a fourth guy in the face. Then, she spilled his intestines all over the floor. I'll give Kane and J'adoube this much. Whatever misgivings they had going into this mess, it didn't show.

As for me, I went old school. I shot my way through a dozen people that had it coming. It probably shouldn't have, but it felt good. It felt righteous. They had come here with every intention of betraying us, of betraying our purpose, and that couldn't stand. I wouldn't let it stand. Command was a facility, interconnected in all kinds of ways and we shot, stabbed, cut, clubbed, punched, kicked and gouged our way toward Magical Practices. We were avenging angels come to judge and we did. We judged them guilty. It didn't come cheap. By the time my team got within spitting distance of magical practices, it was just me and the woman with the olive complexion. One of the non-combat experienced people caught a stray bullet. There was no way to know for sure if it was friendly fire or enemy action. The other non-combat experienced person, a plump woman I didn't know, had beaten a bad guy unconscious with a heavy binder. She stayed behind to stand watch over some people that may or may not have been on our side. The other combat experienced man with us had gotten torn to shreds in a laser web. It was an ugly way to go out, but at least it was over in less than a second.

Based on what I was hearing over the radio, the other teams were taking similar losses. I tried to not feel guilty. I hadn't wanted those people dead, but there weren't many alternatives. Smith *had* to be stopped. If he set some ancient power loose, it would take a hellish toll on the civilian population before the resources could be assembled to banish it. The best bet was to end the threat right then and there, while I had the people best equipped to do it on hand. Plus, if I was being honest, I wanted to make sure Smith died for real this time. Given the opportunity, I was going to cut his damn head off and have it incinerated. Good luck reanimating him after that. Still, the human costs gnawed at my conscience. Sure, everyone in the building had signed on for this kind of thing, in theory, but I doubted that most of them ever believed they'd need to wage a bloody assault inside Command. Up until a day or two ago, even I would have found the idea absurd, if not appalling. How many people had died because I didn't kill Smith hard enough the first time? All I knew was that it was too many.

As those dark thoughts rolled through my head, I stared at the main entrance to Magical Practices. The woman with the olive-complexion was standing on the opposite side of the hall from me. There was blood trickling down the side of her face. Her body armor was pock-marked where she'd taken fire repeatedly. She looked as tired as I felt. Combat drained you physically and mentally and, my little nap aside, I'd spent a lot of time in combat recently. She shifted her gaze to me. Whatever ill-will she had borne me was gone, replaced with something vaguely respectful and definitely fearful. I leaned my head back against the wall and gritted my teeth as I reached inside my coat. The laser web hadn't been the only booby trap. A concealed bomb had turned part of one wall into a storm of shrapnel. My coat had stopped the worst of it, but the coat wasn't a suit of armor with a helmet. A long, thin piece of shrapnel about the size of a pen had ricocheted and found its way into the open space of the hood. It was on just the right trajectory to lodge itself into my right shoulder. I grabbed the end of the metal and started to pull. The metal ground against my collar bone and it hurt so much I almost lost consciousness. I stopped pulling as I gasped for breath. There were noises from across the hall that eventually crossed the gulf of pain and became recognizable as human speech.

"You alright?"

I stared blearily at the woman across the hall for a moment. "Gonna need a hand."

She cleared the corners again and scooted across the hall to stand next to me. I unfastened the top of the coat and pulled it open so she could see the shrapnel. Her eyes went a little wide.

"Christ," she said. "That's got to be painful."

I nodded. "What's your name?"

"Why?"

"I don't let anyone pull shrapnel out of my body before I get a name."

She blinked and then shook her head.

"You're a weird one, Jones. My name," she said and then moved faster than I could track.

My world exploded in shades of white and red. When my vision finally cleared, or maybe it was when I regained consciousness, I was sitting on the floor with my legs straight out. She was applying a bandage to my shoulder. I felt nauseated and it got worse every time she put pressure on the wound. God, I hated getting injured. It left you off-balance, distracted, and adrenaline could only do so much. I hadn't even had the wherewithal to grab another med patch from my storage unit. It was so stupid to have forgotten that little piece of equipment. It weighed nothing and took up almost no room. I'd just been so fixated on offensive capacity, I'd forgotten about injury management. I think I groaned because she looked at me then.

"Maria Torres. That's my name."

"Thanks, Torres. I don't think I could have gotten that out myself."

She nodded and then frowned at me. "Mind if I ask you something?"

"Go ahead."

"I heard Lester say you killed a Linton Worm with magic. Is that true?"

I nodded, but didn't speak.

"So why aren't you using magic now?"

I grunted as I started pushing myself up to my feet. I felt dizzy for a few seconds and used the wall to stay upright until it cleared. It was a fair question. I'd been tempted a few times to go for a magical solution, but common sense won out in the end. I moved my right arm experimentally and almost went down in a second explosion of red and white. That arm was out for the count. Awesome, I thought, because I didn't have enough on my plate. I looked at Torres.

"Too many people moving around out there. I didn't want to kill some of ours while I was killing some of theirs. It's bad for morale."

She nodded and then gave the door into Magical Practices a significant look. "What about in there?"

"In there, all bets are off, which is why everyone needs to stay out here."

"What are you planning to do?"

I didn't answer her. I was too busy fishing around in my coat for the little bottle containing the grey dreamer. I pulled it out and held it in my left hand. I considered that for a moment. I wouldn't be able to carry it and a gun at the same time. I put the bottle into my right hand and closed my fingers around it. I waited. There was no blinding flashes of white or red. That was good news. Torres looked at me expectantly.

"I'll do whatever needs to be done."

Torres considered that in silence for a minute or two. "I didn't think you were real."

"Sorry?"

"I thought you were one of those institutional legends they tell new recruits. One part fact and three parts myth."

"Maybe I am," I said with a smile. "You never can tell."

People started checking in over the radio. It wasn't actually radio, but I'd long since forgotten the official name for the technology. It was some weird hybrid between computer hardware and magic that operated on principles that gave me headaches. I'd fretted about using it. The bad guys had access to the exact same technology and were probably listening in, but it would have taken way too long to rig up some kind of an alternative. It sounded like the home team controlled most of the access points to Magical Practices or were about to control them. I started my mental prep. However cavalier I'd played it off to everyone else, Endgame Smith was profoundly dangerous. I'd gotten Kane to provide me with all the files about the man. He'd done a whole lot of things that even I found impressive. The real problem was that I didn't know what to trust in those files. How many of those things had he actually done? How many of them were simply reported, or set up for him as part of a conspiracy? There was no way to verify most of it, just as there was no way to verify most of what I'd done over the years. I had to assume it was all true.

There was more rapid fire chatter over the radio and then Kane came over the line. "Jones, we're all in position."

"Understood. I don't know what's going to happen in there, but if I say indigo, bomb this place to dust."

All of the intermittent chatter on the radio went dead. It was a sobering kind of thing to hear. Plus, I doubted most of the people under Kane's command really understood the true scope of the danger. I could say "Egyptian god of evil" a hundred times, but it just didn't mean anything to people who had never seen an Egyptian god in action. They didn't have the appropriate frame of reference for the sheer power an incarnate god wielded, even a god weakened by centuries without worship. I hoped that my instruction to level the entire facility helped to drive home some sense of the situation's precariousness.

"Jones," said J'adoube, "we won't leave you to die."

"If it gets bad enough for me to say indigo, I'll be dead before you can do anything to help me. If I give the word, get out and call down the fireworks."

More silence.

"Understood," said Kane. "Good luck."

"Thanks," I said, taking a deep breath.

Torres was watching me from the corner of her eye. "You don't think you're going to survive this, do you?"

I shrugged with my left shoulder while I checked the hallway, which was still clear. "It needs to be done. It was nice meeting you."

She gave me a somber nod. "*Vaya con Dios*, Jones."

"*Hasta la próxima*, Torres."

I slid the Smith & Wesson, Model 27 out and held it in my left hand. It felt strange there. I'd practiced shooting lefty, but I'd never be a crack shot with that hand. There was nothing to be done about it now. I walked across the hall, kicked open the front door to Magical Practices and strode in like I owned the place.

8

I'd braced myself for gunfire, or explosions, or magical mayhem. There was nothing of the kind. A security station to prevent the unwary or uninitiated from wandering into a space where magical experiments were underway stood empty. I frowned at it. Smith should have left people there to stop someone from walking in the way I was walking into the place. There had been some kind of struggle in the entryway that left debris scattered across the floor. I picked up a bit of detritus and tossed it through the air toward the guard desk. I tensed as I waited for a violent response from hidden weapons or traps. Nothing. I made myself stop grinding my teeth. The whole thing felt wrong, but I didn't have much choice. I walked past the security desk, through the blackened space where doors used to be and made my way deeper into Magical Practices. There were no signs of life. There were also no bodies. That made my skin crawl. There should have been bodies. There should have been lots of bodies.

With the possible exception of the Agents in the building, the staff in Magical Practices were the best able to defend themselves. Just because they had, apparently and intentionally, done a half-ass job of teaching me how to use magic, it didn't mean they didn't know how to use it. I fumed a little at that. With nothing to distract me, my thoughts drifted back to what the damn, murderous AI had been saying. I was on something called a "forked variant," which didn't mean anything to me. That was troubling in itself. Command made sure that Agents were well-versed in the possible ramifications of time travel. That I was living in one of those possible ramifications and hadn't even known it existed was just as concerning as the fact they had tried to keep me from learning how to manipulate magic directly. The AI said they had known this was a possibility all along and that I could destroy them all. If that was true, why had they recruited me in the first place? Why risk that when they could have left me to live out whatever life I might have carved out in the regular world? There were too many unanswered questions in my life for my taste. If I survived the clusterfuck of Smith's resurrection, I needed to get some of those questions answered.

The deeper I moved into Magical Practices' inner sanctum, the less I liked the situation. Assuming everything had gone down in a hurry, there should have been experiments gone wrong roaming the halls. I didn't know exactly what kind of experiments, but my brain treated me to imagery of hideous monstrosities and human being deformed into gibbering mutants with a taste for human flesh. The word zombie never crossed my mind, not even once, not even for a second. Gibbering mutants I could deal with, no problem. Zombies, though, those bastards were just scary and stupid hard to kill. Clea had watched a bunch of zombie movies one weekend and I rolled my eyes so much I got dizzy. Those movies would have you believe that a head shot would kill a zombie, or decapitation, or explosions. They wouldn't. In my experience, nothing short of total incineration would do the job. Shoot a zombie in the head and it wouldn't even slow down. Cut their heads off, you just got a headless zombie. They didn't have circulatory systems or even nervous systems to speak of after they became zombies. The bodies were just a convenient house for angry spirits from some awful dimension. At least Archan the Necromancer had the basic decency to bind human souls into human bodies. Those didn't go cannibalistic. They were easier to kill too, since human souls were bound by the rules of this corner of creation. I wondered if the things Archan made were zombies or something else. I decided they probably weren't zombies proper.

I blinked and looked around. I'd been standing in the same place for at least two or three minutes. If I could trust my memory, I'd been talking out loud to myself. I wondered what the hell was happening. Had I walked into some kind of magical trap? I checked my senses and didn't get any of the residual weirdness I'd come to associate with magic. No skin tingles or strange tastes or inexplicable condensation on the skin were present. If not that, than what? I mulled it over for a minute before the answer became apparent. Fatigue. It was just ordinary fatigue catching up with me. I'd been running myself harder than I had in a long time and, with injuries on top of it, I was getting foggy. You can ignore pain, for a while, but it doesn't stop being hard on the body. I'd racked up a pile of minor injuries in the last two days, along with a significant puncture wound. I had the impression that my involuntary nap following the fight with the Linton Worm hadn't been a long one. The impulse to just sit down and close my eyes for a while was overwhelming. I knew that was a terrible ideas and didn't let myself do it. I gathered my willpower and lurched into motion. The fight would either be over or I'd be very dead inside fifteen minutes. No reason I couldn't hold it together until then.

I checked my memory. It'd been a while since I last set foot in Magical Practices, but I was pretty sure I remembered where they kept their dedicated circle. My footsteps sounded too loud in the empty hallways. This is what it'd be like to walk in a city of the dead, I thought with a shudder. I shoved that thought aside, along with my lingering bad feelings about there being no dead bodies, and the growing certainty that things were all wrong. Endgame Smith hadn't won his reputation by being careless or stupid. The only reason that there weren't guards and traps was that he didn't think he needed them. If he thought that, it wasn't good news for me. It probably meant that Clea was already dead and that he'd summoned whatever he planned to summon. I hoped I was wrong. If I wasn't, this was going to be a one-way trip. I couldn't let Smith or anything he summoned get out of the building. It'd be a massacre. The rest of the world wasn't prepared for that level of magical violence. There were probably a handful of practitioners out there who were hiding the true extent of their powers to avoid be drafted into one government agency or another, but I couldn't rely on them to solve this problem. I'd failed to finish the job with Smith the first time. I wouldn't fail again. Smith was overdue in Hell.

I found the room where they kept their dedicated circle. It was pretty obvious from all the warnings not to enter while the red light was on. There were also warnings that unauthorized personnel would be shot on sight. Magical Practices took their security seriously. It made sense, since they could have summoned almost anything into that circle and distractions could prove lethal. The doors were open a crack and a sliver of light shone into the hall. I took one deep breath and tried to steady my nerves. Smith hadn't been ready for me last time. This time, he'd had plenty of time to prepare. I glanced down at the bottle in my hand. He wouldn't have prepared for that, because no one else knew about the grey dreamer. That little tidbit never made it into any of the reports. I extended a foot and pushed one of the doors open. I stepped through it and took stock of my surroundings. The room was absolutely bare, which made sense. Lots of extra-dimensional beings had nifty telekinetic powers. No reason to provide them with handy missiles to throw around.

Smith stood about fifteen feet away. He was directly in front of the dedicated circle, a polished ring of silver set into the floor, and facing me. His left hand was around the back of Clea's neck and he'd positioned her as a human shield. She saw me and there was a flicker of relief on her face. Smith and I pointed guns at each other at the same time. I noted that there was an unnatural shine to his right eye. They must have given him a prosthetic eye when they brought him back, I thought. Other than that, no one ever would have guessed that he'd been brutally murdered. Almost murdered, I reminded myself. Smith gave me a soulless smile.

"Jones, I should have known you'd survive. You always were a cockroach that way."

"Smith, I see you didn't have the good grace to stay dead. We'll have to do something about that. Clea."

"Jones," said Clea in a pain-laced voice. "Took your sweet time, didn't you?"

"Yeah, there was some unpleasantness. Some assholes burned down the house."

Clea's eyes went wide in real anger. "What?"

"Burned it to the ground. Don't worry, I killed them for it."

Smith blinked. "All of them?"

"I don't do things halfway," I said. "Clea, you about ready to blow this popsicle stand?"

"More than, this asshat is worse company than you are."

"You've overestimated your talent and ruthlessness, Jones. You aren't quite cold blooded enough to sacrifice your trainee here just to get me. And you aren't good enough or fast enough to kill me before I kill her."

I nodded thoughtfully. "That's probably true. What do you suggest?"

"You let me kill you. I let her go. I don't care about her one way or the other."

I nodded again. "That's one idea. Here's my counter-offer. Let her go and I'll make it quick for you."

Smith laughed at me. I figured he would. That was okay. He'd made a critical error and didn't know it.

I looked at Clea. She turned her hand just enough to show me what I needed to know.

"Take him," I said.

I'd pushed Clea as hard in hand-to-hand as she'd pushed me on cardiovascular health. She was young and probably as fast as she was ever going to be, and that was unbelievably fast. Her hand moved in a blur and the gun in Smith's hand dropped to the floor. There was a spray of red from his wrist where she'd severed the tendons. In the moment of Smith's utter shock, Clea twisted out of his other hand. There was another flash and a second spray of blood as she cut the tendons in that wrist. Smith screamed and swung an arm at her, but she was already gone, rolling behind him. Her arm swiped in a vicious arc and one of Smith's legs gave out. Before he'd even hit the floor, Clea was on her feet and one booted heel connected with Smith's face. I heard bone crack. I don't think Smith even knew it was happening when Clea slit his throat. She stood and walked toward me. She looked a little sick to her stomach, which was to be expected. Close work like what she'd just done was hard on a person. She managed a grim smile for me.

"How'd I do?"

I put the Model 27 away, reached out and squeezed her shoulder. "You did good, kid."

I got a bad feeling in the pit of my stomach, like I'd made a monumental mistake. I looked at the spreading pool of Smith's blood and then around the room. I reached out with my intuition. I felt it all around us, the dank, terrible presence of something monstrous. Smith had underestimated me and Clea, but I'd underestimated the thing that Smith served. Blood sacrifice. It hadn't mattered where the sacrifice came from, just as long as the sacrifice came. The situation was a win for that thing no matter who came out on top. How could I have been so careless, so stupid, or so blind to the reality? That's what the last few days had been about, I realized.

Smith had pushed me and I pushed back. I did exactly what his master had wanted me to do, I overreacted. I drove myself to exhaustion. I fixated on killing Smith without considering the angles. I'd made the mistake. I'd be the one to pay the price.

"Clea, get out of here. Right now."

She looked around the room and seemed to draw the right conclusion. "Jones, you can't fight this by yourself."

"I won't have to. Now go!"

Her eyes looked a little wetter than usual, but Clea just nodded. "I'll see you after."

I keyed the radio. "Kane, Smith is dead. I'm sending Clea out. Torres, don't shoot her. Once Clea is clear, evacuate. Let me know when everyone is out."

"What about you?" Kane asked.

"There's another problem here I need to deal with. Prep for indigo, but don't go live with it yet."

There was a pause before Kane spoke again. "That bad?"

I felt around with my senses again. "Worse."

"Understood."

I stood rooted in place as I felt the amorphous sense of darkness gather and a figure rose from the pool of Smith's blood.

9

According to Egyptian legend, Apep was a huge, terrifying snake that, by turns, stretched the better part of fifty feet, lived below the horizon or just prior to dawn. It engaged in conflict eternal with the light bringer, Ra. I supposed those stories were as functional a construct for defining evil as any, and, per protocol, bore no resemblance to reality. The figure that rose, sheathed in Smith's blood, was that of a man. He was short by the standards of my society, maybe five and a half feet tall, but that had been the norm in his day. I knew. I'd been there and it had been no mean feat to disguise my height and ethnicity. J'adoube couldn't have gone there if he wanted to, at least not without being mistaken for some kind of god in his own right. Of course, when you're dealing with a god, height was just about the least reliable predictor of the kind of damage they could do. I'd once seen a very minor god of the glen that stood three feet tall vaporize three enormous trolls with one freaking word. Granted, trolls were pretty stupid, but they weren't weak. Apep had been Ra's opposite number at a time when Ra was generally considered to have been the one to utter the phrase, "Let there be light." So scary and appalling was Apep that daily rituals were carried out by an entire society to weaken and banish his influence.

I did take some solace in the idea that he was a very long way and a very long time from his sources of power. That meant that he wasn't invincible, just damned near impossible to kill. On those grounds, I was in no mood to let him finish manifesting before I took my first shot at him. I looked down at the bottle in my right hand and whispered a word. The sigils I'd scratched into the glass flared with blinding light and the cork crumbled. The grey dreamer crawled out of the impossibly small mouth of the bottle with a wail of hatred and hunger that scraped a layer of my sanity away. It flew into the room and whirled to face me. I gave the awful monster a flat look.

"Time to choose. Vengeance on me or feast on that," I said, pointing at the still congealing figure.

The grey dreamer's eyeless gaze slid off of me and toward Apep. There was zero chance that the grey dreamer could actually kill Apep. The grey dreamer probably knew it too, but it had been starving for a very long time. I was a single meal. The half-manifested god across the room was ten thousand meals in a convenient package. If the grey dreamer had been less of an abomination, less of an unspeakable blight upon all of creation, I might have felt guilty for setting it up the way I did. Well, I admitted, future me had set it up. I'd just carried through on his ruthlessness. I wondered if that made it my ruthlessness now. Was there a meaningful difference? I thought that there must be a difference. I'd have never been cold-blooded enough to think of a plan like using the grey dreamer the way I did. Then I considered it a little more and shuddered. The only way future me could have known to tell me was if current me *had* come up with it. Future me just took a shortcut and told me to do what I'd already done. I felt sick. Was my self-knowledge really so flawed? It wasn't a stretch. I wouldn't be the first person to misjudge himself.

As for the grey dreamer, it did what any starving animal will do when confronted with what looks like a feast. It attacked. There was the furious noise of a thousand rags whipping in a wind that wasn't there, followed by sound of those rags slapping against something wet. The grey dreamer had engulfed the bloody body of Apep in its manifold rag strips and appeared to be gorging itself. The grey dreamer swelled and something like a true body seemed to fill out the rags. Then there was a roar of pure outrage and fury so inhuman that I lost time beneath the onslaught. When I regained the ability to process visual information, Apep had the grey dreamer pinned to the floor and was methodically ripping the monster to pieces. I sighed to myself. It had been a longshot. While Apep was busy killing the grey dreamer, I shoved a hand beneath my coat, peeled the bandage away from the wound in my shoulder and worked a finger at the wound. It didn't take much to set the wound to bleeding again and I only grayed out a couple times. With the prep work for plan c in place, I went to plan b. I dug deep inside myself for the magic. I hoped there was still some there to use. I spared a moment of pure hatred for the teachers that had deprived me of the information I needed.

The magic rose to the call, like pressure building behind my eyes. It was hard to wait, but I wanted Apep and the grey dreamer to inflict as much damage as possible on each other. No point in throwing down until one of them finished killing the other. It seemed pretty obvious which way the fight was going to go, but it never paid to act prematurely. Waiting turned out to be the right move. The grey dreamer regrouped enough to drive one of its hands into Apep's stomach and tear away a handful of flesh. Blood flew, sprayed and splashed from the wound. The shock alone from such a wound would have killed a human being. All it appeared to do was piss off the Egyptian god of evil. Apep reached down with both hands and ripped the grey dreamer's head off. I tightened my concentration. I was only going to get one sucker punch and I wanted it to be a solid one. Apep raised the grey dreamer's head into the air and slammed it against the floor with a noise that reminded me a beetle's shell cracking. I raised my left hand, palm out, and aimed it at Apep. The old god seemed to finally take note of my existence and turned toward me. It opened its mouth to speak at the same time that I let loose with fire.

Where the fire I'd used against the Linton Worm had been big and all-consuming, the fire I sent hurtling toward Apep was as tightly constrained as I could make it. In my head, I imagined a beam as fine as a laser. The reality wasn't quite that narrow or contained, but it was no bigger around than a small branch and glowed a retina-scorching purple. I'd aimed with care and the beam slammed into the hole the grey dreamer had torn into Apep's abdomen. The lance of fire punched straight through the god's back and it let loose with a scream that threatened to tear my body apart. I held it together for a few more seconds and dragged the beam of fire diagonally across the screaming god's torso. I meant to cut the damn thing in half, but that scream simply overwhelmed the limits of my sanity and mortal body. Everything went black, and then I was falling through empty space. I'd read somewhere that dreaming about falling was a sign that you felt out of control in your life. I had no idea if that was just pop culture myth or had some basis in fact, but it fit with my circumstances. I saw faces I recognized as I fell. Every single one was an Agent that had been lost in the ley lines. The last face I saw was that of my father. He seemed to notice me and my fall was arrested.

He frowned at me. "You didn't think this one through, did you son?"

"Future me says I survive this disaster, somehow."

"Do you believe that?"

"Not really."

"Might be time to start believing."

"Says the figment of my imagination," I muttered.

My father's head tipped a little to one side. "Might want to check that assumption."

"Check what assumption?"

My father started to speak when gravity took over again. I hit the floor hard and I realized I was screaming in time with Apep. The voice of the agonized god was so painful that I couldn't even escape it with unconsciousness. The enchantments and technology that made up my coat started to fail and the material blistered. I had a horrified moment of realization. The coat was blunting the effects of Apep's screams. If the coat failed, I would die. There was nothing more that I could do. I slid my hand under my coat again and felt the wetness of my blood. I couldn't even hear myself think, but I started to chant.

"Lords of Order, I," and then I stopped when an idea hit me.

The idea was insane. As far as I knew, no one had ever dared to try. Then again, I'd done everything in my power to cleave Apep in two and the wounds were healing right in front of my eyes. Even if Kane leveled the building with explosives, it might not be enough to kill Apep. I also had no idea how many people were still in the building. Sure, the fight had felt like it took forever to me, but I doubted more than a couple minutes had passed. It wasn't long enough for everyone to have gotten clear. I needed to buy more time, but I was out of tricks. It was time for something insane. I pulled my hand out from beneath my coat and stared at the red blood through eyes blurred with pain and tears and utter terror. Screw it, thought some part of my mind that was gleeful at throwing all caution to the wind.

"Lords of Order," I said again and threw the biggest dice roll of my life. "Lords of Order, I *invoke* thee."

Then, there was silence.

10

She and I faced each other. To the left, my body was stretched out on the floor. I looked like I was screaming in terrible, unimaginable agony. Off to the right, Apep's face was contorted in agony of his own. I wondered, briefly, if I'd been stronger, willing to endure just a little more, if I might have banished him on my own. I rolled my eyes at my own hubris. Fat chance of that happening, I thought. The entity I'd come to think of as the representative of the Lords of Order was staring at me in what I suspected was her version of shock. She looked down at my body, then at Apep, and then back at me.

"A terrible risk," she said, "to invoke us is to court absolute destruction."

I nodded. I'd surmised as much before I made the mad gamble. "Looked like things were headed that way already. I figured it was my best shot at taking him out with me."

She regarded me with such intense sadness that I had to look away. "Perhaps, but the cost. Jones, you can't know what it will entail. You will see me as I truly am. I will see you as you truly are. It will change you in ways that cannot be undone."

"If I merely summoned you, could you fight it? Would you?"

"I would, but I could not. There are laws, pacts, that would prevent it."

"If I invoke you? Could you destroy it then?"

"I, no, you do not understand. In terms you can comprehend, yes, it could be destroyed under those circumstances."

"Then I don't see another option."

She looked exasperated and, I realized, afraid. "You speak without knowledge. There are *consequences*."

She said the word consequences the way other people said things like thermonuclear holocaust and global pandemic. It frightened me, which was probably the point. It was clear she didn't want to do what I'd asked, but that she would do it, if I pushed hard enough. I thought about what would happen if I didn't put a stop to the threat. I saw mountains of corpses and a new world order ushered in on an ocean tide of blood. I'd pay a price, that much was obvious, but I was only one man. I'd been prepared to die to stop Apep, so I doubted her consequences could be worse than that. In the end, what was my life compared to saving the damn world.

"People will die," I said. "Innocents will die. My friends will die. If there's a price to pay for preventing that, better that I pay it than someone else."

She stared at me with a face devoid of human expression before I saw something in her eyes that there was no human equivalent for. Based on the way she closed her eyes, it was painful. She nodded.

"My name is Nemeth. You should know it before," she broke off. "You should know it."

She had voiced her true name to me and the power in that name make my bones ache. I stammered incoherently for a moment. I tried to get a grip.

"My name," I started, but stopped as she shook her head.

"I know your true name. I have always known it," she said, glancing down at my body. "I would tell you to prepare you mind, but there is no preparation."

She walked toward me and slipped her arms around me. She rested her head against my shoulder. "Tell me, Jones, have you ever loved?"

"Once," I said.

Simple proximity to the raw power she exuded made me feel like I was drowning in the open air. I felt insubstantial standing next to her, like she was the real person, and I was a mere shadow. That sensation terrified me more than anything else ever had. She lifted her head off my shoulder and looked me in the eyes. She smiled at me. That smile carried infinite heartache and I wondered why she asked me if I'd ever loved. Why would it matter?

"I'm glad you loved," she said.

Then she kissed me. She'd been right. I had not understood. It wasn't my fault. I couldn't have understood. How does one understand a consciousness that spans billions of years? How does one make sense of a duty bequeathed by something older than existence? How does one comprehend a being so immense, so utterly what it is, so inconceivably powerful that you are less than a dust mote? To her, I was something that existed for less than a fraction of a fraction of a moment of time, and she would not have noticed me, save that I had called her. I was rendered nothing before the unimaginable intensity of how female she was and in some abstract way that had nothing and everything to do with sex, nothing and everything to do with love, I wanted her. I wanted us, joined, balanced, and I realized that nothing less was ever going to be enough for me. I was aware of every living thing in the universe. I was conscious of civilizations that humanity would not come to know of for another million years. I was a bug, carried in the wake of universal mind, made more by proximity to it, and made less human. Humanity was defined by the beautiful and terrible brevity of the human lifespan. I experienced the cosmos as she experienced it and would be forever altered by that experience. She had warned me of the consequences. I hadn't listened. I would pay, but that cost was beyond reckoning. Something hard and cold, the thing that let me shoot Endgame Smith in the head the first time, that thing that had allowed me to carry out a suicide mission in World War II Germany and survive, reared up inside me. There was a price to pay.

"So. Be. It!" I screamed.

The world condensed around me, us, and there was no battle for control. There was no Contingency Jones or Nemeth. We operated as a single being. The wound in my shoulder closed because we found it convenient for the wound to close. The chaos thing that called itself Apep ceased its bellowing and glared at us from across the room. We stood and stretched out hand out. A lance tipped in pure, radiant light appeared. Apep rose and a sword appeared in its hand.

"I will kill you both," said Apep.

"You will trouble this world no more, chaos-child," we said.

Apep closed on us with the impossible speed of a god, the sword moving through the air so fast that oxygen ignited as it passed. We ducked and spun, the lance whipping in an arc that would have gutted the foul creature had it not dove and rolled away. It raised a hand and a sphere of black that crackled with pale green lightning shot at us. Our lance pierced the black sphere and, with a casual flick of the blade, the sphere shattered. Apep pointed his sword at us and a torrent of demonic, hooded crows exploded into existence. We opened our mouth and a screech like the god and master of all hawks issued forth. The crows scattered in terror and vanished.

We shook our head. "The tricks of a child. Let us end this."

Apep's face twisted in uncontrolled fury. "A child?"

Apep charged us again, the sword lashing out like the bite of a viper. He had not taken the time to test us, to understand our capacities. By the time he realized that the space his sword was passing through was empty, we were already behind him. The lance split reality as it ripped the wayward god of old in half. There was a spray of red, an immaterial scream of incomprehension, and then Apep was gone, rendered into nothing by the terrible power of the Lords of Order. We stood there for a moment and considered the completed work. We judged it good. A thought from the before us time surfaced and we keyed the radio.

"It is done. Call off indigo."

Kane's voice came over the radio. "Jones, confirm that last."

"Confirmed. Call off indigo. Threat neutralized."

The Clea-child's voice came over the connection. "Jones, are you alright? You sound different."

"It's done," we repeated.

There was a moment of pain and an unbearable sense of loss as we became, less we. When they finally came looking, I was curled up on the floor, sobbing like a lost child. Nemeth had issued the warning. She had said there would be consequences. Now, we understood. I, as I had understood myself, was no more. Nemeth had retreated, but she wasn't gone. The invocation could not be fully undone, because she was so vast and I was so small. Eventually, I retreated into sleep, because it was simply too painful to be awake. Had future me known? Had this been part of the plan all along? There was no way to know for sure and, right then, I simply didn't care.

11

There were a lot of attempts to talk to me when "I" woke up, but I mostly ignored them. The world was different now. I was different now. I reasoned that I would get used to it, eventually. You could get used to anything if you worked hard enough at it, even sharing your consciousness with an immortal transdimensional being of the opposite gender. Sure, I thought, I'd get used to that in no time at all. For her part, Nemeth seemed to be working very hard not to intrude on my part of the consciousness, but she kept bleeding through. I supposed it was inevitable. Her consciousness was just too potent. The only upside was that most of it was completely incomprehensible to me. More like really obnoxious background noise than something I had to pay attention to, so there was that to be grateful for. They'd shoved me into a room with a bed and a shower, and I hadn't made any attempt to leave. Where would I go? When would I go? Did it even matter? More mayfly mortals came and went, some I recognized, some I didn't, but I couldn't muster the energy to talk to them. After a week of that, I woke up one day and felt, for lack of a better term, more me-ish. I asked to talk to Kane.

She came into the room looking uncertain. It was a strange expression to see on her face.

"Jones," she said. "How are you feeling?"

I rolled my eyes. "You're the last person who gets to ask me that. Spread the word. I'm, well, as I'm good as I can be. How are things out in the real world?"

Kane grimaced. "Complicated. There was a lot of confusion after the fact. A whole lot of politicians and bureaucrats have been having "accidents" recently."

"I thought that might happen."

"You did?"

I shrugged. "There had to have been some political support behind Smith and those assholes running around in our coats. There's at least three more of those out there, by the way. Director Worth struck me as the kind of man who could raise vengeance to a high art. They put his granddaughter at risk. What would you do?"

Kane considered that with a thoughtful look. "Director Worth and," she snickered, "Uncle John have been doing employee evaluations. Part of Worth's rather bloody house cleaning, do you think?"

"Probably, though he'd have had to do it anyways."

"True. You're getting a pass on that process, by the way."

"Oh?"

"Apparently saving the world comes with perks," she said, smiling at me.

I nodded. That seemed fair. "So now what?"

"I take a week off and cozy up to a case of hard liquor."

I gave her half a smile. "Sounds like a plan."

"How about you, Jones?"

I shrugged. "Back into the field, I guess. Red Cord is still out there, probably."

"You don't think this nightmare was them?"

I poked and prodded the idea for a little while. "It could have been them, but I'm not banking on it. This was all too obvious for a group that managed to stay off our radar for as long as they did. They might have had a hand somewhere in the background, but I think this was mostly Smith and some politicians making a power grab."

"Above my pay grade and yours too," said Kane, giving me a significant look.

"That ball is in Worth's court now. I'm just speculating."

"Keep it that way. So, you want back into the field. Are you fit to be in the field?"

I glanced at her. Her expression was serious, concerned even, and I guess she had every right to be concerned. Was I fit? Like anyone was ever fit for my job. I shrugged at her.

"Sure, I'm fit."

"Lester," she shook her head, "Chokepoint is having kittens. He keeps saying that Commanders aren't supposed to be field operatives anymore. I think he just doesn't trust you."

"I won't be turning my back on him anytime soon, so the feeling is mutual."

Kane started to say something, but changed her mind. She was quiet for a long time before she finally broached the subject. "Jones, what the hell happened down there?"

I looked her straight in the eye. "We won. That's all I have to say about it. Ever."

"There are an awful lot of people that aren't going to like that?"

"Well, that's sad for them. I'm still not going to talk about it."

She snorted. "Yeah, that's very sad for them."

There was another awkward pause. I watched Kane, curious about her seeming discomfort. She saw me watching her and blushed. I blinked.

"You're different," she said. "You were always kind of intense, but now, it's like you're, I don't know. You're just different. When you stayed down in Magical Practices, I thought I'd never see you again."

She walked over and looked up at me. Her eyes were very blue and very wide.

"I don't want to wait until Red Cord is dealt with to do this."

She reached a tentative hand up and then pulled my head down for a kiss. It was a good kiss and reminded me how very attractive I thought she was. My memories reasserted themselves, the more immediate kind of memory, not the million miles up perspective. I slid a hand up into Kane's hair. It was soft. It was right around the time we broke off from the kiss that I felt a flare of jealousy from Nemeth. So very complicated, I thought. Kane gave me a quizzical look. I smiled at her and kissed her again. We did that for a good, long while. Eventually, duty called and Kane had to go back to the real world. She did her best to straighten her hair. When she got to the door, she kind of jerked a little and gave me a sheepish look. She pulled a slip of paper out of her pocket. I stared at the paper in dawning horror. I knew what it was. I hadn't thought I'd live to have to deal with that particular problem.

"We found this in your pocket," said Kane. "Is it important?"

I nodded. "Yeah, I need to go back. To the day after I left."

"For what?"

"I have a date," I muttered.

Nemeth's flare of even more intense jealousy coincided with Kane's indignant, "You have a what?"

So very complicated, I thought.

Bonus: Episode 10.5 – Date Night

1

Being famous was weird. Granted, it was fame limited to a small organization, but I was at Command, the heart of my fame. Or my infamy, depending on who you asked. So, from one day to the next, I went from being someone that some people knew by name to being someone that everyone knew on sight. The reactions of all those people were less predictable. Some people looked at me with anger. Others looked at me with fear. An unhealthy proportion, in my opinion, looked at me with something disturbingly like reverence and awe. A few misguided souls had even taken to saluting me.

"Commander Jones," stammered one man, hand near his eyebrow, "it's an honor, sir."

I sighed, remembered Kane's admonition to play nice with the rank and file, and gave a half-ass salute in return. "Thank you, son. Keep up the good work."

I did my best not to roll my eyes as he beamed in pride. He couldn't have been more than a year or two younger than me. He should have been insulted and told me to kiss his ass. I'd have to have a chat with the trainers. The newbies needed more backbone. I moved on with some comment about an important meeting before the kid could engage me in a conversation. I did my best not to notice all the repair work being done around the facility. I felt vaguely responsible for it. I transitioned into another hallway and pretended not to notice the hateful death glare a woman from the support staff gave me.

"Asshole," I heard her mutter.

A second later, I heard the sound of a punch landing. I looked over my shoulder. The woman from the support staff was on her ass, hand held against her mouth, staring up at Maria Torres. Torres was on my team when we retook the building, inch by bloody inch. She was also there when I walked into Magical Practices by myself to face down Endgame Smith. Torres was talking fast and low, but I caught a bit at the end.

"...goddamn hero. So you keep your stupid mouth shut, bitch."

I started moving again before anyone realized I'd seen anything. It was becoming clearer by the minute that the best thing for everyone was to get me out of sight, for a long while, preferably in another time. I was too controversial and riled up too many emotions. That little altercation between Torres and the staffer wasn't the first. It wouldn't be the last, as long as I was there to keep reminding everyone of the grim events I'd, in my own way, helped set in motion. It didn't matter that I wasn't the root cause of any of it. I'd been the one who showed up and ignited the bloodshed in earnest. The people who were angry didn't care that it'd probably saved their lives. They just wanted someone to blame, and I got elected. It didn't help that August Worth had swooped in and started an employee review that made the Spanish Inquisition seem like a friendly meet-and-greet. Word had spread that I was Worth's anointed one, despite my rather pointed desire not to be, so I was catching flack for all the summary dismissals that were being handed down. At least, I hoped they were dismissals and not execution orders. Worth wasn't known for half-measures.

I went into what had been designated as "my office," whatever the hell that meant, and closed the door behind me. I leaned my head against the door. "I need to get out of here."

"Agreed."

2

The Smith & Wesson, Model 27 was out and trained on Uncle John's head before I had time to realize who had spoken. If the action bothered him in the least, you couldn't have guessed it from his benign expression. The man's self-control unsettled me more than a little. I slid the gun back into my coat pocket.

I nodded at him. "Uncle John. Kill anyone today?"

"Do you really care to know?"

"Jesus, no," I looked around the room. "I see you're alone."

He sniffed at me. "You're in favor with the powers that be, at the moment. It'd be imprudent to kill you now."

I paused a beat. "But, I see you're alone."

Uncle John actually snickered at the joke. Score one for Team Jones, I thought.

"I'm here on a purely mundane matter," said John, taking a seat on the visitor's side of my desk.

For lack of a better plan, I sat down behind the desk. "Do tell."

"Director Worth is aware, as I'm sure you are, that you are evoking heightened feelings among members of the staff and the other Agents."

"Heightened feelings? That's a hell of an innocuous euphemism for creepy, nigh-religious awe, pant-shitting fear and murderous hate."

"True, but it plays better in official reports. Learn to love those euphemisms, Jones. I expect you'll find them increasingly necessary as time goes by. You've drawn the interest of powerful people. They'll be paying attention to you."

I felt a world of future headaches start to encroach on the now. "Lovely. So, what do we plan to do about these "heightened feelings" that everyone has?"

"The director has decided to approve your requested return to the past." Uncle John gave me a disapproving look. "I understand there is some form of social engagement in the offing."

I groaned and nodded. "I agreed to a date when I wasn't paying attention. The woman provides me useful trinkets from time to time. I'd rather not burn that bridge if I don't need to."

The disapproval vanished. "Ah, a professional decision. You're scheduled to leave in two hours. Arrangements have been made to provide you with a new identity. Same name, but new social security number, bank accounts and so on."

He tossed a clear plastic envelope onto the desk. It was filled with a variety of useful documents, a new wallet, and I even saw a set of keys.

I nudged the envelope with a finger. "Keys?"

"We've arranged a new house for you, as well as temporal zone appropriate transport. The details are in the envelope."

"I assume you've informed Captain Kane about this?"

Uncle John looked bemused. "Naturally not. We knew you'd want to inform her yourself."

I glared at him. "You bastards already know, don't you?"

"If we were aware of any fraternization between you and a superior officer, we'd be obliged to act. In the interest of the organization, of course."

"Bite me."

3

"You're telling me that Worth reassigned one of my people without so much as talking to me about it?"

Captain Marguerite Kane wasn't happy. As the bearer of bad news, that meant I wasn't happy. Those feelings might have been slightly magnified by the fact that Kane was my new girlfriend. It wasn't clear to me whether she was more angry that Worth had stepped all over her command authority or that I was about to leave for another century. My departure had been a brewing inevitability for weeks, but we'd avoided the conversation. It ruined the mood. The whole conversation was made even more awkward because I could feel Nemeth paying close attention. Most of the time, the angelic being that I allowed to bond herself to my consciousness kept her distance. Anytime Kane was in the room, though, Nemeth got very focused. I had the distinct impression that my personal conduit to the Lords of Order considered me to be her property, or possibly her pet.

"Aren't we all his people?" I asked, like an idiot.

Kane's eyes narrowed.

I raised a placating hand. "He didn't talk to me about it, either."

"Of course he didn't. You're his favorite. It gives you plausible deniability."

"I'm not his favorite," I said, not for the first time.

"Uh huh, sure you're not."

"Fine," I conceded, "maybe I am his favorite, but that doesn't mean he actually likes me."

"Fair point. *I* don't like you most of the time."

"The warmth of your affection just fills me to the brim."

She arched an eyebrow at me. "You're damn right it does."

I gave her a smile, enjoying the moment of dysfunctional flirting. I glanced through the glass in Kane's office that let her oversee her staff and did a double take. The outer office was empty. Once the yelling started, the staff's collective survival instinct must have overwhelmed the impulse to eavesdrop. Kane's eyes followed mine. She frowned out at the empty desks, then she giggled. I stared at her. I'd never imagined her as someone who giggled.

"What?" She asked. "It's funny."

"I guess it is. Do you suppose they know?"

She pressed a button on her desk and the glass went opaque. "Of course they know, but who's going to make a fuss about it? You're Contingency Jones. You killed Endgame Smith, twice. You fought a god and won."

"It's a bit more complicated than that."

"I know, but that's how people see it. Bad mouthing you is one thing, but no one wants to pick a real fight with you. Especially not about who you're dating."

We spent a few moments in a quiet embrace. We both knew it was all too possible that I'd get killed in the past, either in the course of my regular duties, or pursuing my off the books investigation into Red Cord. I felt a stab of guilt as I considered all the things I wasn't telling her about that investigation, but she couldn't be prosecuted for things she didn't know about. She pulled my head down and kissed me hard on the lips. She stepped back and gave me a steady look.

"Try not to be too," she considered, "yourself, I guess."

"You mean don't take insane chances that are likely to get me killed?"

"Something like that."

I snorted. "Like the bad guys give me any choice in the matter."

"I know," she muttered, going back around her desk. "But try anyway."

"Yes ma'am."

When I got to the door, I looked back. "Take care of yourself, too, Marguerite. I'm not the only one playing with fire."

She nodded. "I will. One last thing, Jones."

"Yes?"

"If you sleep with her, I *will* shoot you."

"I took that as a given."

What bled through from Nemeth's more powerful and complex mind rarely made sense to me. Even I understood laughter, though.

4

I stood in the transit room and shifted uncomfortably in my new coat. It didn't hang quite the same way. Unfortunately, the damage Apep did my old one was too severe to repair. The techs down at the armory had gathered around that old coat and poked at it for about ten seconds. Then, the head of the armory, a man I knew only as Bill, unceremoniously picked it up and threw the coat into a waste disposal bin.

I grabbed him by his shirt. "What the hell, Bill? I need a coat! I'm going into the field in an hour."

He blinked up at me from beneath enormous bushy eyebrows. "Of course you do. We just need to get you a new one. Michaelson, get Commander Jones the prototype."

I frowned. "Prototype?"

"Yes, we've been working on a version that should protect you from those rail guns used in the untidiness a few weeks ago. Obviously, without a working version of the rail guns they were using, we cannot guarantee the new model's performance."

"Then why give it to me?"

Bill blinked at me a few times, perplexed and owlish. "Statistically speaking, you're the person most likely to come under fire in the field."

"I am? Seriously?"

He nodded. "Yes. According to our records, you are eight times more likely to be involved in a violent altercation than the average Agent. You are the perfect person for a field test," he said, pulling loose from my grip on his shirt.

He walked over to a workbench, dug around in a chaotic mass of paperwork, magical paraphernalia, and loose circuits. He gave a triumphant cry and came up with an honest to god book. He brought it over to me and held it out. I stared at the blank cover.

"What's that?"

"The manual for the prototype. We integrated a number of other improvements that you should find useful. The manual explains how to activate them."

"I'm about to travel to 21st century America."

"Yes?"

"Think about it for a second."

He squinted and then shook his head. "I don't see the relevance."

"I *can't* take that manual back with me. You're going to have to send an encrypted version to my," I heaved a mental sigh, "Quirt."

"There isn't one."

"There isn't? Why the hell not?"

"Experience has taught us that physical manuals provide significantly better retention of material."

I glanced around the room and saw all the techs watching the exchange. "Are you messing with me?"

Everyone burst into laughter. Bill threw the book back onto the table and patted me on the shoulder. "Sorry, Jones, it's a tradition. We do that any time we send an Agent out into the field with a prototype. You all get so squirrely. The manual should already be loaded onto your Quirt."

"You're a mean man, Bill."

The girl assigned to operate the transit room that day interrupted my thoughts. "Commander Jones, if you're ready."

I nodded to her and stepped onto the transit platform. "Beam me up."

"Sorry, sir?"

I waved a hand of annoyance and dismissal. "Send me."

5

When the cab dropped me off at my new address, I spent a solid two minutes staring at the place in disbelief. It was a sprawling house that had be a few thousand square feet and came with an ocean of lawn. After the shock started to wear off, my eyes drifted to the driveway. There sat an Alfa Romeo 4C that was so bright red I could only look straight at it for a few seconds at a time. I shook my head as I pulled the key ring from my pocket.

I muttered under my breath, "No, no, no."

The car unlocked when I pressed the button. I couldn't believe what I was seeing. What moron had done this to me? How the hell was I supposed to be circumspect living in a small mansion and driving a red sports car? The next time I went in to Command, I was going to beat someone senseless. I shook off the distress. I didn't have time to worry about it. At least the stupid, obvious, noticeable car got decent mileage.

I went inside and wandered around the house for a while. It was partially furnished. There was a couch in the cavern that I supposed they thought of as a living room. There was a king size bed in one of the rooms. A bathroom almost as large as the bedroom was attached. I wasn't sure, because I'd never seen one before, but I thought the tub had a whirlpool function. What was missing from the place was everything you need to survive. Stuff like food, dishes, and toiletries. All things I'd owned before Endgame Smith's lackeys had burned my old place to the ground. I felt an irrational surge of anger. The stuff I owned before hadn't been precisely nice, but it's hard not to be pissed off when someone torches your toothbrush.

I checked the time. I still had a few hours before my "date." The device pinpointed some stores nearby where I could get some clothes and the absolute necessities. By the time I got back and unloaded most of the stuff I'd bought, it was closing in on time to get ready. I froze when someone rang the doorbell. It took a moment to decide whether or not to answer the door. I concluded that if it was some nosey neighbor, this was the perfect opportunity to set a precedent that I was an unlikeable prick who was best left alone. I opened the door to find a middle-aged woman standing there. A young girl in a green vest, holding a box of cookies, stood next to the middle-aged woman. I was still wearing my new coat and literally towered over both of them. The girl looked terrified. The mom gave me a pointed once over. Dammit, I thought. The mom nudged the girl with a hand.

"Hi, I'm Jenny and," she stared up at me and trailed off.

I felt a little bad. I hadn't meant to scare the kid. I pointed at the box. "Thin mints."

"What?" The girl almost shrieked.

"I'll take a box of thin mints."

I dug some cash out of my pocket, but the girl was still just staring at me. The mom rolled her eyes.

"Give him the cookies, Jen."

The girl jerked a little and then dug out a box of thin mints. She held them out in a shaking hand. I took them and offered her a twenty dollar bill. She stared at it like it was an alien object. The mom took the cash and gave me some change.

"Thank the man, Jen."

The girl was backing away a half-step at a time. She whispered something that could have been anything and ran to a luxury SUV parked by the mailbox at the end of the driveway. I stared after her, more confused than anything.

"Sorry about that," said the mom. "Jen's a little shy."

"Not a problem. Thanks for the cookies."

I started to shut the door.

"I'm Angie," she said, sticking her hand through the closing door.

I stopped closing the door and shook her hand. "Nice to meet you."

"I didn't catch your name."

I gave her a flat look.

Jones, said Nemeth inside my head. *She's here to kill you.*

I know, I answered. *I'd like to know how she knew when and where to find me, though.*

"They didn't train you very well for this," I said, clamping down on her hand hard enough that her face when white. "You should have left the kid at home."

"I don't know," she gasped as I bore down on her hand.

"Who sent you?"

"You're hurting me," she said, staring at her hand in mine.

"If you reach for it, I will kill you," I said, nodding at her other hand. "Now, if you tell me who sent you, I won't have to kill you and that little girl. By the way, is she actually yours?"

The woman's eyes went wide. "She's a child!"

I cocked my head, like she'd suddenly begun speaking a foreign language. "Children die in wars all the time."

I can sell it, when I have to. While the assassin and her kid screeched away in the SUV, Nemeth spoke up again.

Do you know who Anderson Foley is?

No, I answered, *but you can trust that I intend to find out.*

Would you really have killed the little girl?

No.

Why not?

"Because you have to draw the line somewhere."

6

When I pulled into the parking lot, the car drew a lot of stares. I shook my head. A beating, I thought, someone is getting a damn beating. I got out of the car and walked toward the door.

"John," said someone and I felt a hand on my arm.

I resisted an impulse to bat the hand away. It took me a long moment to realize that the woman standing there was Ruth Quince, my date. At the antique shop she ran, it was always wild hair, thick glasses and cardigans. It was obvious she'd put some time into getting ready for this dinner. The glasses were gone, and I was startled to realize that her eyes were sea-foam green. She'd done something to straighten her hair and it hung around her shoulders. She wore a white sundress that hung to her knees. The dress amplified her thinness and gave her an almost elfin quality.

"Ruth," I said. "You look great."

She smiled. "So do you. Isn't it a bit warm for that coat, though?"

I shrugged. "Force of habit, I guess. It breathes pretty well. Shall we?"

We went inside and I started to realize what an epic mistake I'd made. This wasn't some restaurant she liked. It was her favorite restaurant. The staff all knew her. They smiled, waved, and the owner even came out to talk to her. Everyone gushed about how great she looked. Nemeth sent a little spike of jealous annoyance at me.

Knock it off. It's not a real date, I thought at her.

Does she know that? There was a pregnant pause. *You think she's attractive.*

I think she cleaned up nice. I can appreciate the results without confusing the issue.

I hope so, for her sake.

"So," said Ruth, "what is it that you do for a living?"

"I work as a security consultant of sorts."

"Security consultant? What's that mean?"

"It means that I help people solve unusual security problems. I can't really talk much about what I do. I've signed more non-disclosure agreements than I can count." I patted myself on the back for keeping the lies to a minimum.

"How mysterious. Are you some kind of profiler?"

I laughed. "I suppose I am, in a way. You have to be able to predict what people are going to do, at least a little, in my line of work."

"Hmmmm," she said and pressed a finger to her lips. "Profile someone some for me. Someone in the restaurant."

"Really?"

"Sure. It'll be fun."

"It usually takes a bit of research, but," I started glancing around, "why not?"

As I started processing what I was seeing, my heart sank. Most of the people I saw were ordinary citizens, but four people stood out. There was a couple sitting at a table, but their demeanor was all wrong. They kept watching the doors and the guy actually adjusted a shoulder holster once. Stupid amateur. There was an older guy, mid-fifites, looked to be in better shape than me, with soul-dead eyes. I'd met enough people along the way to know you earn those kind of eyes the hard way. The last one was a guy trying to pass himself off as a punk teen, complete with Mohawk, but he couldn't quite shake the paramilitary vibe. I also spotted the combat knife he'd unsuccessful tried to hide in his boot. A part of me was annoyed, but another part saw this an opportunity.

"Ruth," I said. "You should leave, right now."

Her eyes blinked way too fast and her mouth opened and closed a few times before any sounds came out. "What?"

"There are some people here who are going to try to kill me. I'd rather you didn't get caught in the middle. Did you drive here?"

"What?"

"Did you drive here?"

"No, I took a cab."

I slid my keys across the table. "Take my car and go."

Anger contorted her face. "Look, if you don't want to finish dinner with me, just say so."

"Punk guy at the table to your right. Guy in the gray blazer to your left. Couple in the back booth. Don't look straight at them," I ordered under my breath.

"If this is some kind of joke," she started.

"It's not. I think my last job isn't as over I thought it was."

She looked me in the eyes and whatever she saw frightened her. "What are you going to do?"

"I'm going to get you out of here. Then, I'll do whatever I have to do. Make a scene."

"Make a scene?"

"Yeah, make a scene. Stand up, throw your water in my face, and tell me what a jerk I am."

She was absolutely silent for ten seconds, but I guess she was channeling her inner theater major. She hit the table with her hand.

"You want me to do what?" She almost screamed.

She stood up, grabbed her water and threw it in my face. She snatched the keys off the table. "Dinner's on you, jerk!"

7

I waited until I saw her pull out in my car, before I got up and went to pay the bill. The owner came over and glared at me from across the register. I handed him a couple hundred. He stared down at the money, incomprehension on his face.

"Two seconds after I walk out the door, some of your other customers are going to get up and leave without paying. Do not try to stop them. They don't care about you, but they'll hurt you and your staff if anyone gets in their way. Do you understand me?"

"What about Ruth?" He asked, still holding the money.

"She's fine. She's probably halfway home. Now, do you understand me?"

The man nodded, still looking like he didn't really get what was going on, but it'd have to do. I raised my voice.

"I apologize for the disturbance," then I pointed at each of my four new playmate in turn. "Catch me if you can, assholes."

To his credit, the guy dressed as a punk was quick. He almost intercepted me at the door, but I punched him in the throat. If I'd had more time, I'd have done something else, but I wanted to get these killers away from the civilians. The whole stupid incident was probably doing damage to timeline as it was, and I needed to limit that as much as possible. I sprinted across the parking lot, vaulted a fence and took off down the sidewalk. I took turns at random and did suicidal dashes through moving traffic, always checking behind me when it was safe. Of all people, it was the older guy who kept pace. I moved us toward sketchier neighborhoods, where there were fewer cops and more places to have a nice quiet fight to the death. When I found what I wanted, I stopped and looked around. I spotted the older guy, blew him a kiss, and ducked into an abandoned construction site.

The older guy followed me in, but he was cautious. He cleared corners and kept his gun at the ready. He needn't have bothered. I wasn't hiding. I just wanted to get away from prying eyes. He closed on me, but kept enough distance to avoid a physical confrontation. He cocked his head when he saw that I wasn't afraid. If anything, I was a little annoyed.

"You're Jones," he said.

"Sorry. I'm Smith. Says so on my driver's license."

"Smartass. Definitely Jones," he said, aiming the handgun at my face.

"Did Foley send you?"

The man blinked and shook his head. "I don't do names."

"Oh well, I guess you aren't much use to me."

I released the magic I'd been holding and dropped a steel girder on him from fifty feet up. He should have known that construction site were dangerous places to play. I turned my thoughts to Nemeth.

Do you know where the other three are?

The one you punched slunk away to tend his injury. The other two are approximately three hundred feet that way. She sent a mental impression of the direction I had come from. *They are currently following your vehicle.*

What?

The woman followed you as far as she could. She's looking for you.

Dammit! Why didn't she go home?

Nemeth seemed to consider the question. *Would you have gone home?*

Of course not, but I'm trained for this.

Perhaps you underestimate her bravery.

I sighed. *It's not her bravery I'm worried about. It's her survival.*

I slipped back out onto the sidewalk and, with occasional input from Nemeth, made my way to where I could come up behind the hitman and hitwoman. Ruth, oblivious to the fact that she was in a car worth more than the houses in the neighborhood, was creeping along at about 3 miles an hour. I saw her head swiveling back and forth. The man and woman shadowed the car from a discrete distance. I wondered why they bothered. It should have been obvious Ruth was just searching at random for me. I considered the various ways I could solve the problem of the couple trailing Ruth. The easiest way was just to kill them in an inexplicable, but conceivably accidental way. I started eying lines that I thought might be power lines.

Nemeth, apparently bored, stepped in. *Just stop their hearts, Jones. This grows wearisome.*

It was brutal, but efficient and left no forensic evidence. Let it never be said I can't take good advice.

8

I jogged to catch up with the car. Ruth spotted me in the review and pulled over. She got out and stared at me. I came to a stop a few feet away and gave her an awkward smile.

"So," I said, "that was exciting."

"What happened to," she squinted at my coat. "Is that blood?"

Jones! Go now!

"Get in the car," I shouted at Ruth, as I ran toward the driver's side.

"What?"

"It's not over!"

To my surprise, Ruth ran to the car and got it. I slammed my foot down onto the gas pedal and the car shot down the street with a deafening roar, the automatic transmission gamely moving from gear to gear without complaint. Ruth managed to get her seatbelt on before we took the first corner at a frankly stupid speed. I let go of the wheel with one hand and grabbed at my seatbelt. I managed to get it pulled partway across my chest, when Ruth snatched the belt from me.

"Keep your hands on the wheel!"

She managed to get the seatbelt latched and started looking out the windows. I was checking my mirrors, looking for either pursuit or flashing lights, so I saw them first.

"Behind us," I said. "Two grey sedans and, looks like, half a dozen motorcycles."

She gave me a wide-eyed look. "What the hell did you do to these people?"

"It's a long story, but the short version is a lot. I did a lot to them, if it's who I think it is."

I took us through another breakneck turn and nearly clipped a homeless woman's shopping cart.

"You don't know who it is?"

"I've made some enemies." I glanced at Ruth. "I feel like I should apologize for this."

"You think?"

"It's worse than you know," I said. "They've seen you now. They think you're with me."

She stared at me. "What does that mean?"

"It means I really hope you know how to shoot a gun, because you're stuck with me until we sort this out. Man, she is not going to like this."

"Who isn't going to like this?"

I started to reach for the device.

"Hands! Wheel!" Ruth shouted.

I clamped my hand back onto the steering wheel. "Ruth, there's a phone looking thing in my coat pocket. Will you get it out please?"

"Why me?"

"Because you panic when I take my hand off the wheel."

She blushed. "Oh."

She dug the phone out of my coat and I walked her through unlocking it. I yelled a code in the general direction of the device. A few moments later a face appeared on the screen.

Ruth looked at the other person and said, "Um, hello?"

The face on the other end started screaming, "Who are you?"

"I'm Ruth," she squeaked.

"Sir," screamed the man on the device, "We've got an unauthorized access on Commander Jones' device!"

"Point it at me, Ruth."

She held the device up so the man on the phone could get a look at me.

"Jones! What the hell are you doing? Who is that civilian?"

I spared the device a glare. "Command, we have a problem."

Contingency Jones will return…

Bonus: Contingency Jones - The Original Flash Fiction

Click.

"In other news, the mysterious appearance of a water buffalo backed up traffic for two hours today on Interstate…"

Click.

"The FBI continues to be stymied in its investigation into the theft of the Edward Smith Papyrus…"

Click.

"A child survived a fall into a sewer with only bumps and bruises. City officials are still at a loss to explain the missing manhole cover…"

Click.

I put the remote down and stared at the dark TV screen, my mind moving with all the speed of a sloth in clogging shoes. Even without enough coffee to fuel coherent thought, I recognized the warning signs. Someone was trying to manipulate reality with magic and succeeding. The warped probabilities and appearance of non-domestic animals was the world working to rectify the imbalances.

It was that damned Smith Papyrus, again. These fools thought it was an Egyptian medical text. It wasn't. I should know. I was there when they wrote it. I hadn't understood the code at the time and I'd been banished to the temporal backwater of 21st Century America because of it. The thing was a spell to summon Apep, the personification of evil. Someone was using it and I had an idea who.

*

I looked down at the display and then back up at the shoddy warehouse. The device in my hand insisted this was the place. I shrugged and slid the device into the pocket of my work coat. I pulled up the hood and moved toward the building. The coat wasn't really a coat. It was a tool that let me survive the shear forces that potent magic creates. Thank you 28th century technology. I kicked open the door to warehouse and felt the coat shed off waves of dark power.

I pushed forward and pulled out a fine piece of 20th century tech: a Smith & Wesson, Model 27 revolver. Sure, it wasn't regulation, but practicality matters. The shear forces intensified the closer I got, making it harder to walk, but the coat held up and before long, I saw him standing there, papyrus in hand. His body cloaked in a coat like mine. He heard or sensed my approach and looked up.

"Contingency Jones. So, they really did send you here," he said.

"Endgame Smith. You're two centuries out of your zone," I answered, cocking the pistol and pointing it at his right eye. "Also, you're breaking the law. Summoning of deities is strictly forbidden. You know that."

"Oh please, you're not going to shoot me," he said, looking back down at the papyrus.

"No?"

"You've never had the stomach for bloodshed."

I pulled the device from my pocket and spoke into it.

"I need an extraction team."

*

I plucked the papyrus out of Endgame's hand. I set the stupid thing on fire and dropped it, closing the door on my biggest failure. The firelight danced in Endgame's pristine, left eye.

Made in the USA
San Bernardino, CA
19 June 2016